Praise for Alison Booth's novels

THE PHILOSOPHER'S DAUGHTERS

'A lyrical tale of wild ...
insightful, thought-pro...
                    Ka...

'Two young women in outback Australia in the 1890s, where the brilliant sunlight may illuminate more than the landscape. Booth is superb at the small detail that creates a life, and the large one that gives it meaning'
Marion Halligan, prize-winning novelist

'A delicately handled historical drama with a theme of finding self, both in relationships and art'
Tom Flood, prize-winning novelist

A PERFECT MARRIAGE

'With an intricate plaiting of past and present that both tantalises and beguiles, this novel is a poignant account of a marriage that is not what its title suggests'
Marion Halligan, prize-winning novelist

'Alison Booth captures the magnificence of female friendships and the tragedy of a disastrous marriage in a narrative that has the most satisfying of conclusions, hope'
Nicole Alexander, best-selling author

THE INDIGO SKY

'A charming, big-hearted tale, told with skill and grace'
Madison

'This charming follow-up... captures the heart and soul of a time... you can practically smell the eucalyptus, and picture that titular indigo sky'
Books + Publishing magazine

'Alison Booth's distinctive characters live in Jingera, a small fictional town on the coast of NSW... Booth puts steel into the charm by addressing the harsher realities of the times'
The Age

A DISTANT LAND

'*A Distant Land* is part-thriller, part-romance, and... I found myself engrossed in the drama of Zidra's investigation into corruption in internal security and of the aftermath of Jim's South-East Asian ordeal, all the way to the final page'
The Canberra Times

'*A Distant Land* is a moving story of love set against the backdrop of the Vietnam War'
Aussie Reviews

Other fiction titles by Alison Booth:

THE PHILOSOPHER'S DAUGHTERS

ALISON BOOTH

Red Door

Published by RedDoor
www.reddoorpress.co.uk

ISBN 978-1-913062-14-9

A CIP catalogue record for this book is available from the British Library

Cover design: Emily Caudelle

Typesetting: Fuzzy Flamingo
www.fuzzyflamingo.co.uk

Printed and bound in Denmark by Nørhaven

For my family

*On ne découvre pas de terre nouvelle sans consentir
à perdre de vue, d'abord et longtemps, tout rivage.*

One does not discover new lands without consenting
to lose sight, for a very long time, of the shore.

André Gide (1925)
The Counterfeiters (Les faux-monnayeurs)

PART I

London, 1890

Chapter 1

His Hands Could Span an Octave Easily

'That brings me to my penultimate point.' Dr Bagnall looked up from his lecture notes and peered at Aunt Charlotte, who was sitting next to Sarah in the front row of the packed hall.

At last, Sarah thought. He'd been droning on for a good fifteen minutes and nothing that he'd said was new. Everyone who attended meetings of the Women's Franchise League knew all about the history of the women's suffrage movement. She glanced at her father and Mrs Lydia Buxton. Slumped in their chairs at the back of the platform, waiting their turn at the lectern, their posture could surely not meet with the approval of Aunt Charlotte, who'd nudged Sarah awake only minutes before.

'Get on with it, why don't yer?' shouted a female voice. 'It's about bloody time we 'eard yer last point!'

Sarah felt a thrill of excitement. But alas, Dr Bagnall took no notice of the interruption and continued to develop his second-last point, which seemed indistinguishable from his previous one. Or perhaps it's all too subtle for me, Sarah thought, losing the thread of Dr Bagnall's argument as she vanished into the world of her imagination, a landscape whose features were defined by sound. In her mind she was running through the piano suite she'd been practising that afternoon. She was passing through its valleys and was now uplifted on to a plateau; she was being carried forward towards the peak that was just a few bars ahead when her progress was halted by a harsh sound.

'Give the women a go, why don't yer!' It was the same voice as before. 'We want to 'ear wot Mrs Buxton 'as to say. Get off the stage, yer long-winded burbler!'

Swivelling around, Sarah narrowly avoided bumping hats with Aunt Charlotte. She stood up to see better and – in the instant before the rest of the audience did likewise – saw a tall middle-aged woman in a clinch with two slightly shorter policemen. The woman was still shouting although her words had become muffled, in part by the constabulary embrace, but also by the uproar as fifty or so voices began to talk.

Although Sarah could hear Dr Bagnall continuing with what must now be his last point, no one was listening. All heads were craning towards the performance at the rear of the hall. Surely Dr Bagnall couldn't have failed to notice what was happening to his audience. She turned at the moment a tomato flew towards him. He ducked and it landed on his papers; his shout and the exploding tomato were like a firework on Guy Fawkes Night. Poor Dr Bagnall, how humiliated he must feel. Sarah found a handkerchief and ran up the steps to the platform. While Dr Bagnall wrung his hands, she knelt on the floor and gathered up his notes. She wiped off the tomato pulp as if she were cleaning blood from a wound; her expiation for being pleased, for just an instant, by an act of aggression.

The racket at the back of the hall was becoming louder. People were shouting. Many high shrill voices, mingled with fewer deep male voices, moving towards a resolution of the crisis, as in the final movement of a concerto. Dr Bagnall seemed to have lost all interest in his lecture notes. He leapt down, almost athletically, from the stage and joined Sarah's father and aunt in the side aisle. Sarah absorbed herself in methodically cleaning the pages of the lecture notes. Some of the writing had been washed off with the liquid of the tomato, and her handkerchief was stained with red juice and blue ink.

'That's just not big enough for the job,' said a voice that reverberated like a double bass. Sarah saw a large white handkerchief first, and behind that, a tall figure silhouetted against the harsh lighting. When he squatted next to her, she saw that he had curly blonde hair and a broad, lightly tanned face. 'Such a shame about your handkerchief,' he said.

'Such a shame about the lecture notes. We'll never know Dr Bagnall's last point now,' said Sarah.

'I think we can predict it, don't you?' the man said. 'You have some tomato on your sleeve. Use my handkerchief.'

His hand holding out the handkerchief was large, with long fingers. They could span an octave easily. As she took his offering, her fingers accidentally touched his. She felt a shock as if she had felt something very hot and withdrew her hand so quickly that his handkerchief fell on to the floor. Each of them went to pick it up simultaneously and again she felt that electric touch. She was blushing now and didn't want to look up. As she wiped up the few tomato seeds clinging to the sleeve of her pale-grey jacket, she noticed the monogrammed initials HV on a corner of the handkerchief.

'I'm Henry Vincent,' the double bass man said. 'Delighted to meet you, Miss Sarah Cameron. Charles Barclay told me who you are.'

She wound the handkerchief around her fingers. Sarah, the eighteen-year-old younger daughter of widower James Cameron, that was how Charles might have described her. She wasn't usually shy but she didn't know quite what to do or say next. To offer to return the handkerchief after having it laundered seemed forward, as if she were proposing a future meeting, while to return it covered in tomato seeds seemed inappropriate too. She wished that Aunt Charlotte would join them to offer some guidance but most of all she wished her blushes would subside.

The fuss at the back of the hall was now over and people were resuming their seats. Henry Vincent said, 'Let me take that from you. You've bandaged your left hand expertly. With all those bits of tomato pulp, it looks like a shocking injury.'

She laughed and unwound his handkerchief. His eyes seemed yellow in the artificial lighting, as yellow as the eyes of next door's cat, Lucifer. But people didn't have yellow eyes; they must be hazel or light brown. She forgot her earlier embarrassment and stared at him, almost mesmerised by the yellow. He stared back, unblinking. 'Your eyes are a light brown,' she said at last, as if making a scientific observation, when what she was really expressing was a startling new discovery: that golden blonde hair and light brown eyes were the acme of male beauty.

'And yours are blue,' he said.

She recognised this as a declaration of sorts and not a statement of the obvious. Their eye contact was broken by the appearance of her father, who was puffing slightly after his climb up the stage steps.

'Such an unpleasant incident. This sort of thing should never happen,' he said, nodding to Henry. 'Though Dr Bagnall did go on too long. We'll have to schedule him last next time.'

'Or not at all,' said Sarah.

Henry followed her down the steps. 'There's a lesson to be learned from every incident, our old parson used to say,' he said.

'Let's hope the good doctor has learned his,' Sarah said.

'Up with brevity.'

'And down with repetition.' She stopped and grinned at him. He smiled back. The gap between his two front teeth reminded her of a rodent, of the endearing mole variety. Before she sat down next to Aunt Charlotte, she observed him moving along the line of seats several rows behind, and sitting next to Charles Barclay. Charles, a man of average appearance in every regard, looked slight next to Henry's tall figure.

'I wouldn't have missed this for the world,' she said to Aunt Charlotte, whose hat had become tilted at a jaunty angle in the excitement.

'Nor I. But the most interesting talks are yet to come. Do try to stay awake, Sarah dear!'

There was no chance that Sarah would fall asleep; she had too much to think of, including her father's speech. His words were as carefully reasoned as always, but he dropped the calmness of his usual conversation and adopted the language and cadences of the natural orator. The subjugation of women was political and psychological in origin. It was based on emotion and not reason, on prejudice and not logic, on feelings and not the intellect. And it was prejudice that had led to the creation of institutions and customs that perpetuate this subordination.

After the applause – the standing ovation that her father often received – Sarah couldn't resist turning around, and there was Henry, clapping along with the rest. He caught her eye and smiled. And then the audience sat down to hear what Mrs Buxton had to say. Sarah's father and Mrs Buxton were a double act. Her father roused the audience while Mrs Buxton described how the enfranchisement of women could be achieved.

After the meeting was over and the Camerons were heading into the street, she found that Henry was by her side. He told her he was to dine with Charles at his club. She calculated that, if they walked very slowly, they'd have about ten minutes of conversation before reaching the junction of Wimpole and New Cavendish Streets and the parting of their ways. She was acutely conscious of his presence but the wide brim of her hat, only inches from his shoulder, hid his expression.

'Is this the first time you've attended one of these meetings?' She tilted her head so she could see his face and almost tripped on an uneven paving stone, slippery in the damp. She caught her breath and coughed. The air was smoggy, heavy with soot. He held her elbow until she had righted herself and she was sorry when he let go.

'Yes,' he said. 'Of course, I do think that women should have the vote,' he added hastily, 'But I'm just not a political animal. Never have been.'

'My sister Harriet is a political animal, and so's my father, of course,' Sarah said. 'It's a shame she's at home with a bad cold.' But she was being hypocritical; she was glad Harriet hadn't been there, glad that Harriet wasn't accompanying her as she strolled beside Henry Vincent through the dense fog. 'Tonight wasn't typical,' she added. 'But at least you learned the history of the movement, or did you know that before?'

'I'm afraid I can't remember a word of what Dr Bagnall said. The other talks were different. Your father was downright inspiring. Mrs Buxton was short and to the point. I'll never forget this evening.'

She wondered if he meant their encounter or the riot at the back of the hall or the talks. After a moment's thought she decided he meant all three. 'I'll never forget it either. What brought you here?'

'Charles invited me.' Henry explained that he'd been back in England for only three months and that most of that time had been spent with his people in Suffolk. Indeed, this was only his second trip to London since his return. He was here on business for his father, and what a stroke of luck running into Charles at his club five days ago. He'd been at school with Charles' youngest brother and had often spent part of the school holidays at the Barclays' place in Scotland, so when he'd bumped into Charles it had been almost like meeting a member of his family. School friendships were like that, they lasted, especially for boys who'd been packed off to boarding school from the age of five. It must have been a good three years since he'd last seen Charles, just before he'd gone to Australia. Charles had immediately invited him to dinner but insisted that he first accompany him to the WFL meeting. But he was boring Sarah, he'd been babbling on like a brook in full flow, he really must apologise. He bent to peer under her hat. His face was framed with little tendrils of hair, curling in the damp air.

'Charles can be quite persistent,' she said. 'Father says that's why he's doing so well at the Colonial Office. What were you up to in Australia?'

'I worked at a stock and station agents in Sydney for a bit. That involved a lot of travelling around. Then I spent some time on a sheep station in the High Country of New South Wales.'

'The High Country. How lovely that sounds!' She estimated they were now about thirty seconds away from New Cavendish Street.

'They call the southern tablelands the High Country. Or the Monaro. I loved it there. So much space.' He paused and seemed to be struggling to express his thoughts. 'The light's harsh there. You can't escape it but it clarifies things somehow. It makes you see what matters and what doesn't.' He was speaking so softly that she could barely distinguish the words. 'I've never been good at explaining myself.'

'But you are. That's how I feel about music.' She wanted to continue but there was no time; her father and Charles Barclay had caught up with them.

'Charles tells me you've just returned from New South Wales,' Sarah's father said to Henry.

'Queensland too,' said Henry.

'We mustn't forget Queensland,' her father said, smiling. 'Would you like to come to tea next Sunday and tell us all about it?'

'I'd be delighted to.' Henry spoke with such haste that he almost stammered the words.

'Charles can show you where we are.' Sarah's father shook Henry's hand and then gave her his arm. She turned once, when they had gone ten yards, and saw Henry watching them as they walked down New Cavendish Street towards Bloomsbury. She nodded at him and he waved back.

She couldn't wait for next Sunday.

Chapter 2

Of Sunlight Slanting through Eucalypts Like Messages from God

The grandfather clock struck the quarter hour before four. Sarah sat for a moment on the sofa opposite the fireplace and smoothed the folds of her dress, before jumping up again to check her reflection in the mirror over the mantelpiece. Harriet had said the dark blue velvet suited her. But perhaps it was too severe; perhaps it emphasised her pallor. She looked critically at her face. It was too oval and her upper lip too short. She pinched her cheeks to redden them.

Next she glanced around the drawing room, wondering how it would appear to Henry Vincent. The furnishings were a little shabby, although the proportions of the room were fine. She loved the deep red walls, the ornate ceiling cornice and the skirting board that was easily a foot deep. One window overlooked the communal gardens behind the house. The trees were mere skeletons and the lawn looked unkempt. The laurel shrubbery was so darkly absorbent that it appeared to bleach the sky of all colour although it had been a vivid blue only an hour before.

Maybe Henry wouldn't turn up with Charles. He might forget. Or, even if he did remember, she might have imagined what had happened between them at the WFL meeting. She'd spent much of those five days struggling to suppress her excitement and was convinced that time had slowed down.

Once more she went to the mirror. She looked so pale. She

pinched her cheeks again, and then wondered if she might have overdone it. Five minutes to go. She sat down in an armchair and tried to keep still.

'All alone?' said her father, appearing at the door. 'I thought Harriet would be here too.'

'She's out walking with Violet. I'm sure she'll be here soon. She promised.'

A bell pealed and Sarah's stomach lurched. She heard Rose's footsteps followed by the click of the front door. She imagined Rose staring suspiciously at Henry, as she always did with any newcomer. But he must have passed muster, for Rose was beaming as she opened the drawing-room door and ushered in Henry and Charles Barclay.

At first Sarah didn't dare look at Henry, for she knew that she was blushing. Instead she focused on Charles. Dressed in a dark suit and with his black hair parted austerely in the middle, he might have been attending a funeral. His set expression was probably because Harriet was not yet here; it was really too bad of her to be late. Then she noticed that Henry was regarding her intently. As she gazed back she felt a deeper blush suffuse her neck and cheeks, and her heart became a thumping thing in her throat.

At this moment he bolted towards the chair next to her. Although he knocked into Charles, he didn't allow his apology to slow him down. Once seated, he stared at his hands, awkwardly clasped on his lap. Charles sat next to her father, an amused expression on his face that she barely registered.

She saw how the lighting illuminated the planes of Henry's face and his golden skin. He seemed almost tongue-tied, although Father had just asked him a question about the move towards federation of the various Australian colonies. Fortunately, at its second repetition, Henry seemed able to respond, but her own powers of concentration had vanished and all she heard was the lovely timbre of his voice. After a while she wondered if he was going on for too long. Knowing her father disliked people who blathered, she interrupted the flow to say, 'Do you play the piano, Henry?'

He looked at her with a grateful expression, and explained that, although he played, he wasn't very good. In a couple of minutes, they were sitting side by side on the long piano stool and playing the duet by Fauré.

Henry's fingernails were cut short, like hers, so that as he played she didn't hear the clicking of nail on ivory, a sound she hated; it so destroyed the quiet passages. He played with feeling, though not always accuracy. She decided that she was technically more proficient, before abandoning herself to the music. They were going too fast, she knew, but she felt overcome with the thrill of the passage. The faster she went, the faster he went; she was unsure quite where they were heading. At last they finished the piece and she was almost shocked to realise that she was sitting on a piano stool in a London drawing room. She turned to look at him. His pupils were dilated and his cheeks flamed red. She felt her own face burning and raised her hands to cool them.

'Bravo!' said Charles.

Neither Henry nor Sarah got up from the stool. No longer looking at each other, they stared at the music on the stand in front of them. Her father and Charles began to talk again. Their topic of conversation didn't seem to have changed while Sarah and Henry had been transported elsewhere.

'What was it like in Australia?' she eventually said.

'My favourite place is the High Country.' He began to tell her about it, his words pouring out, as if they'd been waiting for her question, waiting at the ready, perfectly formed and arrayed in coherent lines like the bars of music on the sheets in front of them. He told her of the early morning frosts, of waking up to find the fences white and the sunlight slanting through the eucalypts like messages from God. He told her of the smells of the bush and the heat in the middle of the day, even in winter, and the sky a vivid blue and so deep one could drown in it. And then in the evening the fingers of shadows creeping down the hills from the Brindabella Range, and one by one the stars appearing. The sky was at first dotted with a sprinkling of them, but as the night wore on, great streamers of stars stretched across the sky, so bright you could travel by night without a lantern, even when there was no moon. If only you could see it, he concluded.

'You've made me see it, Henry.'

He flushed red again.

'And you've made me want to visit it,' she added. 'You spoke like a poet.'

He murmured something and she had to ask him to repeat it.

'I'm no poet. It's the music and you.'

Her limbs felt weak, as if her bones were dissolving. It was a shock to discover that Charles was now standing next to them and reminding Henry of their dinner engagement with his youngest brother.

'So soon!' Sarah said. 'Harriet's still not home and I'd so hoped she'd meet you today, Henry.'

'She tends to forget the time.' Charles' voice was tight.

It really is too bad of her, Sarah thought. But then she dismissed all such thoughts from her mind as Henry suggested they should walk in Hyde Park some day soon, with Miss Cameron, of course.

She spent the next few hours contemplating her own good fortune and Henry's handsome face, etched like an engraving into her mind.

PART II

London, 1891

Chapter 3

Sarah Dealt the Cards with a *Thump-thump-thump*

Never would Harriet forget the day that Sarah packed for the voyage. Sitting on her sister's bed, she watched her roll up their mother's red and orange Persian carpet and secure it with string before heaving it into her trunk. Nothing could be more final than the thudding of the rug as it landed in the bottom. When Sarah began to hum softly to herself as she opened her wardrobe, Harriet turned away and stared at the patch of grey London sky framed by the window sash.

After a few minutes, Sarah stopped humming. 'Henry and I won't be away for long,' she said.

Harriet felt as if there was a tight band around her throat.

'We're just going to look around. You know that, Hattie. It's a honeymoon, not an emigration.'

'Two years is a long time.' Harriet watched an isolated strip of dark cloud drift across the uniform grey. How strange it would be with Sarah gone, and how empty the house would seem.

'It might be for as little as eighteen months.' Harriet felt Sarah's arms envelop her. Even when blurred by anxiety, Sarah's face looked affable and her short upper lip gave the impression that she was about to smile. 'Anyway, we're not leaving until after the wedding and that's not for another week.'

Harriet, struggling to smile, let herself be pulled to her feet and whirled around in a waltz. Only when the grandfather clock in the hall struck five did Sarah let go of her. She dashed out of the door and skidded on the carpet runner on the landing, before clattering down the staircase.

Harriet followed more slowly. By the time she reached the drawing room, Sarah was at the piano picking out the tune she'd been humming earlier. Their father was sitting in his favourite armchair with a pile of galley proofs on the occasional table in front of him. Proofs that Harriet would be asked to check through later, although today she felt little inclined for that task.

A cough made her jump. Rose was standing behind her with a tray of tea-things. Harriet darted to the table and swept the papers to one side. Rose's face might have been constructed out of dough, Harriet thought, the features added like daubs of pastry; a dear piecrust countenance that she'd known all her life.

Sarah finished her piece with a flourish. 'How did you like that?' she said.

Harriet wished she were like Sarah, never frustrated with the notion that her talent might be limited, never bothered that she was good but not brilliant enough to be a concert pianist. 'Lovely,' she said. 'You played it beautifully.'

'It *is* a lovely piece, although I stumbled over it a bit.' Kneeling on the hearthrug, Sarah flexed her fingers in front of the glowing coals. 'Strange that when I first met Henry he told me that Satie was one of his favourite composers. And only the day before I'd decided to learn these new pieces.'

Satie his favourite composer indeed! He had so many favourites: Satie one day, Fauré the next. Whatever was in vogue with Sarah – and it varied week by week – was Henry's favourite too. He must have known right from the start that music was the way to Sarah's heart.

Harriet poured the tea. Several months ago, she'd thought that Sarah's interest in Henry would prove to be a short infatuation. After all, Sarah had never before come across a young man who had spent several years travelling in the colonies, and it was hardly surprising that she should initially find this fascinating.

But Harriet had been proved wrong.

It was true that Henry was also good-looking. The combination of brown eyes with fair hair was pleasing, although the blonde curls would probably have dropped out by the time he was forty, and his ears were too large and stuck out a little. Early in their acquaintance she'd made a sketch of him. It was more caricature than likeness: all big ears, big teeth and big smile. She'd burned it in her bedroom fireplace before Sarah could see it.

Shivering, Harriet tipped more coal on to the fire and began to pace up and down. Now that tea was over, her father was reading his proofs with as much concentration as if alone in his study. She thought how tired and thin he looked; there was no spare flesh to camouflage the sharpness of his high cheekbones and the pronounced bridge of his slightly asymmetric nose. Although she took after him in appearance, what was considered handsome in a man was regarded as plain in a woman.

She stopped in front of her mother's portrait that hung above the mantelpiece. Sarah's likeness to her was striking: pale oval face, deep-set blue eyes, strongly arched eyebrows and thick blonde hair. Eighteen years ago, their mother had died of pneumonia. This painting and a few early childhood memories were all Harriet had to remind her of what she looked like, and she knew that those childhood memories might be no more than the crudest representation of the truth.

'Do sit down, Hattie. You're as restless as can be. Would you like a game of cards? That'll calm you.'

Sarah dealt the cards with a *thump-thump-thump*. Harriet,

remembering the thud of the Persian rug into Sarah's trunk, reminded herself that Sarah took the rug with her wherever she travelled. Its disappearance into the bottom of the trunk had no extra significance beyond the fact that it was an essential part of Sarah's luggage. She packed it for weekend trips. She'd even taken it with her when they'd first visited Henry Vincent's parents at Stour Lodge.

That stay in Suffolk had irrevocably changed the lives of the Cameron sisters. It was during that stay that Sarah and Henry had become engaged.

After the card game was over, Harriet stood up to stretch. On the whatnot behind the door was a cut-glass vase filled with white roses and green-tinged water. She picked it up and carried it into the kitchen. Everyone loves Henry except for me, she thought, as she turned on the tap to change the water. Afterwards, she buried her nose in the brown-tinged petals of one of the blooms. Was she jealous because Henry was going to take Sarah away, or was he simply not good enough for her beautiful sister? The rose petals gave off a slight odour of decay. The trouble was that nothing lasted.

Chapter 4

The Air was Thick with Paper Ribbons

Sarah, keeping a firm hold of her father's arm, watched her husband's back as he forged along the wharf with Harriet. Everywhere there was noise, everywhere confusion. There were people shoving and pushing, people shouting, whistles blowing, seagulls screaming, tugs hooting. Luggage littering the wharf seemed to belong to no one. Around these obstacles, porters trundled trolleys laden with suitcases and trunks. Now Henry and Harriet had stopped and Henry began to talk to one of the stewards, a smartly dressed man in a brass-buttoned jacket, who was ticking passengers' names off lists. Other stewards ushered passengers and friends towards the gangway and on to the SS *Oceana*. Still more helped with cabin baggage and directed people to their accommodation.

Their cabin was far more spacious than Sarah had expected; it had a porthole and a proper bed, on which Aunt Charlotte was already sitting. Like their father, Aunt Charlotte was tall, but her frame was more generously upholstered, and there were several rolls of fat around her neck that the garnet necklace she was fiddling with did nothing to hide. On the chest of drawers next to her was a vase of yellow and white flowers bearing the message: 'With all my love.'

'Nothing but the best for the Vincents,' Harriet said.

The sourness in Harriet's voice was because she was tense, Sarah told herself. 'Why shouldn't we have a good cabin?' she said. 'It's Henry's wedding present.' She couldn't bear it if

Harriet were to be cross today and spoil everything.

'It's a beautiful cabin and you're very fortunate,' Aunt Charlotte said. She took hold of Harriet's arm while smiling at Sarah.

Too soon a bell rang. Another steward appeared at the cabin door and reminded them that it was time for the visitors to leave. 'You will write, Father,' Sarah said.

'Of course, my dear. And often.' Although he smiled, there was a tremor in his voice. She threw her arms around him and hugged him. Indistinctly she heard him say, 'If I were a young man again I'd go with you but I don't think Henry would be too keen on that.'

'We must leave,' Harriet said. 'They're calling us ashore.'

Sarah let go of her father and he began to fumble in his coat pocket, eventually pulling out a rather battered book: Charles Darwin's *The Voyage of the Beagle*. 'It belonged to your mother,' he said as he handed it to her.

Sarah felt tears pricking her eyes but she wouldn't cry. She unwound from her neck the canary yellow scarf she was wearing and gave it to Harriet. 'Wear it on the wharf,' she said. 'It will help me spot you easily.'

Afterwards, leaning on the ship's rail and peering down at the crowded pier, she feared she would never be able to distinguish the faces she was looking for. All she wanted was one more sight of them but they were nowhere to be seen in this sea of anonymous dark-coated figures. And Henry was being more hindrance than help. 'There they are,' he said half a dozen times and each time was a false sighting.

At last she made out the waving figures of Father and Harriet, standing to one side of the crowd, and behind them the nodding plume of Aunt Charlotte's hat. Harriet was wearing the bright yellow scarf. Father looked like a heron, with his long thin legs and bulky black coat that was too short. Even from this distance Sarah could see how alike their faces were, each with high cheekbones and a sharp-bridged nose.

Now Henry had spotted them, he hurled streamers in their direction. Soon the air was thick with paper ribbons connecting passengers to the crowds ashore. People began to cheer, and wave handkerchiefs and hats. A brass band struck up a polka while a tugboat gently pulled at the ship's bow. As they moved away from the dockside, the streamers tightened, and then finally broke. Sarah's last link to England was ruptured. She was alone with Henry in this mass of hopefuls travelling to a new world.

She felt that her hope and her courage were being washed away by tears that she couldn't stop, even though Henry had his arms around her, even though he was gently kissing her. Weeping, then sobbing against his chest, she wondered what on earth she was doing. She'd been mad to let Henry persuade her into a lonely two years in Australia.

Yet she would never be alone, not while she had Henry by her side. He needed her and she him. After drying her eyes on his handkerchief, she took his hand, that large comforting hand with its strong fingers. They watched the wharf and its waving figures recede, and that last spot of canary yellow vanished from sight.

An hour later they were still on deck. Only the ship's wake and Sarah's memories remained to connect her with home. The light was fading and the sky to the west was patterned in swirls of pink and grey. The salty air began to feel damp as the evening quickened. A few seagulls flew alongside them, but their cries were all but drowned out by the throbbing of the ship's engines.

The SS *Oceana* was starting to rock and Sarah hoped she wouldn't be seasick. Averting her eyes from the choppy Thames water, muddy brown and opaque, she focused on the horizon. A cool breeze had arisen but she didn't want to go inside. Going inside would mark the termination of their departure and the start of the voyage, and she wasn't yet ready for that.

Despite Henry's attempts to distract her, the image of her father and Harriet, standing side by side on the wharf, wouldn't leave her. She was abandoning that stooped old man in the shabby black greatcoat. She was abandoning her only sister, that slender young woman wrapped in the yellow scarf and skeins of brightly coloured streamers. And she was leaving behind Aunt Charlotte, who had been almost a mother to her for so many years.

It would be eighteen months to two years, Henry had said, and it seemed like an eternity to her now. Yet people did make the return journey from New South Wales. Henry had done it, and Henry had inherited money enough to pay for as many trips as they wanted, and more. Although she was nineteen now, she'd never before been on a long sea voyage; the furthest she'd been was crossing the Channel to Calais, when it had been so rough that she'd been seasick all the way there and back.

'Look at the geese,' Henry said.

They were flying overhead, fifty or so, in a low V formation. Sarah watched them wheel along the estuary, following its curves as if they were using the river as a navigational aid, until finally they were out of sight.

'Do you remember the day I proposed?' Henry said.

'Of course I do.' Sarah couldn't resist adding, 'And the day after we had our first argument.' She didn't want to look at him, not when there was a harvest moon newly visible in the eastern sky, not when she was still blaming him for the separation from her family.

'Was that an argument?' he said. 'I thought it was a discussion.'

'Perhaps you need training so you'll notice when I'm arguing with you and when we're discussing.'

'I don't think we've ever argued, Sarah, and I hope we never will.'

'It was when you suggested going to Australia for our honeymoon.'

'I thought you wanted this trip.'

'I know I agreed, but right now I'm feeling sad about leaving Gower Street and my family.'

'But didn't you find living in Gower Street claustrophobic at times? Always together in that tall terrace house. It was a narrow life.'

She felt his words relentlessly cutting into her. 'You're wrong, Henry. It wasn't narrow.'

Close to tears again, she twisted away to hide her face. 'It's true that we were educated at home. But that was so we wouldn't be tainted by what Father calls "girls' nonsense".' Her voice was nothing better than a croak and she coughed to clear her throat. She felt that she and Harriet had been lucky to be taught by tutors who were subject-experts and by their father too. He'd been a tough teacher, tolerating no lapses in logic. He'd insisted they learn to swim, and at one stage had thought that fencing would be good exercise for them until Aunt Charlotte had talked him out of it. And how proud he'd been when Sarah began to excel at the piano, and especially proud when Harriet had shown a flair for his subject, political economy, although her obsession with painting seemed to leave him unmoved.

Now her hurt feelings morphed into anger and her cheeks began to burn. Her upbringing had been broad and she wouldn't tolerate Henry's criticism of it. She'd say nothing more until he apologised.

At last, Henry spoke. 'Please look at me, Sarah.'

She turned when he put his hands on her shoulders. Gazing into his warm yellow-brown eyes, she felt her anger ebb away.

'I'm sorry I was insensitive,' he said. 'Your family's so different to mine.' He pushed a strand of hair off her forehead and took her hand. 'I know my parents love me but we're not close. We don't really know one another, even after all this time. So we don't miss one another when we're apart.'

The steamer was pitching more as it moved away from the shelter of the land, and she tightened her grip on the ship's rail and Henry's hand. A flock of seagulls was wheeling so low overhead that their shrieking could be heard above the ship's engines. Although the sun had sunk below the horizon, there was enough light remaining to see that the water appeared cleaner.

The harvest moon continued its advance up the eastern sky, ripening visibly. By the time it had evolved into a glowing red disc, she found she was beginning to look forward to the future.

Chapter 5

Measuring Out Time

Harriet stood in Sarah's old bedroom in Gower Street. Not even a week had passed since Sarah's departure but already it seemed like months. She watched raindrops lash at the windowpane and slide down the glass, soon to join the pool of grimy water on the sill. Idly she traced the path of one of the drops with her forefinger, and then another. If she concentrated hard on this task, she might forget the emptiness that she felt. The house was too silent; all she could hear was the clock in the hall, measuring out time. She breathed on the windowpane, watching it mist over, and with a handkerchief wiped away the smudge left by her fingertip. She continued polishing the entire pane until her handkerchief was black with soot. The end of an era, she thought as she folded up the handkerchief so that the dirty bits were hidden. Time to get on with her life.

She ran downstairs to the drawing room and stood in front of her mother's portrait, the painting that might almost have been of Sarah. But today she didn't feel soothed by the picture: for the first time she noticed its failings. The paint was too flat. It wasn't glowing as her memories of her mother glowed. And it was not how she remembered Sarah either. The composition was too static, too posed.

She would paint her sister as she'd seen her on their last shopping trip in Argyll Street, when Sarah had paused for a moment under an awning, waiting for Harriet to catch up. Wearing her bright red coat, Sarah had seemed almost incandescent against the dull background of the wet afternoon. Drably dressed creatures flitted around her like moths around a beacon. At that moment Harriet had seen the street as if it was a revelation; the glistening of the raindrops and the stick figures of pedestrians huddled against the drizzle. Grey on grey, everything appeared at first drained of colour. Yet the almost infinite number of greys were not grey at all but built up from the refraction of many colours.

She would try to construct this street on her canvas with colour upon colour, with small dabs of paint to create the appearance of flickering as the rain fell, drop after relentless drop; small splodges of paint that taken together would give an impression of a London street.

After this, Harriet often spent the afternoons in Sarah's room. She and Rose pushed the bed against the wall and brought down from the attic an old deal table that had been put there years ago. Harriet used this as a workbench and she set up her easel next to it. This was her first experience of having a studio of her own and it was no small consolation that it was Sarah's space that she was using.

Even with this distraction, Harriet thought several weeks later when she was painting in Sarah's room, the house still seemed too quiet without her. Without her endless piano playing, the whistling and singing and, most of all, her laughter. Harriet felt almost as if one of her senses had been turned off and she was left not quite whole.

It was true that she had become aware of noises she had never noticed before: the rumble of carriages in the street, the shouting of hawkers, and the conversation of pedestrians wafting up to the second-floor window. Yet those are the sounds of silence, she thought, this is what emptiness sounds like.

She put down her brush; she'd allowed her emotion to

obscure her judgement of the quality of the light. She'd made the sky much too dark and flat; the pavement was too grey. And nowhere did the canvas hint at the shimmering of rain.

She was at that stage when she couldn't judge whether what she'd done was – accidentally, serendipitously – a brilliant impression of an autumn London street or was instead a flat, dull painting, the clumsy rendition of an amateur.

She felt it was the latter. The trouble was she had no talent.

After cleaning her brushes, she shrugged off her smock and threw it over a chair. She had to get away from her failure. In a few days' time she would return to it. In a few days' time she would be able to face the truth.

Chapter 6

'Why Not Think of Standing for Election as a Poor Law Guardian?'

Harriet pulled her coat more closely around her. Although the afternoon was sunny, the breeze was cool. For the past few days she'd done nothing but help her father out with his papers and had barely found time to paint. Yet one couldn't be cooped up inside all the time and her friend Violet was a wonderful walking companion, the only woman in Harriet's acquaintance who walked at the same pace as her.

She watched Violet slam the front door of her Islington house behind her, blocking out the shrieks of her small children, who were overjoyed at the prospect of being left with Violet's husband and their nanny. Violet, who had a weakness for hats, adjusted her latest – a veiled confection of cherries perched on a flimsy-looking straw frame – before seizing Harriet's arm. 'It's time you embarked on your own life instead of doing your father's work,' she said. 'You could be writing your own articles, not checking his.'

Harriet braced herself for one of Violet's lectures. 'He always acknowledges my contribution. Far more generously than I deserve.' The two women marched at high speed around Thornhill Square towards the Caledonian Road. 'And I'm learning so much from him. It's like an apprenticeship.'

'You're his unpaid secretary. You've got your own life to live.'

Harriet flushed with annoyance but decided to keep her peace.

'Are you still painting?' Violet released Harriet's arm and strode ahead down a narrow, cobbled alleyway, raising her voice so that it reverberated off the high brick walls on either side.

'Yes, but not seriously.' Harriet didn't know whether to give it up or to carry on, but she mustn't tell Violet this, or reveal her doubts about her talent. Practical Violet would tolerate neither indecision nor introspection. 'I paint when I feel like it and find the time.' She glanced at her left shoe. Something that looked like orange rind had become attached to the toe. When they emerged from the alleyway, she kicked it into the gutter; she wished she could kick away her self-doubt like that. 'Father isn't demanding and I can't paint for too long at any one time.' She didn't mention the conclusion she'd reached that morning: that her painting of Sarah in Argyll Street was the best she'd ever done. And that she was looking forward to finishing the picture that Charles had commissioned.

As they walked towards Somers Town, the streets became grimier. They passed a group of small children playing with a rotten fish-head, using it as a ball. One of them picked it up to throw at a boy holding a stick of wood as a bat; he hit it high into the air and it just missed hitting Harriet. 'Good stroke!' she shouted. 'Great style!' The boy looked pleased and scampered around like a clown while the other children stared. Their feet were bare. Two little girls, identical twins, had pieces of red rag tying back their greasy fair hair. Thick yellow snot decorated their upper lips like small moustaches.

'If you want to do some other work instead,' Violet said, undeflected from her train of thought, 'why not think of standing for election as a Poor Law Guardian?'

'Thank you, but I'm much too young.' Harriet really meant that she wasn't cut out for it. Even Violet, ten years older than she, often found this work harrowing.

'You're twenty-two. And you'd have lots of backers. You've got all the right credentials.'

'Maybe I'll stand in a few years' time. At the moment Father needs me and he's likely to need me more as he gets older.'

'Or less,' said Violet. 'Don't sacrifice your life for your father.'

'It's no sacrifice. It's what I want.' Yet Harriet was no longer sure of this. Since Sarah had left, it seemed that some of her old certainties had gone as well.

'There's marriage too. What are you doing about that?'

'I don't want to marry. I've told you that before. Have you been talking to Aunt Charlotte?'

'No,' Violet said. 'I'm perfectly capable of thinking up that question on my own.'

'I don't want safety and respectability.'

'Why ever not?'

Harriet decided not to tell Violet that she found most men physically repulsive. There'd been a couple of exceptions: that male model from the life drawing class, for instance. She could never have brought him home despite Father's broad-mindedness. And she certainly wouldn't want to marry a man like that: he had a beautiful body but no conversation. She would marry no one. She said, 'I don't want to lose my freedom.'

'It's easier to be free with the right man than it is to be single,' Violet said.

'I'm not so sure. Married women fritter away their time making life pleasant for men. I don't think we evolved for that purpose alone.'

Violet laughed, but Harriet was tired of her well-meaning advice. She added firmly, 'We're all different, Violet. You're like a new convert. You want everyone to follow your beliefs.'

'I'm interfering, I know. Why do you put up with me? You

should cut me off. Do what you want.' Violet seized Harriet's arm again; she was domineering even when she was telling Harriet to stop her from being so. Harriet wasn't sure if she was holding her elbow out of affection or because she wished metaphorically to propel her along the path of her life as she was literally propelling her along the street.

'You're advising me what to do now,' she said, laughing. 'And you're steering me as if I were a boat.'

Their route took them through more squalid streets, smelling of rubbish and sewage, and lined with shabby terrace houses; blank-faced tenements with unpainted window frames and sometimes no front door. Harriet peered through these yawning openings and saw ramshackle staircases, often stripped of banisters and balustrades: probably burned for firewood like the front doors. Those of the residents who didn't look at them in open hostility begged instead; begged them for money, begged them to buy what they had to offer: *everything of the best*. Matches, pencils, useless pieces of scrap picked up from some rubbish heap or less useless objects stolen from the back of a delivery cart or lifted from someone's pocket.

'How can we run a country like this?' Violet said, when they emerged into a wider street and were able to talk again.

'That's one of the things Father writes about,' Harriet reminded Violet, in part to lessen the guilt that she often felt for having too much. 'He has ideas about how to make things better.'

'The pen is mightier than the sword and all that.' Violet's tone was dismissive. 'I never get time to read and I can't bear to sit still.'

They walked over the iron pedestrian bridge spanning Regent's Canal. It was a popular place for suicides; only the previous week two bodies had been fished out of the water. Paupers who'd tied bricks around their necks and gone under,

33

like unwanted cats or dogs. The canal water, as black as oil, was so viscous it looked almost solid. Once underneath that surface it would be hard for a body to rise again.

At last they were at Regent's Park and Harriet filled her lungs with the scent of recently mown grass. Crowds of people, drawn outdoors by the unusually sunny weather, thronged the paths; women in fine dresses and hats and even the occasional parasol; men in suits and tall hats; well-dressed, well-scrubbed children; all enjoying the almost carnival atmosphere induced by the rare coincidence of a blue sky with a Sunday in late October. And sauntering too; Harriet and Violet were forced to slow down to the leisurely pace that Harriet found exhausting. She saw a break in the crowd and accelerated, only to ram into the back of an elegantly dressed woman who had suddenly stopped in front of her. She felt her legs slam into the light timber frame of the woman's bustle and rubbed at her thighs while both women apologised profusely.

'Stupid fashion,' Violet said once they were out of earshot. 'But I suppose no more stupid than my hat.' She patted at the cherries, as if to reassure herself that they were still there, before returning to her account of her work. They were still discussing this when they reached the Euston Square entrance to the Underground Railway where they were to part.

'Do let me know if you change your mind about standing for the election,' Violet said as they came to a halt. 'It would be wonderful to work together.' She tried to kiss Harriet but their hats were so wide brimmed that she succeeded merely in kissing the air.

Harriet gave her a hug instead, and in so doing knocked her hat slightly awry. Its rakish angle suited her. A middle-aged man coming up the stairs, distracted by the sight of Violet's lovely face, tripped on the top step and bumped into Harriet. Although he *regretted it deeply*, his words were addressed to

Violet rather than to Harriet, as if she were one of Violet's accessories like an umbrella or a pet poodle.

Violet seemed to feel this more keenly than Harriet. 'It's my friend to whom you should apologise,' she said. She smiled at the man, the sweetness of her expression tempering the sharpness of her words as she added, 'Please don't treat her as if she were invisible.'

Then she straightened her hat and pattered down the stairs, cutting a swathe through the ascending throng. Together with the man who had bumped into her, Harriet watched Violet in admiration until she was out of sight.

Chapter 7

Yellow Silk Slippers and Sunlight

It was stupid to wonder if Charles Barclay mightn't turn up at the time they'd agreed upon. In all the years Harriet had known him he'd never been unpunctual. Not long before he was due to arrive, she set up, on an easel in her father's study, the painting he'd commissioned from her several months before.

This was her second commission. Her first was for Aunt Charlotte, who had initially wanted a portrait of her beloved spaniel. Harriet had eventually persuaded her to settle for a painting of an interior in which her spaniel was seated on a red velvet armchair looking quite anthropomorphic; indeed that had been the point. Charles had been present when Aunt Charlotte had collected her painting and had appeared captivated by either the painting or the spaniel. It was several months after this that he'd placed his commission. A view from the house in which his friend and mentor James Cameron lived and wrote, he'd said. Not of her father but of what her father saw when he looked over the gardens; what visitors to the house saw when they sat in the drawing room. A symbol, Harriet had concluded. Inside looking out. The interior world and the outside stimulation.

After Rose let Charles into the house, Harriet took him into the study, where a coal fire was burning in the grate. The painting was shrouded in a white cloth over which firelight fluttered. She hesitated, not wanting to remove the cover. The scent of witch hazel, in a vase on the desk, filled the air and overpowered the usual musty smell of the books in the cases occupying all the available wall space. The curtains hadn't yet been drawn over the window and a half moon was visible through the top sash. Completely framed in one of the panes, it looked almost as if it were stuck there, immovable.

Glancing at Charles, she saw he was jiggling his thick black eyebrows, raising first one and then the other in that comical fashion that had always made her laugh when she was a child. But she was a child no longer, and although she recognised his intention was to make her relax, she felt a heightened apprehension. She stood facing him so she could watch his expression. Poker-faced he undoubtedly was when it came to his own feelings, but maybe she would observe him showing some emotion; disappointment maybe or, if she were lucky, satisfaction. His opinion mattered to her; for years he'd been a part of their lives, almost a part of their family, more uncle than older brother.

'It's not as I intended,' she said, whipping the cloth off the painting. 'Not at all.'

After a moment, Charles said, 'I love it. You've framed it perfectly by including the window frame. You've made it clear it's the view from James Cameron's drawing room and not just a view of the gardens.'

Harriet felt her spirits lift. Charles liked the painting; perhaps he'd understood what she was trying to convey. Yet suddenly his expression changed and she was shocked by what she saw. He was showing emotion: he was showing affection but not of an avuncular or brotherly kind. He bent towards her. Surely he wasn't going to try to kiss her. She stepped back and busied herself folding up the cloth that had covered the painting, into smaller and smaller squares, anything to avoid that needy look in his eyes.

'Let me paint you another view of the gardens.' She wanted to distract him, wanted to apologise, although she was unsure for what. 'From Father's study this time. That's the outlook we should have chosen first.' She laughed and realised her laughter sounded like that of Aunt Charlotte when she was unamused; tinkling social laughter, not spontaneous.

She went to the window. Putting her hand on a pane of glass, she felt its coldness. Charles moved to her side. They stood together, looking out at the view. The half-moon had shifted slightly and illuminated the garden and cast deep shadows on the unkempt lawn. Harriet shivered and closed the curtains, shutting off the view, closing off what had happened.

To end the silence, she seized on the first thing that came into her mind. 'I should like to travel,' she said. 'On my own, dressed as a man. I should make a handsome man, don't you think?'

'You must dress as you wish. But you should realise that you're now sounding just like Mrs Smythe.'

She knew that Charles was really saying that she was being silly.

'That's not kind to Mrs Smythe,' she told him. She thought of Mrs Smythe and her volumes of exquisitely sensitive poetry, published under the pseudonym of John George, the names of her two boys. Mrs Smythe wasn't silly but she tried to conceal her identity behind a carapace of youthful playfulness. Harriet knew that Charles liked her poetry but this was the first time he'd revealed his opinion of her frivolity. It was also the first time he'd revealed he had emotions. He must be very provoked indeed.

She had always thought of him as rationality personified.

* * *

38

Harriet washed her face in the basin in her bedroom, and removed the hairpins restraining her hair. In the dressing-table mirror she watched her reflection as her hair fell across her cheeks like smooth brown curtains. She bent forward so her hair completely concealed her face and then flicked it back.

What had happened with Charles that afternoon was bothering her still. He had become overfond of her, the sort of attachment she thought she'd never inspire. Of course, she was fond of him too; for years she'd held him in the highest regard. When she was small, he'd been her father's pupil at Oxford and a regular visitor to their house. Later he took a civil service job in the Colonial Office. Some years afterwards, when Father had become a professor of moral philosophy at University College in London, Charles had continued visiting the house in Gower Street.

She wondered if her affection for him could ever develop into something stronger. She doubted it. This was not through any flaw in Charles' character: he was a good man, an intelligent man. It was simply that she didn't want love of that kind. It was too constraining.

But she would hate any misunderstanding to jeopardise their friendship. Perhaps she'd been mistaken when she thought Charles was about to kiss her. Yes, that must be it: she'd been mistaken. He'd simply been leaning forward to get a better look at the painting. No wonder he'd appeared perplexed by her behaviour. Perhaps he was afterwards mortified to think she'd misinterpreted his action, that simple inclination towards her.

Yet he'd been too close, his lips barely a couple of inches from her own, until she'd moved away. And there was his expression too; was that what desire looked like? Or perhaps it wasn't desire at all but need, as she'd thought at the time. If only she had more experience, or someone with whom she could talk over such things. A mother would surely notice, as would Sarah. But Sarah had gone and she certainly couldn't talk over such matters with Father, nor did she want to with Aunt Charlotte or with Violet.

On the dressing-table top was the old ivory-backed hairbrush that used to be her mother's. She picked it up and began to brush her hair, sweeping away her cares, in 200 long smooth strokes, until her scalp was tingling. Though it was pointless yearning for her mother, logic couldn't banish those memories that had come to her more frequently since Sarah had left. She remembered her mother as a lively loving person. But perhaps her memories might be no more than a crude caricature of the truth. Or worse, even a misrepresentation of the truth.

No, surely she was wrong. The last memory of her mother was unchanged, it was unchanging, a constant in her life. The sunlight, slanting across the room, illuminated her mother, who was lying in bed, laughing. Four-year-old Harriet crawled across the floorboards to the Persian rug to retrieve the decapitated doll's head that had landed there. Her carefully choreographed puppet show wasn't going to plan. She hadn't intended that the main character should literally lose her head in mid-scene, but her mother was enjoying the diversion so much that Harriet abandoned her original plan and began to improvise. She pretended that her crawling across the floor was an intended part of the play, that she was actress as well as puppeteer. While her mother clapped, she crouched down again out of sight at the end of her bed and restored the doll's head to its torso before resuming the scene. The more her mother laughed, the more improvisations Harriet introduced. She lifted the dolls up and down and had them turn up in surprising parts of the bed, now one side, and now another, the slanting rays of the sun illuminating the dolls like spotlights in a theatre. Her perspective of the room was child's-eye. She saw the detail of the floorboards, the enormous fireplace, and even some balls of dust under the bed, next to which her mother's yellow silk slippers were neatly lined up, taking the shape of two disembodied feet.

The twenty-two-year-old Harriet felt soothed by this memory. And she still had those slippers. She took them out of the drawer where she kept them and carefully removed the layers of tissue paper wrapping. Putting one hand inside each slipper, she held them up to the light. For a moment she felt comforted by them, comforted by the memory of yellow silk slippers and sunlight, her last recollection of her mother.

Then her vision blurred. Yellow silk slippers and sunlight were all very well. But with Sarah gone, she had no one left to talk to about the things that mattered. Irritably she wiped her eyes. She was strong, and would weep for no one, least of all for herself.

Chapter 8

'I'd Put Money on Rationality Any Day'

It was early December before Harriet received a letter from Sarah. There were a couple of postcards from Aden and Colombo, and Sarah telegraphed as soon as she and Henry arrived in Sydney. Yet you didn't learn much from a telegram. Especially one that simply stated, 'ARRIVED SAFELY STUNNING SCENERY BOTH WELL LETTER FOLLOWS LOVE SARAH.' Even the most imaginative mind could only guess at the nature of the stunning scenery and wait with growing impatience for the letter.

At last it arrived. On a cold bleak Monday morning, Rose deposited the morning post on the breakfast table next to Harriet's plate and stood there, breathing heavily. Harriet glanced at the pile of letters, on the top of which lay an envelope embellished with Sarah's neat copperplate writing.

'It's come,' said Rose and coughed.

'I'll read you the news later,' said Harriet. 'As soon as breakfast's over.' She shuffled through the pile of letters to see if her father had also received one from Sarah. There was another slimmer envelope addressed to him and she put it next to his plate. Then she sliced open the top of her envelope and pulled out the closely written sheets.

Dearest Harriet,
     You'll be wondering about us, so I'm sending this to you right away, even though it's a rather brief affair.

We've been in Sydney for a week and have been busy every day. To begin with, we stayed with the Arnotts, who were so kind to Henry when he was here before. They've been kind to me too, treating me as if I'm a member of their large family. Before we'd even arrived here, Mrs Arnott went to the trouble of finding several possible places for us to rent.

Last week we visited all of these and have now taken the loveliest rooms in a house right next to the harbour. We fell asleep last night to the sound of water lapping against the sandstone shelf not far from our window and in the morning we awoke to hear magpies carolling. Then we heard the strangest sound, like a rusty door creaking, and Henry told me it was probably a gang-gang cockatoo, a rare sight even in Sydney.

You would love the light here. Clear and bright, it makes the eucalyptus leaves shimmer in the early mornings and evenings, although in the middle of the day – or when the sky is overcast – they can look a rather drab olive-green. The harbour too sparkles and I'm sure, if you were here, you'd want to paint the light and the waves, and become frustrated immediately, because even you can't convert paint into pure light, although you're so talented!

The voyage out seemed to go on for ever, to begin with. I was seasick for the first week and although Henry was most attentive, I missed you and Rose terribly. Then I rallied and spent much of my time on deck with Henry, at first keeping my eyes firmly fixed on the horizon until I was confident that the seasickness was a thing of the past, and then we began to read those books you thoughtfully provided before we embarked.

Henry and I took turns reading to each other. He has such a lovely voice and reads so expressively, and we passed many happy hours that way. I have to confess, however, that we haven't yet finished Charles Darwin's *The Voyage of the Beagle*, although we read a little bit of it each day while we were at sea.

We made several friends on the ship but were glad on the whole to be left alone to get to know each other more, and how happy we are, although we're so far away from family and friends. Henry has decided to work as a stock and station agent for a while. Mr Arnott has offered him employment, and he has accepted. He'll start next week. Mr Arnott's office is in an old sandstone building in Sussex Streets, not far from the wharves at Darling Harbour, a useful location because most of the produce is transported by ship. We visited the office this morning, and it seemed delightful, although very messy with paperwork everywhere, not to mention samples of grain and corn of various types that are quite foreign to me. I fear this work will involve much travelling on Henry's part, which will mean absences from home (I am already calling these rooms home, although I haven't yet had time to unpack all our things).

The Arnotts held a party in our honour four days after we got here. I'm writing separately to Aunt Charlotte to tell her of the success of my blue silk dress, for I don't want to bore you with details of the impression created by her good taste. Indeed, were I to tell you, I fear your prejudices about the divisive nature of fashion might be reinforced, for it became clear during the evening that the blue silk excited more envy than admiration from some of the younger women I met. However, since I intend to wear the same outfit to all possible events in future – a piece of information I shan't be revealing to Aunt Charlotte – I'm sure that habit will breed indifference – if not contempt. After that I'll wear some of the other outfits, but by then they will be so out of date that pity will come my way.

Fortunately, Henry didn't notice any of these niceties and we were united in our warm appreciation of the Arnotts for their kindness in every detail. I have never met such friendly and generous people; it must be something to do with the climate here that makes these people so.

Last week we had a most enjoyable evening dining with Father's old friends Professor and Mrs Morgan at their house near Mosman Bay. You would remember them from when we lived in Oxford, which the delightful Mrs Morgan talks of a lot, although she's glad they emigrated. The good professor is shielded from the harsher realities of life by his wife and his great intellect. (Is this harsh? Perhaps people say of me that I'm protected by you and Father and Henry and my own musical fantasies!) Mrs Morgan is one of the kindest people I've ever come across. Once she learned where Henry and I met, she invited us to accompany her to the next meeting of the local equivalent of the Women's Franchise League. I didn't have the heart to tell her what you, my beloved sister, know – that Henry was at that WFL meeting entirely by accident. Mrs M certainly makes me feel connected, and I'm more than happy for this connection to extend to the entire WFL membership, whose cause is undeniably of the greatest importance.

There are just two things that mar my happiness –

the absence of my family and the lack of a piano. While the latter can be easily fixed (and indeed a piano will be arriving next week), the former can't, unless you can be persuaded to pack your bags and come to see us in this new city. A city that seems, even after over a century since settlement, to be sitting precariously on the edge of this vast continent whose interior is, according to the books you gave us, still so little understood.

I must finish – the mail will be collected in two hours and I have yet to write to Father and Aunt Charlotte. I promise I'll write again soon. I'm looking forward so much to hearing from you and I hope a letter will be arriving any day, although it would be unreasonable to have expected correspondence to have got here ahead of us! It seems so long, dearest Hattie, since I last heard from you.

With all my love,
Sarah

Harriet read the letter through twice. Her immediate desire was to dash off a reply but she felt so cold that she dragged her chair closer to the coal fire and huddled over it while imagining Sarah living by the water in a country where winter was summer. Shutting her eyes, she visualised herself sitting in Sydney on a sandstone ledge by the harbour, watching triangles of light flicker off the surface of the sea below an enamelled blue sky. Try as she might she couldn't conjure Henry into this little fantasy, though it was easy to picture Sarah inside the stone house a few yards away from the water's edge.

Distracted by an unexpected sound, Harriet opened her eyes and was surprised to see Charles Barclay smiling down at her and asking how she was.

'Perfectly well,' she said, struggling with difficulty out of her reverie, or perhaps it was a dream, and noting with surprise that she was still in Gower Street. She offered Charles a chair and some tea. Afterwards she read him selected passages from Sarah's letter.

'She sounds very happy.' Charles stared at the coals in the grate, as if they were the reason for his visit.

Harriet felt she was a poor hostess this morning, transported so suddenly from Sydney where she'd been on the verge of discovering the meaning of light on water. 'I expect Father will be down shortly,' she said at last, to break the silence.

'It's you I've come to see, Harriet.'

She folded up the pages of Sarah's letter while waiting for Charles to begin. Although not displeased to see him, she wished he hadn't arrived quite so early. Since he was still staring at the fire, she was moved to drawl, in an imitation of an affected mutual acquaintance, 'I never talk about Father's work until at least half an hour after breakfast. It does upset my digestion so.'

Charles smiled. 'I'll remember that in future, but I haven't come to talk about work.'

She rang for fresh tea. Sarah's letter had made her feel more reconciled to the prospect of crouching over a coal fire on a bleak London day. They talked about the weather until Rose brought in the teapot. As Harriet passed Charles a fresh cup, he said casually, 'I do hope you might consider marrying me, Harriet.'

She was too astonished to do any more than stare, and certainly too astonished to relinquish her hold of Charles' saucer. For a long moment they each had hold of it, one on each side. A symbolic moment, Harriet thought, and at once let go, so suddenly that Charles almost spilt the tea although he managed to juggle the cup and saucer so that only a small amount of liquid collected in the saucer.

Harriet took a deep breath. She glanced at Charles' hand holding the teacup and then at his thin brown wrist emerging from the white cuff of his shirt. There was something vulnerable about the slenderness of his wrist, but she recoiled from the sight of the black hairs growing there. For an instant – for even less than an instant – she had been tempted to reach out and touch him. She must avoid hurting Charles; she must reply gently and at once.

'Thank you for doing me the honour of making this proposal.' Her words were too formal but she couldn't think of how else to reply. She continued, faltering now, 'You know I hold you in the greatest regard. You've been part of our lives for so many years and I feel you're part of the family. But Charles, I'm so very sorry, I'm unable to accept.' Despite her good intentions, she felt her words had emerged cold and sharp. They might be arrows so wounded did he look.

'You could never love me?'

It was a moment before Harriet realised this was a question rather than a statement and she struggled to find the words to express how she felt. She did love Charles in a fashion but she didn't want any of the trappings of love or marriage on the voyage she was beginning. Quite what she would do with her life she still had little idea, but she wanted to travel through it alone.

'Romantic love is responsible for much unhappiness,' Charles said, almost as if he were changing the subject and starting one of his abstract discussions. 'It's a bit like religion, it clouds the judgement. I'd put money on rationality any day in a race between reason and romance.'

Harriet couldn't tell if he were right or wrong. She knew that when she painted she thought logically, rationally, beforehand about what she wanted to do; but once she started applying the paint, intellect vanished, and passion – or perhaps it was

48

intuition – took over. Yet romance was neither of those things; it had more to do with fantasy.

'Maybe you're looking for romantic love and you don't feel that way about me.'

Charles was generous almost to a fault. He was offering her a way out but she wouldn't take it. 'That's not the point,' she said. 'You know I regard you with the greatest affection.' It would be misleading to tell him that the affection she felt for him was love. 'I need freedom and marriage wouldn't suit me. I'm going to remain single all my life.' Only after speaking these words did she wonder if she were happy at this prospect. Wouldn't it be better to share her journey with someone she loved? Sarah's departure – her absence – had made her realise how daunting loneliness could be.

The fire sputtered and a lump of coal fell to the front of the grate. Charles pushed it back with the poker while Harriet stared at the blue and orange flames. Eventually he said quietly, 'There are other ways of preserving female independence. For example, we could sign a special marriage contract. Or we could even live together, with my assignment to you of additional rights.'

His brown eyes were so dark that it was almost impossible to distinguish pupil from iris. He would make a good husband if she were looking for one, but she wasn't. She said, 'You're so thoughtful, Charles. But I can't do that. I want to make my own way through life.' Yet this wasn't right either. She didn't want to give up working with Father, helping Father, and she'd always view this as privilege rather than a burden.

Despite her refusal of Charles' proposal, the exposed blue vein on the underside of his wrist moved her. She might have touched this as a penance for hurting him if she hadn't been distracted by a sudden draught. Her father was standing in the dining-room doorway, silhouetted against the bright light from the hall.

'Good morning, Father,' she said, struggling to disguise her relief. 'Charles and I have been discussing all manner of things. And look, we have letters from Sarah at last!'

Her father's face lit up and he seemed ten years younger. She poured tea for him. 'More tea, Charles?'

'Thank you, Harriet.' Charles' hand was steady as he held out his cup. Perhaps he had anticipated her refusal before making the proposal of marriage. Having known her opinions for years, he surely couldn't have expected that she'd accept. Not only had his declaration surprised her, it also brought home to her that she really had little idea what lay behind his phlegmatic façade. For just a few moments the mask had slipped but now it was firmly back in place.

Sipping her tea, she listened to her father engage Charles in a debate about the coupling of liberal reforms with Irish home rule. Unusually, she didn't wish to participate in the ebb and flow of their conversation. She had too much to think of, but it was no longer Charles' proposal that preoccupied her. Instead she thought of Sarah's letter.

A vision came to her of her own future and it didn't include Charles. She saw it as iridescent, patterned with light and shade, and punctuated with form and colour. Converting drabness to colour and light: that would be her mission.

PART III

London and Sydney, 1892

Chapter 9

The Woman's Costume Looked More Like a Bag than a Dress

Sitting on a bench in Sydney's Botanical Gardens, Sarah stared at the patch of scuffed lawn in front of her. Better to focus on the grass than on the harbour and all that water separating her from Henry. Ten long days since she'd seen him off on the steamer, and it might be weeks before she saw him again.

Only when the creeping fingers of shadows touched her bench did she become aware of the passing of the afternoon. A westerly breeze had arisen and little waves of harbour water were arguing with the incoming tide. A ferry steamed towards Mosman, its plume of smoke tinted orange and lavender by the sinking sun.

After walking to the water's edge, she rested her elbows on the sandstone balustrade and listened to the slip-slap of waves on the wall, to the mournful cries of the seagulls wheeling around the rocks on the point, and to the distant hoot of a tug conducting a ship away from one of the wharves at Darling Harbour.

Presently she pulled from the pocket of her jacket a wad of rather crumpled paper and began to reread Henry's letter. 'It could be anything from three to four weeks before I get back,' he'd written; 'you must appreciate that the purchase of millet for the Arnott stock and station business is more time-consuming than I'd imagined, for so much depends on connections of one sort or another.'

Three weeks seemed like an eternity to Sarah, waiting in this city that was not her home for her life to begin again. Without Henry, she felt as if a part of her had been amputated. In his letter he upbraided her for not writing to him, making her misery even worse. For she'd written her first letter to him the day after he left and had walked all the way into town to the GPO to post it, to speed the progress of the letter as well as the passage of that first lonely afternoon.

Henry had caught a steamer up the coast to Brisbane and had travelled overland to Gympie. He'd waited there two extra days in the hope that he might receive some word from Sarah but none had come, so he was forced to travel on. He hadn't actually put in writing that he was feeling lonely and unloved. Yet Sarah knew him well enough to read the hidden message. She gave the stone seawall a little kick with her boot, and wondered how Henry could be so obtuse as to think she wouldn't have written, to think she was not missing him as much as he missed her. But by now he surely would have received her letter, her letters, for she'd written every second day since he left.

It was harsh of Henry not to understand that it was as bad, if not worse to be left behind. She felt as if she were condemned to an inactivity that was exacerbated by the isolation of this place. The tyranny of distance was how Mrs Morgan had described it and that was what she was suffering now. Distance from Henry, distance from Harriet and her father, and from dear Rose and Aunt Charlotte too.

She missed them so terribly, and that was why she'd made such a fool of herself at the Barracloughs' dinner party the previous Saturday.

* * *

Determined that she shouldn't be left alone while Henry was away, kind Mr and Mrs Arnott had conducted her to Potts Point. The Barracloughs' garden was dense with exotic semi-tropical plants. The curtains hadn't been drawn across the tall French windows facing on to the wide front verandah of the house. From each window a shaft of golden light lit up the lawn, which formed a narrow terrace before the garden rose steeply to the street.

Sarah's exposure that night – for that was how she thought of it now – didn't occur until after dinner. Several young women had been induced to play the piano that occupied one corner of the opulent – if not quite tasteless – drawing room of this Potts Point mansion. The perfectly tuned piano had a resonance that wasn't spoilt by the proficient, if rather mechanical, execution of the women induced to perform. Afterwards Mrs Arnott, almost as proud of Sarah's accomplishments as she was of her own children's, had insisted that Sarah play.

Although Sarah had at first refused, the piano was so much better than the upright in their lodgings that she soon decided to seize the opportunity. Sitting on the stool, she spread her fingers across the piano keys, while she stared for a moment through the French doors. The garden was brightly illuminated by the marbled full moon and several shafts of light from the drawing-room chandeliers. The moonlight reminded her of Henry's tales of the outback, and she elected to play the Consolation No. 3 by Liszt that she'd started to learn not long before Henry had set off on his trip to Queensland.

She began to perform, quietly at first, as she experienced the sensation of the worn keys and the flow of sound around her; and then she was reminded so much of Henry that she poured into her interpretation all her commitment to him. The narrative of the music became tied up with her own story of passion, in which she was able to ignore her not infrequent mistakes because of the grander aspects of the tale. Then her interpretation changed, and she moved into a quieter passage of such gentle reflection that it might almost be mistaken for grief. Perhaps that was what it was, for she felt the tears coursing down her face: her grief at Henry's absence, her longing to see her family and her home, her isolation and loneliness in this roomful of strangers who – she felt sure – were judging her for this want of self-control, which culminated at last in her sobbing aloud and being unable to finish the piece.

Mrs Arnott was quick to take charge. She extricated, from somewhere about her person, a bottle of smelling salts and waved it under Sarah's nose. 'It's the heat, dear,' she said, apparently clutching at the first excuse that came into her head, inappropriate though it was on such a mild evening. Her kindliness made Sarah weep all the more. 'Sniff, Sarah,' Mrs Arnott exhorted and thrust the bottle closer to Sarah's nostrils so that the ammoniacal fumes were impossible to avoid.

The other middle-aged women began crowding around, competing with one another in their ministrations and in their hypotheses as to what could cause her lapse. Perhaps she wasn't yet used to Sydney's weather, or the stuffiness of the room, or conceivably she was getting a cold or – and at last one of them was brave enough to suggest it – maybe dear Sarah was in the family way. Sarah felt too tired to deny anything and, although she was sure that the last explanation wasn't possible, she didn't want to announce this to the company at large. Let them think what they wanted so long as she didn't have to speak; she felt too tired, too drained.

Not long afterwards, Mr Arnott ordered the carriage to take her home. As the party made their farewells, Sarah was aware of how much they loved her after her exposure. The suspicion – or even active dislike – that she'd felt at first had now dissipated. They loved her because she was weak, because she needed protection. However, she suspected that Maisie Cunningham would never forgive the success of her blue silk dress.

* * *

Sarah shrugged away memories of that evening as she leaned on the harbour wall and watched the setting sun cast a ladder of reflections on the darkening water. After pulling on her gloves, she smoothed down the soft leather and smiled to herself. Something good would come out of Henry's absence, for this afternoon she'd come to a decision. Never again would she allow Henry to go away for such a long time. In the future she would accompany him. They had money enough and she wouldn't have to sit around Sydney waiting for his return.

At this moment she realised the Botanical Gardens were empty. The sun set so quickly here and it would soon be dark. The last thing she wanted was to be anywhere near the Domain at night. It was dangerous, Mr Arnott had said, full of desperate and homeless people. Only yesterday she'd read of someone being murdered there. She should hurry away, to the Exhibition Gates on the Macquarie Street side of the gardens.

Her route took her under some dense, spreading trees, whose foliage was made darker by the fruit bats. There was not quite enough light to allow her to make out the colour of their fur, although she knew from previous sightings that they were almost gingery. The colony was starting to break up to begin their nocturnal activities; several creatures swooped down towards her. She had no idea if they were dangerous and wouldn't wait to find out. Propelled by fear, she flew up the path, at last arriving breathless at the gates.

They were locked. The large bolt was fastened by a padlock the size of her hand. With sweating hands, she shook the heavy bars of the gate. The bolt rattled against the uprights. Her heart quickened as panic gripped her. The gates were cast iron and at least ten feet high at their lowest point. The fence around the gardens was much lower; it couldn't be any higher than five or six feet but it would be impossible to climb over. It was constructed from vertical, cast iron railings, with no intermediate bar that might form a foothold, and each upright was crowned with a sharp point, like a palisade.

Yet if she couldn't escape the gardens, others couldn't enter them either. She mustn't lose her nerve. The worst that could possibly happen was that she might have to spend the night here. But the gardens could be full of desperate people who wanted to be locked in, who wanted a secure place to spend the night, who wanted the contents of her bag. And who might get hold of it by banging her on the head or sticking a knife between her ribs.

She had to try to get out.

Quickly she ran her hand over the solid sandstone wall that curved up, from the top of the iron fence, to the massive gateposts. Although it was impossible to see clearly in the dark, she could feel narrow joints in the ashlar. They might support her but climbing up would be a precarious operation since she couldn't see where the joints were. The gates were a possibility: she'd have to climb over them. There were many toeholds in their intricate pattern that she might be able to use. First, she'd have to remove her tightly fitting jacket or else she'd split it with the exertion of climbing the gate, or even just with lifting up her arms. She experimented with raising her arms and felt the constriction of the fabric around her shoulders and back, and the seam in one armpit creaked slightly. There was her handbag too, of almost carpet-bag construction. She couldn't throw this over the fence ahead of her; the fence was too high, the bag too heavy. Nor could she clamber up the gate holding it; it was too bulky. She put the bag down on the pavement and took off her jacket while considering the remaining option – removing her bootlaces and using these to tie her bag to her shoulders, knapsack fashion.

As she began to unfasten a boot, she heard a sound behind her. Too frightened to move, she waited for the blow.

'Want a hand with them things?' said a soft voice.

Sarah turned, startled. A sliver of moon, veiled in a shred of cloud, cast little light, and at first she couldn't make out the source of the voice. Then she saw a gleam from dark skin and distinguished the features of an Aboriginal woman standing perhaps two paces behind her. 'We're locked in,' she said, her words sounding strangled as she stepped back a pace.

'I'll give yer a leg up. You climb them rungs and I'll hand yer bag up.' The stranger's voice was friendly.

Sarah wondered if she could trust her to relinquish the bag once she was on the top of the gate. The woman could easily run off with it then. To delay making a decision, she said, 'How will I get it down the other side?'

The woman laughed. 'Toss it down when yer get to the top.'

'How will you get over?'

'I won't.'

'You'll stay here all night?'

'Yee'mm,' the woman said, and laughed.

'It's getting cold.' Sarah looked at the stranger at the moment that the moon cast aside its veil of cloud; there was now no disguising the fact that the woman's costume looked more like a bag than a dress. 'And your dress is so thin,' she added, and at once regretted that her words sounded critical.

The woman took no offence. 'I'd rather be in than out. I sometimes stay if I don't leave enough time to get back to La Perouse.'

Sarah had heard of the reserve at La Perouse but had never met anyone from there; indeed had never before met an Aborigine either, in spite of the fact that she'd been in Sydney for five months. Although consumed with curiosity she didn't want to ask any questions, nor did she want to be questioned either. They were both illegals in the gardens after dark, but Sarah had read enough reports in the *Herald* to know that, if they were apprehended, this woman would be treated with less courtesy than she would.

I'll trust her with my bag, she thought. She had no other alternative.

The woman stood next to the smaller of the gates. She began to giggle as she linked her hands together to form a stirrup, into which Sarah stepped, resting her hands lightly on the woman's shoulders. From here it was an easy stretch to the intermediate bar of the gate, and then a second to the top. At this point Sarah's boot got caught in the hem of her skirt and she almost toppled back down again. The woman gave her a hard shove and Sarah regained her grip on the top of the gate, while the woman started laughing. Sarah teetered at the top, finally regaining her equilibrium.

Clutching the top of the gate with one hand, she looked down. The woman had gone and so too had her bag. She'd been such a fool; in the bag were her money, door keys and return tram ticket. She would have to walk home now.

'Here!' said a voice from the other direction. And there was the woman holding up her bag. With relief Sarah took it and tossed it on to the pavement of deserted Macquarie Street, where it landed with a resounding thump.

'Scarf now,' said the woman, reminding Sarah of what she had forgotten.

Afterwards Sarah swung both feet on to the street side of the gate and slid down, slightly tearing the fabric of her blouse in the process. When she was standing on the pavement, she peered through the bars of the gate for her helper, to whom she'd decided to offer her scarf for some warmth for the night.

But the woman had gone.

'Thank you,' Sarah called out. 'Thank you!'

There was no one to be seen. At this moment Sarah remembered her jacket. The woman was welcome to it, she thought, and wished she'd offered it before it was taken. So deserted did the gardens now appear, she might almost have imagined the incident, although without her jacket she was beginning to feel cold. This worried her less than being alone in a deserted Sydney street on a Sunday evening. Shivering, she began to hurry up Macquarie Street towards the Edgecliff tramline. After a few hundred yards she started to hum as she skipped along the street and stopped only when she joined the crowd of people waiting at the tram stop.

Chapter 10

Before We Settle Down on Our Own Place

The wharf was damp and the humid air tasted salty on Sarah's lips. While she waited, she imagined Henry bracing himself on the ship's rail. He would be looking out for Darling Harbour wharf, just as she was looking out for the steamer, although with the rational part of her mind she knew that she shouldn't bother yet, for there was still some time to go before it was due to arrive. She and Henry were like two distinct strands of rope that some unstoppable force was pulling together into an entwined and stronger whole. Like that cable coiled up on the wharf, thicker than her arm.

When at last she saw the steamer, her heart began to flail against her ribcage like a heavy cockatoo about to launch into flight. Struggling to calm herself with deep breathing, she couldn't suppress her feet. As if worked on by a puppeteer, they began a little jig, her new boots tapping out a rhythm on the weathered planks of the wharf.

But the steamer was approaching so slowly and where was Henry? Eventually she spotted him leaning over the ship's rail, waving a red handkerchief. Almost here, almost home; her feet continued to tap and she laughed out loud.

'I've missed you so much, Sarah,' Henry said when he was safely on shore and squeezing the air out of her lungs in a great bear-hug.

'And I you. I'm not going to ever let you go away again for so long.' She was about to tell him more when a discreet cough distracted her attention. An elderly man and woman, who seemed to know Henry, stood next to them.

'You dropped these.' The kindly faced woman handed Henry a packet of letters tied up with a blue ribbon. 'A steward found them and asked us to give them to you.'

Sarah recognised them at once: her letters and her hair ribbon.

'I was reading them on deck.' Henry's golden skin was slightly flushed and Sarah realised he was blushing.

She took his free hand and squeezed it. 'I have your letters too, Henry. In my bag.'

From Henry's introduction, she learned that the elderly man was a grazier from central Queensland. 'I always get lost in Sydney,' he said, squinting at the city from under his broad-brimmed felt hat. 'It looks so easy from the water but once on dry land I'm bushed.'

'It's very simple when you know,' said his wife.

'It helps that you grew up in Sydney,' the grazier said. 'Visitors like me find it confusing.'

Sarah sympathised with him; at first she too had got bushed in Sydney. If Henry and the grazier hadn't embarked on a lengthy discussion, she might have explained that the geography of Sydney could be understood by a knowledge of the waterways, the fingers of rivers cutting through the surrounding land, the inflow of streams and creeks that determined the configuration of the town and the serried ranks of houses creeping ever outwards through the surrounding bush-land.

Several words in the conversation now caught her attention: cattle drives and the Barkly Tablelands. Henry exclaimed, 'I'd love to travel to the Barkly Tablelands!'

She watched him carefully as he hung, almost open-mouthed, on every word the grazier uttered. He was talking of a trip he'd been on many years earlier, as a young man, driving cattle from Cloncurry through the Barkly Tablelands and eventually to a new cattle station on the Roper River. What an adventure that had been. He could see why some men never wanted to leave. The country was beautiful though you wouldn't want to be there in a drought. 'The isolation gets to you,' the grazier concluded. 'You either hate it or love it; you never feel indifferent. I love it, though it's a bloody lawless country.' Here the grazier apologised to Sarah and his wife.

His wife nodded pleasantly, if slightly absently. Although she was probably used to this little exchange, her husband waited for her absolution before continuing. 'A lawless country,' he repeated, 'With hardly any police and some of them crooked, and the black feller and the white feller not always getting on. You can see why the black fellers get upset. The stock affects their tucker and drives out the wallabies, so who can blame the Abos if they kill a steer or two? But some white blokes don't understand this and shoot the blacks. I've heard some terrible tales, and the murderers never brought to justice either. Talk about one law for the rich and one for the poor in the cities! Out west there's almost no law. What governs men is just what's in their heads.'

'Good or evil,' his wife said.

'That's about the long and the short of it,' the grazier added, nodding sagely.

'Before we settle down on our own place,' Henry said, 'I wouldn't mind seeing a bit more of the country.'

Although Sarah kept her expression tranquil, she vented her irritation with a quick tap-tap-tap on the jetty with her left foot. *Before we settle down on our own place*; she wondered what this could mean. Surely Henry wasn't thinking of staying in Australia. And if he were, why hadn't he broached it with her first rather than confiding it to someone he barely knew?

Or perhaps he simply meant settling down on our own place in Suffolk.

At that moment a porter arrived with their luggage and they made their farewells.

'What did you mean about settling down on our own place?' Sarah said once the grazier and his wife were out of earshot.

'Only that at some point we'll want to buy somewhere.'

'And do you have a *somewhere* in mind?' she said coldly.

'No, not yet. Well, I thought perhaps somewhere near Braidwood or even Eden. You loved Eden when we took the steamer down south.' His face was acquiring that determined expression that she'd seen a couple of times before, when he'd wanted something very badly. The first time was when he'd asked her to marry him. The second time was when he'd pushed her into travelling to New South Wales for their honeymoon, and what a long honeymoon this was proving to be.

Well, she could be determined too. She said, 'Those places are in southern New South Wales.'

'Yes.'

'In Australia.'

'Yes.'

'In *rural* Australia.'

'Yes.'

'Before we left England, we agreed we'd spend at most two years here. This was to be our honeymoon trip and not our home.'

'But you love it here. You've told me that a hundred times.'

'I do love it here but that doesn't mean I want to live here.'

'You would get used to it.'

'Is that all you can say, *you would get used to it*? Don't you even want to discuss it, Henry?'

'Of course I do, but not when you're being so emotional.'

'Me emotional? I can't believe you wouldn't understand. I've just spent nearly a month on my own while you've been swanning around Queensland. I know all about loneliness. Is it any wonder that I'm emotional?'

'I missed you too, Sarah. More than you're willing to believe. I thought I'd finish Arnott's work in a couple of weeks. It wasn't my fault it took longer than I expected.'

She looked him in the eyes. Though she saw the hurt, she wasn't going to give in. 'I don't want to settle down yet, Henry. I haven't seen anything much of this country apart from that trip to Braidwood and Eden. I want to see more before we discuss whether we're coming or going. I want to travel with you when you go about your business.'

'You stamped your foot just then, Sarah. I've never seen you do that before.'

'You scowled at me, Henry. You looked quite anthropoid.'

'What does that mean? Did you intend it to be terribly insulting?'

Henry was smiling and she began to see the ridiculous aspect of this argument. 'Like an ape,' she said.

'I don't think that's quite right, Sarah. You're forgetting I had to study Greek at my school. *Anthropos* means human being.'

'A shame you didn't study zoology as well. Anthropoid includes all of the higher primates such as apes, monkeys and human beings.'

'Why can't you simply be straight with me and say I was scowling like an ape?'

'We've moved right away from the point, which is that I'm not yet ready to discuss where we will live. I want to travel about with you more first and see what this country is like. And then I want to go home.'

'Sure. What are we arguing for then?' Henry put his arm around Sarah's shoulders.

'And I'm not letting you go away without me again,' she said, 'wherever it may be.' She suspected that her natural lightness of voice made even her firmest statements appear no more than a gentle expression of preference and wondered if she should stamp her foot again.

'I don't want to go away again without you either,' Henry said. 'There's really no reason why you shouldn't travel with me. The company won't mind, so long as I pay for your travel. Oh, Sarah, I've missed you so much!' He began to fumble in the outside pocket of his coat and eventually found what he was looking for, an oblong object wrapped in tissue paper. 'A present,' he said. 'I bought it for you in Brisbane.'

She unwrapped it. It was a Hohner harmonica: small and light, she'd be able to make music anywhere with this. 'I'll take it with me when we travel,' she said firmly. 'It will be perfect for our return journey to England.'

Chapter 11

'Thank God for Charles'

Perched on a stool in front of the dressing table, Harriet examined the three images of Rose in the triple glass. Biting her lower lip, Rose the trinity was bending forward to fasten the strand of pearls around Harriet's throat. The clasp of the necklace was small and fiddly, and Rose kept repeating that her eyes weren't what they used to be. Yet she looked hurt when Harriet suggested that she fasten the necklace herself.

'I always do them up,' Rose said.

Harriet kept very still while she continued to watch Rose, for whom fastening the pearls was fastening on to the past. To Harriet the pearls had no sentimental value, even though they'd been her mother's, for she had no recollection of ever seeing her wear them. Before her mother, they'd belonged to Harriet's maternal grandmother, whom Harriet had never known. She was merely a custodian of the necklace, she thought. She'd wear them until it was time to hand them on to the next generation, to the daughter she hoped that Sarah would one day produce.

Meanwhile, she watched the triptych of Rose achieving grace of a kind as she struggled with her sacrament. Perhaps she looked a little Flemish; a little like a Rembrandt. She was homely but the years had been kind to her – or she to the years – for her features revealed, from all angles, the goodness that was her nature.

Squinting at her own reflection, Harriet wondered if it was

the rather harsh electric lighting or the glow from the pearls that made her features look less sallow. The shape of her face could be represented by geometrical shapes in black, grey and white. Or perhaps just black and white. A sharp triangle for the dark shadow cast by her nose. Two white ovals where the light fell on her cheekbones. A black elliptical shape under her jaw line, and a small dark oval in the middle of her chin. Rose's face, all soft curves with no strong contrasts, would be harder to represent in only two or three shades. As Harriet regarded Rose's features in the glass, in such close proximity to her own, she repressed a desire to find a piece of charcoal and start sketching. It would be a challenge to capture this composition, this juxtaposition of soft curves with angularity; this representation of love.

'Done,' said Rose, when she had finished fastening the pearls. 'That dark red silk suits you.'

Harriet glanced at her dress, the one she had worn to Sarah's wedding. It was cut too low in the bodice and was too tight in the waist and lower sleeves. The dress had more to do with Aunt Charlotte than Harriet, but she felt pleased by Rose's compliment. When she smiled at Rose in the glass, she beamed back. Then Harriet caught herself unaware. She saw, as she might a stranger, her own reflection in one of the side mirrors; the tiny triangles of shadow forming under her cheekbones as she smiled made her cheeks look almost rounded. Almost pretty, she thought for a moment, before laughing at her folly.

The grandfather clock in the drawing room chimed seven. Father would be growing impatient. They were to dine with Violet and her husband in Islington and had yet to order a hansom cab. She collected her coat and ran down the stairs, two at a time. The drawing-room door was ajar; she peered around it, expecting to see her father pacing up and down. But he was seated in his usual armchair by the fire, with his eyes shut and his head lolling slightly to one side. An open book lay upside down on his lap. He must have picked it up when she hadn't appeared as agreed at ten minutes to the hour, and dozed off. He appeared so tranquil that for a moment Harriet was reluctant to disturb him, but they were already running late.

'Father,' she said. 'I'm sorry I wasn't ready in time.'

He didn't stir. He must be very tired indeed. He'd eaten nothing at teatime, despite having a metabolism that required four meals a day.

'Father,' she said more loudly. 'We must go or we'll be very late.'

She crossed the room to his chair and gently placed her hand on his.

His skin was as cool as marble. She rubbed it lightly. Poor Father had got cold while he was dozing by the hearth and hadn't had the energy to get up to stoke the fire. Tenderly she chafed at the cool dry skin. She had to warm him; he couldn't be allowed to catch a cold.

He didn't move. His eyes remained shut.

It wasn't possible. It couldn't be possible. He'd been well at teatime, although he hadn't eaten. He'd been well before she'd gone upstairs to change.

Her hand shook as she rang the bell on the wall. 'Rose! Rose!' she shouted. 'Come quickly!' Kneeling on the floor in front of her father, she began to massage his hands.

'My father's sleeping,' she explained, when Rose rushed into the room a moment later. 'I expect he'll wake up soon. But I think he's too tired to go out tonight.' She coughed to clear her throat before adding, 'We must telephone Violet to let her know we're not coming.'

'I'll contact Mr Barclay too,' Rose said, her voice shaking. 'I think he'll know what do.'

Harriet continued to rub her father's hands. She couldn't bring herself to look at his face again; instead she examined his gnarled fingers, cold but still flexible. The index and middle fingers of his right hand were marked with ink; she'd never known him not to have these stains.

Of course, he wasn't sleeping. He would never wake again. She would never talk to him again. She observed his dead hands but felt nothing. It was the shock, that was all. A brief respite. And then who could know what might happen.

She steeled herself to glance at his face once more. He looked peaceful. It was as she thought: he had gone peacefully.

He had gone.

Now she understood what she'd lost, and tears began to stream unchecked down her face. 'How can he have gone like this?' she wailed when Rose returned from making her phone call. 'Where has he gone?'

Harriet felt Rose put her arms around her. Leaning into Rose's embrace, she let herself be enveloped by her warmth, her bulk. Then Rose said, 'I'm sure he's gone to heaven, Miss Harriet. He always was a good man.'

'There is no heaven, Rose!' But if only she could retrieve her words, for a belief in heaven might sustain Rose even if it were of no comfort to her. She burst into shrieks of what might be interpreted as laughter were it not so hysterical. Though Rose remained silent, her arms tightened around Harriet. Soon they heard the ringing of the front door bell – Charles' characteristic four rings.

'Thank God for Charles,' said Harriet, as they both struggled to their feet.

Her remarks showed religious inconsistency; she could hear her father's voice saying this to her, with the teasing – if not detached – amusement that he always displayed when correcting any lapse of logic. His comments would for ever be in her head. Despite her shock, she was able to see in sharp clarity this simple truth.

Rose showed Charles in. Without thinking, Harriet flung her arms around his neck and rested her face against his shoulder. After a few seconds she became aware of his reserve. She stiffened and withdrew her arms; she quelled her display of emotion. She wasn't behaving like a lady; she wasn't behaving like one of her class. She stepped back a pace and looked at Charles' face. Shock and sadness were displayed there. Perhaps he was as devastated as she, so devastated that he had nothing to give and was unwilling to take anything either. For an instant she felt a surge of anger. It was her father who had gone and not Charles. Surely he could show some warmth. But then she looked into his sad, dark eyes and felt compassion for this man who was unable to reveal his feelings.

This emotion was quickly overwhelmed by desolation. She felt it wrench at her stomach, as if she were going to vomit up all that she had absorbed in the past hour or so. She needed to purge herself; she wanted to go back to life as it was when she and her father were about to go out for the evening. 'I'll phone Violet and Aunt Charlotte,' she said.

'Would you like me to take care of the funeral arrangements?'

'Yes, thank you Charles.' This was how Charles gave, she thought. He'd loved Father too and could only show this in practical terms. She was more grateful than she could say for his offer.

Chapter 12

'The Telegraph Boy is Waiting'

Afterwards, years afterwards, Sarah would be able to remember every detail of the moment before she received the news. The image she would carry was like a picture postcard: the breakfast table on the lawn a last supper, the sky a too-deep blue, the magnolia tree covered with plump white buds and the azaleas already in flower in the dense shrubbery behind Henry, although the season was autumn and they shouldn't come out until spring.

And the maid Emily, dressed in black, standing immovable in front of Sarah, a part of the tableau. Holding out her hand with the telegram resting flat on her palm, as if it were a tray of seed for the birds, as if that were the reason she was extending her arm. Sarah kept perfectly still and waited for the little blue wrens darting through the bushes to land on Emily's hand.

'The telegram is for you,' Emily said.

'I can't open it,' Sarah said to Henry. 'You do it. It's bad news, I know.'

'You can't know that.'

'I have a feeling.' Hoping she was wrong, she watched Henry rip open the envelope and read the contents.

'It's from Harriet,' he said, and hesitated.

She listened to the laughing of a kookaburra from a eucalyptus tree further up the point. 'Go on, Henry.'

'She says, 'DEAREST SARAH FATHER DIED PEACEFULLY IN HIS ARMCHAIR STOP FUNERAL NEXT WEEK STOP PLEASE ADVISE.''

'Please advise what?' Sarah was so pervaded with a sense of unreality that she could focus only on that part of the message over which she had some control. Although she'd expected bad news, she hadn't anticipated this. Aunt Charlotte was what she'd thought, not Father.

'I suppose if you've got any opinions about the funeral arrangements.'

Sarah glanced at Henry, who was standing next to her chair looking rather anxiously at her. When she held out her hands he pulled her up and drew her close.

The maid coughed. 'A reply-paid telegram,' she said. 'The telegraph boy is waiting.'

'We'd better tell him something,' said Henry. 'Shall I do it?'

'Yes. You'll know what to say. Send all my love to poor darling Harriet and say that I'll leave the arrangements to her judgement.'

'I suppose your Aunt Charlotte is helping Harriet,' said Henry. 'And Charles too.'

Sarah, watching him pace up and down the scrappy lawn, thought of how devastated Harriet would be. Her whole life revolved around Father. She worked for him, she worked with him. Sarah wished she could be with her to share this loss. But it was impossible. This distance was impossible.

Henry was still struggling to compose a reply. 'Perhaps I'll say "Letter follows." No. "Message follows. Message and letter follow. Sympathy and love. Arrangements to your judgement..."' Something like that. Maybe that will do.' He hurried inside to deal with this response before its form escaped him.

Sarah held on to the edge of the breakfast table and looked at her hands. Her father's hands; perhaps the only physical characteristic of his that she had obviously inherited. She inspected them dispassionately while she thought over the news. One minute she had a father, the next minute she didn't. Just like that. And for the moment she had no reaction apart from heightened powers of observation.

After finishing her cup of cold coffee, she walked down to the water's edge. Still she felt nothing but saw everything. Small waves were slapping against the sandstone shelf, the wake from a ship that was being towed down the harbour towards the heads by a fussy little tug. A water bird with lanky legs and a bowed black beak inclined its head at her approach, before ambling away.

Father had gone. She thought of the passage of the seconds, the minutes, as if they were almost tangible. Time ticked relentlessly on while she remained behind, stranded beside the harbour in a state of disbelief. It was impossible to believe, it was impossible to admit, that she'd never see him again.

When she saw Henry come out of the house, she ran across the grass, almost tripping in her haste. She desperately wanted to hold him, to have him hold her. She didn't at first notice the wine glass he was holding, until he said, 'Whoa, girl,' as he sometimes did, as if she were a horse. 'Have a spot of brandy,' he said, and held the glass up to her lips. 'Drink it all at once.'

It was a hug she wanted, not a tot. She might have batted his hand away if she hadn't felt too weak. Swaying slightly, she swallowed the brandy that he forced between her lips and spluttered at its harshness.

Almost immediately she began to feel light-headed, with a wilting sensation in the small of her back, as if her spine might suddenly give way. 'You should rest,' said Henry. 'We'll lie down together for a while.'

He led her inside, out of the sunlight that she now found too stark, that was exposing too much, and into the darkness of their bedroom, where the curtains were still drawn. He gently pushed her on to the bed, on to the white counterpane, and lay down next to her. He held her close until at last the import of the telegram penetrated her brain, penetrated her defences, and she began to cry, quietly at first, the sound muffled against his shoulder.

Afterwards Henry began to talk. Sarah rested her head against his chest and listened to the reverberation of his voice. Soon she fastened on to his words too. They emerged at first haltingly but then he began to shape them into a eulogy, into an interpretation of her father's life. He told her of her father's delight in his daughters, and of his work that was so clever it had influenced a whole generation of thinkers. Here Henry faltered for a moment and then took an enormous breath – Sarah could hear the air swishing into his lungs – before carrying on with his words of comfort. Her father's legacy was in his daughters and in his books, and in his former students too. His memory would live on in them.

Sarah no longer wondered at the difference between Henry's communication with her and his more casual and sometimes inarticulate conversation with acquaintances. Together they could achieve a rapport that was impossible with others. She tilted her head back so she could look at Henry's face. His eyes were closed in concentration and his forehead slightly furrowed.

She listened to Henry repeat some of the anecdotes that he'd heard from her in the past, and then to elaborate on some of his own experiences of James Cameron from their first meeting. After a time, she felt herself drifting off. Like a boat in a deep river, she was insulated by his meandering conversation, by his love, from what was happening on the shore. Later she would have to deal with it, but for the moment she would escape into sleep.

Chapter 13

'I Am Reminded of Father'

In her father's study, surrounded by his books, Harriet felt closer to him than anywhere else in the house. Though his presence was strong in the drawing room, there was always that empty chair with the hollow in the middle that no amount of plumping and shaking could remove. There was that absence of papers too; no books or drafts of articles piled up and waiting to be read. Sitting at his desk now, she was partway through writing to Sarah. For once she wasn't finding it easy. Again she read what she had written.

My dearest Sarah,

How I long for a letter from you but still none has come, although I know you will have written to me as soon as you heard the news, as you said you would in your telegram.

Everyday things are so painful now. One forgets for a while that Father is dead, and then it all comes flooding back. I'm reminded of him each time I go into the drawing room and he's not there in his usual chair, although there's still a dent where he used to sit, so that it seems as if he will return to the room at any minute, as if he has merely gone into his study to take down another book.

I'm reminded of him when I walk the streets, as I often do now, feeling the need to walk myself into a profound exhaustion so that I can get some sleep at night, and then I remember that he won't be at home when I return. I'm reminded of him when I walk through the parks, past the clumps of daffodils that are flowering so very late this year. Daffodils that remind me of being a child in Oxford, secure in Father's protection, the spring there so sweet in my memory, with the great swathes of narcissi that grew in our garden that you and I picked in armfuls – do you remember?

When I think of our past, our childhood, my memories of Father are intricately mixed up with places, are firmly attached to places. As I grew up, I was always profoundly aware of my own changes, each stage an apparently unique development; but I was less aware that Father was changing too, that he was ageing. And I never thought, I never thought much at all, about changes within Father, that he too might have been changing, maturing, evolving, the way you and I have been all our lives, always in a state of flux.

The people one loves grow and mature, deteriorate and then they must die. People are in a state of flux, the world is in a state of flux. But in my memory the places of our childhood are fixed points. These are sacred places, seen with the innocence of youth, in the security of Father's protection and love; these are hallowed places to me. These past few weeks I have been remembering Father, deliberately pulling out my memories to cherish, and to construct the average memory of him in which I want an equal weight to be given to all the precious components of his life as I knew it, and to reduce the weight given to that last dreadful evening when I found him in the drawing room.

What I saw in Oxford as a child, with Father as my early interpreter of the world, was not a fixed point, although I would like it to have been. I returned there with him several months ago, as I told you in one of my letters. What I didn't tell you was that I was devastated at the changes that had occurred in the ten years since I was last there. There was a big gap between my memories of childhood places and what is there now.

I would have liked Father to be a fixed point too; to have avoided ageing, deteriorating then dying, leaving the world to you and me as a lesser place. I have been preparing myself for months for losing Father, since I realised over a year ago that he seemed suddenly so much older, but I still feel so diminished, as if a part of me has been painfully wrenched out. And indeed it has.

Putting down the sheets of paper, Harriet wondered if she should tear them up and start again. These words were not what she had intended to write; they simply flowed from her pen like autonomous writing and had nothing to do with her conscious thoughts. But she decided to let them be. She picked up her pen and carried on writing in a less emotional vein, giving Sarah an outline of the funeral service and the warm letters of sympathy that she would post to her to read, and of Aunt Charlotte's support at all times. And then there was the will. After much thought, she wrote:

Father made a new will not long before he died. The solicitor has sent you a copy. He made it after I refused Charles' proposal of marriage and I think he did this because of my decision. Dearest Sarah, I know you won't hold this against me or against Father, but he left me most of his estate, including this house. He knew how well provided for you are, with Henry and his inheritance, but he did note that if anything were to happen to Henry I should look after you, which of course I would. He left me a letter in which he explained why; that he wanted me to be able to stay single.

Harriet paused; she had been about to write: 'I am plain and ugly and only Charles would want to marry me' but it sounded so full of self-pity and that was not how she really felt, or at least not most of the time. Anyway, it was still the case that she didn't want to enter the state of matrimony. Nothing that had happened to her since Charles' proposal had led her to change her mind about that.

Her father had been very considerate of her wishes but she wondered, not for the first time, how Sarah would feel when she learned that her father had left her a few hundred pounds and the portrait of her mother. She suspected Sarah wouldn't mind, for she was so unworldly and she had no need for extra money as long as Henry didn't squander his inheritance.

At last Harriet finished the letter and left it on the table in the hall for the post. She felt relieved that this task was over but debilitated too. The house seemed quiet.

The house seemed dead.

Chapter 14

Her Resolve Was Fragile

Harriet continued to feel paralysed by indecision and by grief. While the days were flashing by like the view from a train window, she'd felt at a standstill for all those weeks since Father's death. It seemed she was always inside looking out, never a part of the life outside.

Now, standing in the hallway of her house in Gower Street, she felt acutely conscious of the sounds of traffic from the front and, from the communal gardens at the back, the shrieks of next-door's children, whom she hadn't seen for months. The clock in the hallway chimed the hour and then continued relentlessly counting down the minutes.

It was time for her to get out of this living tomb.

She couldn't see any of the children when she entered the garden. But she could hear them crashing around in the laurel shrubbery, somewhere behind the dark, glossy leaves, their screaming waxing and waning as they moved about. All at once she was a part of the game; she was the centre of a ring of laughing children who linked hands and raced around her, shouting, until eventually the smallest child tripped over and the entire circle collapsed on to the grass, convulsed with giggles. The oldest child, the only boy, recovered first. He stood up and brushed down his clothes – twigs, dried leaves, a couple of strands of spiders' webs, and possibly even a spider or two. Harriet caught his eye and at once his smile was replaced by a solemn expression.

'So sorry to hear that your father passed away,' he said gravely.

He could be an adult, Harriet thought, and a mature one at that. She was touched by his words, touched that he'd even noticed her. 'Thank you,' she said, in tones of equal seriousness. 'It was so sweet of you to mention it. Many people don't bother.'

'Lots of people don't notice anything,' the boy commented. She saw he was trying hard not to look too pleased.

'You do, though, Clive,' said the youngest girl.

Clive treated this tribute with the disdain of an older brother. He gave his sister a little push. She giggled, perhaps recognising this as a sign of affection rather than abuse, whereupon all four siblings discarded their serious expressions and smiled at Harriet.

'When's your sister coming back?' said the oldest girl.

'Not for ages yet,' Harriet said. 'Perhaps she never will.' It was only after she'd spoken these words that she realised this was the most likely outcome. Sarah and Henry would never return. Maybe Sarah would want to and Henry wouldn't let her. He had a knack of getting his own way. People called that his charm. Her sadness returned, and it was all the stronger after its brief absence.

'Where is she?' The oldest girl resumed her serious appearance and regarded Harriet with deep concern, almost as if she imagined there'd been another death in her family.

'In New South Wales.'

'You must visit her,' said Clive.

Could he have any idea of the distance? Probably not, but he certainly had the ability of his class and sex to make decisions for others. Yet he had a point. There was nothing to stop her visiting Sarah now. Nothing to stop her travelling, nothing to stop her doing all those things she'd dreamed of doing and never thought might be possible.

Nothing apart from those other commitments that had once given meaning to her life. The Women's Franchise League. Charles, whom she knew was missing Father too. Aunt Charlotte and Violet. How could she tear herself from those connections and head off into the unknown? She didn't have the courage to do that. Not now, not so soon after Father's death. Yet she found herself saying, 'Perhaps I shall visit her there. Such good advice.' She said this to keep Clive happy, she told herself, that was all.

Clive grinned back, delighted at being thought helpful. Then the four children, as if they had a collective mind, remembered their usual – and important – mission of having fun and flew off in pursuit of it, shrieking.

* * *

'My dear Harriet, I bumped into Mrs Next-Door just now in the street, and she says you're going to the antipodes to see Sarah! Is it true?' Aunt Charlotte asked breathlessly after Rose had shown her into the drawing room, where Harriet was sitting in front of the fire.

'It was merely a passing thought. I haven't made up my mind to do anything.'

'What a marvellous adventure it would be, but really you simply mustn't rush into anything too quickly so soon after poor James' death! And without talking it over first with your family too.'

Aunt Charlotte sat down in Father's chair and fanned herself. Harriet didn't need to ring for tea; Rose had anticipated her and appeared with a tray.

'Are you going to marry Charles?' Aunt Charlotte asked, when she'd drunk a cup of tea rather quickly. She picked up a napkin and fanned herself with it.

'I don't know. Probably not, but who can say? Anyway, he hasn't asked me again.'

'You could revive his proposal, that's something we women know how to do. Or you could ask him yourself, after all you're a liberated young woman.' Aunt Charlotte laughed as she helped herself to a scone.

'I'm not at all sure that I want marriage. You know that, Aunt. Surely you haven't forgotten our conversation before Sarah married Henry.'

'People do change, my dear. But why not go to the antipodes anyway? There's nothing like a prolonged absence to help decide. You'd soon learn what was important after six months away. Charles is a good man.'

'I know. People are always telling me that, although I'm quite capable of observing it for myself. You said I shouldn't rush into anything and now, barely two minutes later, you're talking about marriage and long voyages.'

'I was simply thinking aloud. Or perhaps talking it through with you is a better description. Actually, the more I think about it, the more I am of the opinion that a sea voyage would be good for you. You've often said you'd like to see the world.'

'There are my speaking commitments at the WFL.'

'Lydia Buxton won't mind finding a stand-in. There are plenty of others she can call on, you know. The number of supporters is growing all the time.'

'Then there's my painting.'

'Dearest girl, you're very talented but that's simply an excuse. You can do that anywhere. I'm sure they have canvas and paints out there. You're always talking about the light. Just think of what it would be like in New South Wales! And you could check up on Sarah first-hand, you girls have always been close. The Morgans are in Sydney too. You knew them very well when you were a child. They were almost like family.'

'I'll make up my own mind.'

'I'm sure you will, my dear. But just remember I can help you with the house and anything else if you decide to let it out.'

After Aunt Charlotte left, Harriet glanced around the drawing room. She loved this house but how shabby and unloved the furniture looked. And how vacant the room: it was lost without her father, as she was too.

Through the window she could see the pale washed-out sky, bleached of all colour. How drab it all looked. She thought of Sarah's letters, her descriptions of the light and the landscape, of a country she would love to see. Perhaps she should go to Sydney, for a year at most. She could reassure herself about how Sarah was faring.

The next day she found out that there was one berth left on a steamer leaving Southampton in two weeks' time. She booked it at once, before she had a chance to change her mind. That evening she wrote to Sarah and the following morning sent a telegram to Sarah and Henry advising them of when she would be arriving in Sydney.

Her remaining days in London were frenetically busy, filled as they were with packing her trunks, sorting out her father's library with Charles' assistance, arranging to let the house, seeing the solicitor, making the myriad little arrangements necessary before a long absence from home.

Her resolve was fragile though. The sight of Charles closing the last box of books moved her almost to tears. She wondered how she could leave behind this good and dear friend, and for such a long time. He'd always been a part of the family and now she was throwing that friendship away, as if it counted for nothing.

His head was bent over the box, and amongst the smooth dark hair were several silver streaks that she'd never noticed before. Leaning towards him, her heart full of tenderness, she was about to touch his head when she thought better of it. It was too soon to commit, far too soon. And she wasn't throwing away his friendship, she was simply testing it a little.

Chapter 15

'You've Never Managed a Cattle Station'

Sarah was reading the front page of the *Sydney Morning Herald* when Henry returned to the breakfast table, twirling his hat around his forefinger.

'You're leaving early today, Henry.'

'No, I'm simply ready early. There's something I want to talk to you about. I forgot to mention it last night.'

She put down the newspaper and offered him more tea.

'When I was up in Queensland,' Henry said, absent-mindedly placing his teacup down on her saucer with a loud rattle, 'I heard that the manager of Dimbulah Downs is looking for someone to run the place for six months over the winter. I thought nothing of it at the time, but Arnott told me yesterday that they still haven't got anyone to do it. Would you be interested in coming with me if I did it?'

'You've never managed a cattle station.' Surprise was Sarah's dominant emotion, with apprehension a close second.

'No, but I've had plenty of experience with mustering and droving.'

'So you have, but perhaps you should tell me where Dimbulah Downs is.'

'In the Northern Territory of South Australia.'

'That's a long way from here. You didn't mention Dimbulah Downs in your letters from Queensland.' While the name conjured up an image of a substantial stone dwelling set in lush green countryside and ringed with green hills, she suspected the reality would be different.

'It wasn't worth mentioning. I have no intention of going.'

'Why did you bring it up then?' She might have felt irritated with his lapse in logic if she wasn't more worried by his restlessness.

'I thought it might be a distraction for you. Something completely different.'

She knew he was referring to her grief. She'd been touchy for several months and couldn't settle to anything. Perhaps if she'd been able to attend her father's funeral it would have been a little easier to accept that he'd gone. Again and again an image returned to her, of a stooped old man in a black greatcoat, standing with Harriet on the wharf the day she left England.

She said, 'A distraction before we go back to England, you mean?'

'Yes. If we go back to England.'

'*I'm* going back, Henry.' Sarah wasn't going to be tricked into agreeing to stay. She would leave Henry if she had to. At this thought, tears pricked her eyes. Since her father had died, she'd felt even closer to Henry. The trouble was that she couldn't bear to be apart from him; his trip to Queensland had shown her that. He would be the ideal husband if only he would be more reasonable and do exactly what she wanted him to.

'The conditions up there would be primitive,' Henry said. 'And the climate would be too harsh for you, even for six months.'

She bristled at this. 'I'm not some little weakling.'

'I know. You're as strong as an ox. Stronger sometimes.'

'And anyway, you're not going on your own.'

'Of course I'm not going on my own. I'm sorry I mentioned it. I thought only that you needed taking out of yourself.'

'*Only?*' she said. 'Do you mean to say that you yourself don't want to go to Dimbulah Downs?'

Henry's laughter was misplaced, she felt. When he'd sobered up, she said, 'How far is Dimbulah Downs from Port Darwin?'

'I'm not sure. Maybe a week's ride.'

'A week's ride!'

'Through glorious country, so I've heard.'

'And what would the manager's wife have do?' she asked.

'Nothing. The manager doesn't have one. That's why he wants to go south for six months. He'll never find an unmarried woman up there.'

She knew how this translated: harsh conditions and very little female company. She said, 'Is Dimbulah Downs like Old Finch's place in Queensland?'

'How do you mean?'

He avoided her eyes and fiddled with his watch chain. She guessed he knew exactly what she was referring to. She said, 'Mr Arnott must have told you about Old Finch.'

'Perhaps he did.' Henry opened his watch and examined its face, although she could see from the dining-room clock that he didn't have to catch the tram for another fifteen minutes.

'I overheard the Arnotts discussing him weeks ago, Henry. I was playing the piano at their house and they thought I couldn't hear. Old Finch is a sunburnt chap with gingery hair, Mr Arnott said, who looks a bit like a Viking. There were at least twenty gingery children in the Aboriginal camp next to his shack, he said, and all of them under the age of eight. You can draw your own conclusions about that.'

Henry looked embarrassed. 'I've heard good reports about Dimbulah Downs. Apparently it's a well-run station, with separate quarters for the stockmen and the manager, and a separate Aboriginal camp.'

'You know a lot about it.'

'I saw a plan,' he said.

'Where?'

'The bloke in Queensland who told me about it drew it on the ground.'

'You were thinking, even then, of going without me?' She picked up the Hohner harmonica that was resting on the sideboard and blew into it several harsh chords.

'Never, Sarah. Never without you. We are *not* going.'

She swapped the harmonica for the newspaper and peered at its front page with unseeing eyes. When Henry said he was leaving for work, she did not look up. 'Goodbye,' she said coldly when he kissed the top of her head. 'I'm so glad we've agreed that neither of us is going to Dimbulah Downs.'

* * *

The thing about not making peace before parting is that it hurts you as much as it hurts the other person, Sarah thought as she wandered around the garden in the late afternoon. Lunch with Mrs Arnott and some of her daughters hadn't cheered her at all; she'd felt like an actress playing the role of the happy wife when she'd had no mind to.

She watched the water lapping against the sandstone shelf below the garden. A horn blast from a steamer broke into her reverie; a sound that usually made her feel excited, evoking as it did the glories of travel, of seeing new places, of heading off over unknown waters. But today it made her feel melancholy.

An hour before Henry was due home she began to wonder if she'd been too hasty. The whole point of their honeymoon in

Australia had been to see a bit of the world and so far they'd seen very little of it apart from the colony of New South Wales. Perhaps six months at Dimbulah Downs in the Territory was an opportunity. There would be wonderful new scenery to see and people to meet. She thought of Father's words the day she and Henry had sailed from England. *Be cheerful, my dear. This is the beginning of a great adventure. You will see such wonderful things.* He was right. She had seen such wonderful things. And she wanted to see more.

Perhaps she and Henry should go to Dimbulah Downs. Maybe after six months in the Territory they could take a steamer to Singapore and then on to England. And then she could see dear Harriet again, and Aunt Charlotte too.

She could certainly do with a diversion now, she thought; Henry had been right. Would this be a holiday though? Hard work, more likely, and the north of Australia was hot. Yet in winter it would be a dry heat and she loved the heat. She thought of the reports she'd read of wild blacks in the Kimberley, but she knew that the Territorian cattle industry was already established. She thought of what the grazier she'd met at Darling Harbour had said about the lawlessness of the north. It was a dangerous place, but he'd been referring to more than a decade ago. She thought of how she and Henry had travelled all the way from England but still she hadn't been into the outback. And she really wanted to see it for herself before returning home.

Dimbulah Downs was such an evocative name. Last week she had been with Mrs Morgan to an exhibition of photographs taken by the former Government Resident of the Northern Territory. The countryside had looked wild and exotic, the gorges dramatic, the Aboriginal faces full of character. At the prospect of seeing the place for herself she felt a squirm of excitement in her stomach.

When Henry returned that evening she was waiting for him in the living room.

'I think we should go,' she said after they'd hugged and made up.

'You mean go...?'

'To Dimbulah Downs.'

Like a slideshow displaying the gamut of emotions, his expression changed from disbelief to doubt to a joy that she found irresistible. He took her in his arms and whirled her around the room in a waltz, murmuring into her hair words that were hard to distinguish, though their meaning was clear enough. She was someone who could be counted on. She was the best friend a man could ever have. He was the luckiest man in the world to have her as his wife.

'And I you,' she whispered. 'I'm lucky too.'

Part IV

Sydney and the Northern Territory of South Australia, 1893–1894

Chapter 16

Perhaps the Flaw Was in Herself

Again and again Harriet scanned the faces of the crowds thronging the wharf at Darling Harbour, searching for Sarah and Henry. Again and again she saw no familiar face. Fingers of anxiety squeezed the life out of her excitement and beckoned in despair. Sarah was always so reliable. Something dreadful must have happened to her. But if it had, surely Henry would be here. Perhaps they were simply running late.

The shadows lengthened and the air began to feel cool. Seagulls screeched overhead, a melancholy sound, and the water slapped and sucked at the massive timber piers supporting the wharf. Harriet sat on her cabin trunk and wondered what to do.

Finally, the purser rescued her. He told her about a hotel nearby that he stayed at when in port, on the corner of Sussex and Market Streets, and arranged for the transfer of her luggage.

The streets were crowded with horses and carts, horses and carriages, and everywhere the smell of wool from the nearby stores, overlaid with the odour of horse manure. But the hotel was clean and had a telephone in the lobby. Thankfully Mrs Morgan was at home when Harriet called her that evening, her voice choked with worry that a fit of coughing couldn't dissolve. It was only after several attempts that she managed to explain who and where she was.

'You're in a hotel in town?' Mrs Morgan said. 'You don't

need to worry about Sarah, she's fine. But it's such a pity you missed her, and by only a few days too. She had no idea you were coming. You must come to stay with us first thing tomorrow.'

Now, sitting in the Morgans' drawing room in Mosman, Harriet watched kind Mrs Morgan pour her a cup of tea. 'My dear Harriet, of course you must stay with us as long as you like, or at least until you decide what you want to do.' Mrs Morgan was short, with dark curls that bobbed about when she talked, and a voice so deep and carrying that one couldn't help but wonder where it came from. 'We have a little apartment under the house that would be perfect for you. Don't you agree, Percival?'

'Yes, dear. Perfect.' Professor Morgan was tall and so stooped that he appeared concave. His face looked vacant, perhaps because his attention was directed inwards to the realms of higher mathematics, a subject that he taught at Sydney University. Or maybe it was to the question of whether or not he should have a second piece of the lemon sponge cake, a large slice of which he now slid on to his plate.

'I'm sure Sarah will telegraph as soon as she gets your message. The Victoria Hotel in Port Darwin will hold it for her until they arrive. It was fortunate that she and Henry told me they were going to stay there for a few days. But so very unfortunate that you missed them by such a short time. By the way, you did carefully word the telegram you sent them just now, didn't you?'

'Yes.' It was not surprising that Mrs Morgan was worried about this. The telegram that Harriet had sent Sarah before leaving England had either not reached her in time or had arrived garbled. Or at least that was Mrs Morgan's theory; it was the only plausible explanation for Sarah's failure to mention it.

'It's so easy for these telegraph operators to get things wrong,' Professor Morgan said around a mouthful of cake. 'It happens all the time. Last week a friend told me how his instructions had been misinterpreted. It was his handwriting, you know. The operator couldn't read it so the message was transmitted as some gibberish.'

'Not now, Percival. Don't get poor Harriet worried. She has enough to think about without fretting what else can go wrong. Come with me into the garden, Harriet. Several of my camellias have just come into flower and I'm sure you'll be interested in seeing how well they flourish here.'

Outside, the narrow strip of lawn was fringed by a dense row of camellias pruned low. Below this the land fell away steeply and the late afternoon light struck gold from the sandstone ledges descending to the harbour foreshore. Harriet struggled to interest herself in the pale pink blooms of the camellias, their veined petals edged with white, and their centres dense and creamy.

'Why Henry should want to take up the position of acting manager at Dimbulah Downs I really can't fathom,' Mrs Morgan said, breaking off a dead camellia flower. 'And it's a mystery why your sister Sarah seemed almost as keen about it as he did, heaven only knows why. The place is a veritable outpost. My guess is that it was on the recommendation of Mr Arnott, who has a lot to answer for. Not to mention the letter of introduction from Henry's father.'

Sarah and Henry on some remote outpost, Harriet thought. How typical of Henry, intent on spiriting Sarah away.

Mrs Morgan said, 'But you mustn't fret, Harriet. I'm sure they'll be perfectly safe. It's the dry season up there so there won't be any floods to worry about. Now, let's talk of other matters. Your pearls, for instance. They're very beautiful.'

'They were my mother's.' The last time Harriet had worn

them was the night her father had died. At the time Harriet had felt that the pearls had no sentimental value, but she'd been wrong. Fingering them now, she felt she was fastening on to her memories of Father, her memories of home, her memories of Rose.

'They're lovely,' Mrs Morgan said, smiling. 'They show your complexion to advantage.'

She means they make me look less sallow, Harriet thought, while thanking her hostess for the compliment.

'Now, let me show you this other camellia. See how different it is? Vermilion and with a double row of petals.'

'Very striking, Mrs Morgan. And what are those strange cones on that shrub below?'

'That's what they call a banksia. Hairy little brute, isn't it? Do watch your step, dear, the rock falls away quite sharply here.'

Rooted on a lower ledge, the tree was taller than Harriet had thought, its dark green leaves serrated and showing a silvery underside. The feathery new blooms were upright cathedral candles, while the hard and woody old fruits were something you might throw on a fire if you didn't think, as Harriet did, how splendid they looked on the tree.

When she rejoined her hostess, Mrs Morgan took her arm and said, 'It will be lovely having you to stay. Shall we go inside again? The afternoon is getting chilly. We'll see if Percival has managed to eat up all the cake in our absence.'

* * *

At least Port Darwin was easily accessible by wire; the telegraph line had opened up the north around three decades before. Several days after moving into the Morgans' flat, Harriet received a telegram that read: 'DEAREST APOLOGIES

98

NOT THERE WONDERFUL ADVENTURE PERHAPS FOLLOW US SOON BUT AWAIT CONFIRMATION ACCOMMODATION UNCERTAIN LETTER FOLLOWS.'

The next day Harriet remembered that Charles Barclay had an old friend who was the Government Resident of the Northern Territory, so she sent a telegram to Charles. If she were to decide to follow Sarah to Port Darwin, it would be good to have another contact there.

But she was unlikely to go, she thought. She could stay in Sydney until the Vincents returned.

* * *

Some weeks later, Harriet was sitting in a cane chair on the brick paving bordering the Morgans' lawn. Her travelling desk on her lap, she picked up her pen and began to write.

Dear Charles,

Thank you so much for your interesting letter. It was dated three months ago so you must have written not long after I left, and it was so lovely of you to do this.

Thank you also for the telegram you sent introducing me to the Northern Territory Resident, Mr Richardson. How convenient that you and he were at Oxford together! I have received a wire inviting me to stay with them if I should decide to visit Port Darwin.

I haven't had a letter from Sarah yet, although she did telegraph me. In the meantime, I am kept busy with the Morgans. Mrs Morgan has taken me to visit the artists' camp at Balmoral and she's absorbed me into her work for women's emancipation when I'm not painting. You know how you introduced Sarah to Henry at the Women's Franchise League? That was an accidental meeting if ever there was one: Henry there solely to fill in time before his dinner engagement with you! Of course, life is a series of accidents. I live at the Morgans' because the telegram I sent Sarah from London was either lost or incomprehensible. Sarah and Henry are travelling to Dimbulah Downs because, so Mrs Morgan asserts, of the random encounter Henry had with someone in Queensland.

I spend my days painting and my evenings fund-raising – and consciousness-raising – for the suffragists. There is much poverty here: people without jobs, banks collapsing, depositors losing their life savings. But at the Colonial Office you would know all about that.

The light here is harsher than I ever imagined. It cuts unrelentingly through the surplus dross to reveal the truth beneath. The structure, the shape, the meaning. Whether I can capture this on canvas remains to be seen. I can only try.

She paused, wondering if she should start the letter again. Charles might find her struggle to paint dull. On the other hand, he was a good and loyal friend. After putting down the pen, she massaged her aching fingers. Rather than tell him of the dozen canvases she had painted – and repainted – in the weeks since she'd arrived, it would be better by far to tell him about politics here. Although Charles would certainly be getting detailed reports through the Colonial Office, she knew he would appreciate her perspective. She picked up the pen again and rapidly covered several pages. I might be a journalist, she thought, or an academic, if I were a man and not obsessed by converting light into paint.

* * *

Although the apartment under the Morgans' house proved to be a delightful place in which to live, Harriet still felt alone. But she'd chosen this way of life, and one couldn't be independent without being occasionally lonely. Sometimes she thought that Mosman was so isolated that she might be living on an island, even though it was served by ferries. And although she loved the sparkling water of the harbour and the coruscating light, she seemed unable to translate this into paint, let alone use it to illuminate the nature of existence. Everything changed too fast. The light altered too quickly. Nothing stood still; only herself, stationary on the northern edge of this beautiful harbour. She was going nowhere.

Perhaps the flaw was in herself. Perhaps she would quite simply never be happy, wherever she was, whatever she was doing.

Feeling in need of a day out, Harriet took the ferry to Circular Quay and wandered through the Rocks area. Up narrow steps and along terraces, where life seemed to be lived as much in the streets as in the houses. Children were charging up and down, couples were shouting at one another through open doorways, men were propped up against pub walls while they set the world to rights. Harriet viewed herself as unseen. Her lack of looks was equivalent to a cloak of invisibility that gave her the confidence that prettier women might not feel on their own and allowed her to wander about as an observer of life rather than a participant.

After a while, she realised she was lost, although she wasn't concerned, for she could always ask for directions. She came at last to a long flight of stone steps opening into a vista of the lower street that she decided she must sketch. It was only when she'd stopped to pull out of her bag a pad and pencil that she realised the two young lads behind her had stopped too, ostensibly so that one could do up his bootlace. Yet they were too close to her for comfort and at any second they could grab her bag and make off with it, or with her pearls. One tug at her necklace and it would be gone.

And there would be no one to whom she could call for help. The alleyway was deserted. She raced down the steps two at a time, hearing as she did so the thud of boots as the boys pounded down behind her. Her heartbeat pulsing in her ears, she accelerated, but they seemed to be gaining on her.

Halfway down, she saw another figure enter the alley from the bottom: a middle-aged man in a shabby suit, surely an accomplice. He began to run up the steps towards her, and she shifted her bag to her other side, away from where he would pass. Behind her sounded the thump of the lads' footsteps; they were closing in on her now. She would relinquish the bag if they snatched at it. Better by far to lose her money and her sketchbook than to feel a knife sliding between her ribs. She took a deep breath and prepared to hand it over.

The lads overtook her a second or two before the middle-aged man was level with her and carried on galloping down the staircase, still laughing. 'Gidday,' said the man as he passed her, doffing his hat. 'Good-day,' she replied, her voice unsteady.

Emerging into the bright sunlight at the bottom of the alleyway, she walked fast towards the crowds milling around the quay. Although she was unharmed, the incident – if you could call it that – had unnerved her. The price of independence wasn't just loneliness, it was also fear. Yet it was a low price, she decided as she strolled through the stream of passengers disembarking from several ferries that had recently arrived. The fear she was likely to feel and the need to take precautions were costs she was willing to pay to live alone. Yet despite this rationalisation, she started to experience once more an unwelcome detachment.

When the Mosman ferry pulled into the wharf, she was the

first on board. Sitting on a slatted wooden bench towards the front of the boat, she stared at the dark choppy water. No one knew where she was at this moment. Not a soul. If anything were to happen to her, it might be days before the Morgans noticed, so separate was her little apartment under their house. It might be months before Sarah would find out.

When she looked up, she saw that the formerly brilliant blue day had metamorphosed into an evening suffused with a strange yellow light. The bruised-looking sky promised a later storm, which she hoped to watch from the security of her sitting room, and she willed the boat to depart.

Yet later, sitting by her harbour-side window and watching the lightning perform, Harriet experienced no security. Instead, she was overcome by a feeling of depression so overwhelming it was almost paralysing. It was the incident in the Rocks, she thought; that moment when she'd felt she might be attacked and robbed made her acutely aware of how isolated she had become. She began to shiver. If only she could talk to her father again but that would never be. Nostalgia was negative; she must be positive. If only she could talk to Sarah.

And to Charles. Reluctantly she admitted that she missed him. Her teeth began to chatter, and it was with the greatest of effort that she was able to force herself out of her chair, to find a warm shawl and to light the kindling in the open fireplace.

The blue flames flickered around the logs and grew rapidly into a strong red blaze that spurted up the chimney, as if to find a way out. As she watched the progress of the fire, Harriet felt as if she was on the wrong side of the ocean, the wrong side of the world.

It was tempting to take the next available ship home, and there were plenty of departures. But she couldn't possibly do that. She would be leaving Sarah behind; the only family she had left apart from Aunt Charlotte, and she'd give anything to see her sister again. She couldn't possibly leave without doing that.

After throwing another log on the fire, she went to the window to close the curtains. The storm had passed and, as she watched, a thin moon slipped out from behind a cloud. She observed it for a time as it almost imperceptibly sliced through the dark velvety sky.

The following morning the long-awaited letter from Sarah arrived, and not merely one letter but four. Sarah and Henry were at Dimbulah Downs Station, Sarah wrote, and she was expecting Harriet to take a steamer north. Harriet's spirits lifted when she read Sarah's words: 'Write at once to let us know what steamer you will take. We can't wire you yet as we are days away from the repeater station and Henry can't spare a man, so do please write as soon as you receive this letter. I am so much looking forward to seeing you again!'

Chapter 17

'A Louis Lot Flute, Sarah.'

The homestead was deserted, apart from Ah Soy's chickens. These scrawny creatures, impervious to the midday heat, were scratching around in the dust in the yard next to the kitchen. After finding her hat, Sarah clattered across the wide verandah surrounding the three rooms forming what was grandly known as the manager's residence. Shed would be a more accurate description, she considered, not for the first time. Dimbulah Downs consisted of a collection of corrugated-iron sheds in a large paddock sparsely treed with eucalypts: the manager's residence, the kitchen block, the stockmen's quarters, the horse yards, and a miscellany of assorted shelters housing tack, horse feed, stores and equipment. About a quarter of a mile north lay the Aboriginal camp, close to the billabong.

To the west, between the furthest building and the track to the river, were several coppers. Behind this, a small army of trousers and shirts hung limply from several clothes lines strung between ironbark posts. Nearby was a windmill that, on a breezy day, pumped water into a tank and some troughs. Today the windmill's blades were still, apart from a shimmer as they dissolved then reformed, dissolved then reformed, in the blinding sunlight. Sarah wandered across to the kitchen block, and then past the fenced-off vegetable garden, the greenest part of the homestead.

Eventually she found the cook sitting on the ground in the shade of a stringybark tree, with his wide straw hat pulled low over his eyes. Ah Soy, usually so active, seemed to be in a kind of heat-induced trance, or perhaps he was soundly asleep despite the smouldering pipe gripped between his teeth. He appeared almost frail, she thought with surprise. It was his ebullient personality that gave him stature when he was awake.

'Ah Soy,' she said gently. He opened his eyes and began to struggle to his feet. 'Don't get up,' she said, but it was too late.

Smoothing down the wrinkles in his navy-blue trousers and jacket, he smiled at her around the stem of the pipe. 'Missee wash plenty muchee clothes.'

'There's a bit more to do yet.'

'Missee swimmen river.'

She laughed; on washday she always kept the best part to the end. 'Have you seen Bob?' A stockman on light homestead duties while recovering from a riding accident, Bob found the presence of a white woman on the station confronting, and she guessed he was avoiding her.

'Over there.'

She looked where Ah Soy was pointing, and saw Bob crouched low behind the woodpile, stacking logs.

'Bob!' she called. Unable to pretend deafness in front of the cook, he sauntered towards them. A tall thin figure, he had a thick grey moustache whose ends drooped down to the jawline, giving him a mournful expression. The visible part of his face was a parched landscape, and his eyebrows small ledges that cast his eyes into shadow, making them appear deep set.

'Can you saddle my horse please? You can tether her to the verandah rail. I'll be back in an hour.'

She headed towards the river track. The stream meandered over the plateau until the ground started to fall away steeply and the water was channelled into a series of rock pools. When she'd first seen this place, she'd thought it looked almost like the sequence of locks on the Grand Union Canal, but less even, less regulated. Some of the pools were short, some were long, some were curved, some almost rectangular. As the water flowed into these various receptacles, it altered its tempo, from adagio to allegro, and it varied its volume too, from pianissimo to fortissimo.

Her favourite spot for swimming was the long pool with twin waterfalls. The Aboriginal women were here already, splashing about in the water. She watched Bella, who was perched on a rock, and rubbing a bar of soap into a piece of clothing. Though Sarah still didn't understand why Bella viewed her as kin of the absent manager of Dimbulah Downs, she was glad of the friendliness this had brought her.

When Bella tossed the garment into the water, it swirled about for a few seconds before vanishing under the surface. The other women started diving for it, naked black bodies flashing through the white foam, and emerging faces whooping with joy. One of them retrieved the garment and tossed it around like a ball, until eventually another seized it and wrung it out, before putting it on to a small mound of clothes on a flat rock at the side.

After taking off her shoes and stockings, Sarah hitched up her skirt and tied it into a loose knot above her knees. She picked up a bundle of dry clothes and stepped on to a broad rock above the pool. 'Next!' she shouted and flung a cotton petticoat down to Daisy balanced on the rock below.

When the last piece of clothing had been washed and rinsed, Sarah slipped off her skirt and blouse, and undid her corset. Wearing only her chemise and knickers, she dived in a clean arc into the pool below, emerging some yards further down. Shaking her hair off her face, she began to float on her back, feet pointed downstream. What heaven it was to be in the water, to feel its softness caressing her skin. Far above was a circle of harsh blue sky, ringed with the dark foliage of casuarina trees. She was swept a few yards further downstream before she started vigorously kicking with her feet and moving her arms in a kind of backstroke – in which she raised both arms simultaneously then lifted them backwards and down into the water. Slowly she inched towards the women, her arms working furiously as she struggled to make progress.

After hauling herself on to the rocky ledge, she sat in the sun to dry her underwear. Soon she was joined by Bella, who was now wearing one of the shapeless cotton dresses that were found in bulk in the station store. 'Missus too much white feller for sun,' she said, lightly touching Sarah's bare shoulder.

'I'll move in a minute.' When Bella grinned, she showed all her teeth, top and bottom, like an advertisement for high quality dentures. Sarah was glad her own smile was narrower, concealing the slightly crooked lower incisors and revealing solely the even upper teeth. Idly, she watched the beads of water dripping from Bella's wet black hair. Trickling down her neck, they darkened the blue fabric of her dress.

* * *

Sarah would never forget the first time she met Bella and Daisy. It was the morning after she and Henry had arrived at Dimbulah Downs, and the two girls had turned up at the homestead to work. She'd been shocked to see what they were wearing: calico flour sacks with holes cut for the arms and neck.

'Where are your dresses?' she said.

'Boss no givem dresses. Just bags.' Bella's voice was soft and friendly, and it reminded Sarah of the young woman who'd helped her climb over the locked gate of the Botanical Gardens in Sydney. That evening she hadn't been quick enough with her offer of clothing, but that wouldn't happen again.

'We'll go to the storeroom and see what we can find.' She led the way across the dusty ground to the store and unlocked the door. Cobwebs and rows of sacks and cans and bottles confronted her. Flour, sugar, tea. Tins of jam, butter, Worcester sauce. Not to mention the supplies of tobacco, pipes, boots, blankets and mosquito nets. Months' worth of provisions were stacked methodically on the shelves. Eventually she spied some clothing in a corner and pulled out a bundle of cotton dresses. Unfolding one, an ugly shapeless garment, she held it up for inspection before draping it over her blouse and skirt.

Bella and Daisy began to shriek with laughter. At first Sarah thought they were pleased at the prospect of having such a dress, but soon she understood that they thought these garments ridiculous. Bella, catching sight of Sarah's astonished expression, struggled to contain her mirth. She pulled off the flour sack – she was wearing nothing underneath – and slipped the dress Sarah handed her over her head. After smoothing the voluminous garment over her hips, she sashayed up and down between the rows of stores. Tall and slender, she looked beautiful even in this travesty of a dress. 'It's far too loose,' Sarah said, controlling with difficulty the urge to find pins, or a needle and cotton, to take in the fabric.

Bella shrugged and smiled, and Sarah guessed she would strip off the garment as soon as she finished work. For a moment she felt disconcerted. She looked down at her own long skirt, laced at the hem with cobwebs, and her long-sleeved high-necked blouse, edged at the cuffs with red dirt. Wasn't her own clothing ridiculous in this climate? Would these girls laugh at her garb when they were out of her sight? But like a vulnerable creature – a snail perhaps or a tortoise

– she needed a carapace to protect her from what the climate had to offer. And to protect her also from the appraising eyes of white men.

* * *

Sitting in the sunlight now, with Bella by her side, she thought how easily she had come to terms with the Aborigines' nakedness here at the river. When bathing in these rock pools it seemed right to be without clothes, rather than wearing a silly costume that dragged you down. She touched the fabric of her chemise and knickers. Already it was dry.

'Time for me to go, Bella.' Sarah stood and began to dress. She knew that, unsupervised, the women would take hours to peg out the washing, but she wanted to ride out to meet Henry.

'I have to tell you something, missus.' Bella's smile had gone and she looked unusually serious.

'Can it wait until tomorrow?' Sarah brushed a few twigs from her clothes.

'Tomorrow.' Bella turned her head so that Sarah could not see her expression. 'Day after.'

'Is it important? You can tell me now if you can make it quick. I promised the boss I'd ride out to meet him. What did you want to say?'

'It's about bad man Carruthers.'

'What about him?' Carruthers held the leasehold of Empty Creek Station a week's ride away. Sarah had met him only once, a big man with legs that were too short for his heavy body and hair like grass in the dry season. She hadn't much liked him; it was the queer way he'd looked at her, like a buyer at a horse sale. In the first five minutes he'd let her know that he'd been to one of the best public schools England had to

110

offer, but she knew what her father used to say about such an education: *good in parts*.

'Mebbe Carruthers come take me,' Bella said.

'How can that be? He's too far away.'

'He send someone or come himself.'

Sarah said, 'I don't think he'd abduct one of our people.' She had been going to say 'our Aborigines' but that made them seem like slaves. *Our people*; the English term for *our family*. 'But I'll let Henry and the others know.'

Bella nodded and kept her face averted.

'Is there anything else you want to tell me?'

With a faltering voice, Bella began to describe what Carruthers did on Empty Creek Station. Each morning at first light he went to his Aboriginal camp and laid about with a stockwhip. Men and women alike. 'I'll shake you buggers up a bit,' he would bellow, as they sprang away from the lash.

'That will never happen here,' Sarah said, struggling to keep calm, though she was beginning to feel a deep anger. 'Never at Dimbulah Downs.' She put an arm around Bella's shoulders. 'Unfortunately, he can do what he likes at Empty Creek, but not here. This is not his leasehold.' And thank the lord that Empty Creek's a week's ride away, she thought. There are some advantages to distance after all.

Bella kept her eyes down, her face expressionless.

'Is there something else that's worrying you, Bella?'

'No, missus.'

'You can tell me if there is.'

'Nothing else, missus.'

Sarah began to make her way back to the homestead. Away from the river, the flies were a nuisance. In a vain attempt to discourage them, Sarah fanned her face with a branch torn from a bush, and walked faster. By the time she reached the homestead she was feeling hotter than before she'd swum, and more perturbed.

111

Not far from the kitchen, Ah Soy and a young Aboriginal girl were milking the goats.

'Any visitors while I've been away?' Sarah asked. The mailman was due that evening. A delivery once every six weeks was an event not to be missed.

Ah Soy took the billycan from the girl and inspected the frothy milk. He turned to Sarah. 'Plenty good tucker tonight,' he said. 'Paper-yabber night special night.' He looked as if he might have expanded on the culinary theme, but they'd discussed it earlier, so she simply nodded before striding across the yard to the verandah.

Her horse was tethered to the verandah rail. As usual there was no sign of Bob. After mounting, she rode out to meet the muster. Far up in the azure sky three or four brown-winged kites wheeled and circled. One suddenly dropped, talons outstretched and wings uplifted, and vanished from sight beyond the treetops. A goanna or a small marsupial or a snake would be no more. Not a dead steer though; that would have attracted all the kites.

Before Sarah and Henry had arrived at Dimbulah Downs, Henry had thought he knew everything there was to know about cattle, but he'd been wrong. The leasehold was vast and supported only a low density of cattle. Most of the stock were wild. To begin with, he'd been almost entirely dependent on the guidance of Mick, the leading hand. The taciturn head stockman, known as Smithy, hadn't been at all forthcoming and Henry had initially been left in little doubt that Smithy resented his presence. But Mick had taught his boss how to manage and the irony of this had not been lost on Henry. Although mustering wasn't one of the manager's duties, Sarah had soon realised that Henry was prepared to try even the most dangerous tasks. She guessed that Smithy and Mick had both grown to respect him because he was willing to ride in front to keep the cattle in the mob; he was willing to pursue and tail the wild cattle to head them back into the mob. He'd known that he couldn't afford to show any physical weakness and that was why he'd been accepted.

Mick, who'd seen Sarah before she saw the mob, galloped to meet her to tell her Henry was riding behind the muster. When he'd finished talking, he smiled. A handsome black face, with strong features that would be the envy of any fellow, black or white or yellow.

People in Sydney and Palmerston had cautioned her about the Aborigines. *The Aboriginal problem* was how some of them phrased it. Others – a minority – had told her of their generous nature and their deep affinity with the land. Their land; she knew it was their land and she didn't know what to think of this conflict between cultures, this invasion of country. Because she felt there was no easy resolution to this tension, she'd adopted the pragmatic approach of avoiding thinking about it at all. But what Bella had told her just now about Carruthers had disturbed her equanimity. She felt she would no longer be able to focus only on living in the present; on finding happiness in the small things of life: in the sounds of the bush, in the Aboriginal music, in the play of light on the distant hills as each day unfolded.

'The mailman will come in two hours,' Mick said. 'That way sun.'

'How can you be sure? Why not an hour and a half? Or three hours?'

Mick grinned and pointed across the plain.

At first she could see nothing but after a moment of squinting she distinguished a faint plume of dust far into the distance. 'How do you know that's the mailman and not someone else?'

Mick tapped the side of his nose.

Sarah smiled. Plenty of time to ride with the muster to the camp north of the homestead, where the men would put the cattle to water. Plenty of time to ride back, to welcome the mailman with his string of packhorses and the bags of mail that they had been looking forward to for weeks.

When months before she'd agreed to accompany Henry to Dimbulah Downs she hadn't anticipated that the mail would be so slow, or that she would be so dependent on Frank O'Connor to keep her in touch with the outside world. Of course, before they left Sydney, and before they left Palmerston, she'd been warned of the isolation but she hadn't really taken much notice. Then she'd had no conception of the distances, of how much rivers and gorges could slow down communications. There was always the telegraph, of course, but that was so expensive, and hard to reach too, for they were several days' ride from the nearest repeater station. And you couldn't have the newspapers telegraphed; you couldn't receive sheet music over the wires. Yet most of the time this didn't matter, she thought, as she and Mick galloped towards the muster: every day here was busy.

* * *

Sarah poked her head through the open doorway of the kitchen, located across the yard from the main house. Ah Soy had his back to her and was cutting up something with a large cleaver. His pigtail was jiggling in time to his movements. Or perhaps slightly out of time, she thought, watching in some fascination: a syncopated rhythm. 'Supper on the verandah please, Ah Soy,' she said very gently. It would never do to surprise a cook with a cleaver.

'On verandah, missus,' Ah Soy repeated, without stopping his chopping.

Sarah made her way back across the yard. To the west the orange disc of the sun was sinking so swiftly it looked almost as if someone were lowering it on a piece of string. The ground around the homestead needed watering to keep the dust down, but she'd worry about that tomorrow. She felt so excited she broke into a skip and the dust eddied in little swirls around her ankles. The mail bags were waiting for her in the living room. She had a choice: to run straight inside and cut through the seals – and what a delightful thought that was – or she could deliberately extend this delicious feeling of anticipation, she could deliberately delay opening the bags.

The corner of the homestead verandah nearest the kitchen was completely encased in mosquito netting. Inside, seated at the long trestle table, Henry and the mailman Frank O'Connor were absorbed in conversation. Yarning, Henry called it, following local custom; but Frank seemed to be doing all the yarning today. A lean, sun-dried Irishman with pale blue eyes and a self-inflicted haircut, he could turn the most insignificant incident into a spellbinding tale. When she'd first met him, she'd wondered how such a sociable man could stand the lonely life of delivering mail to these remote properties. But then she realised how well the job suited him. He had an audience at every cattle station, an audience at every telegraph repeater station. And always an audience desperate to hear his tales. In between these performances he had time to transform into a grand epic any new anecdote he heard along the way. Lots of time; the distances he travelled were vast.

Sarah stood on the verandah for a moment watching the two men. Henry, nodding his head from time to time, appeared totally immersed in Frank's conversation. She felt a rush of tenderness for him. Everyone loved Henry, and not just because he was so interested in them. He never tried to impress them. He never tried to raise his own value by lowering someone else's.

Frank finished his story. Henry noticed Sarah watching them and smiled. 'Not opening the mail bags yet, Sarah? I thought you'd have already consumed the contents.'

'If I do it slowly it will last longer. Any moment now I'm going inside.'

'That reminds me,' Frank said, 'about the man who'd staked out a gold-mining claim out by Maude Creek.' And off he went on a tale about a man who never opened his mail, who'd come to the Territory to get away from his mail. Still it found him, and when he'd died they'd discovered bags of the stuff, eaten away mostly, by termites. But inside had been a letter from England saying he'd inherited a fortune back home. 'So it goes to show,' Frank concluded, 'that you should always open your mailbags.'

Sarah laughed. As she was about to move, she heard the screeching of the white cockatoos. They flew in every evening at around the same time. She hesitated for a moment to watch them jockeying for position in the branches of the dead gum tree down by the billabong. This was a complex ritual that they could never resolve harmoniously, no matter how many times they practised it.

The light was beginning to fade. She went inside and lit the lamp, before breaking open the seals and tipping on to the table the newspapers, packages of books and the sheet music she and Henry had ordered. At last, buried under everything else, she found the bundles of letters she was looking for. She flipped through these as through a deck of cards, sorting them by sender. There were several from Aunt Charlotte, one from Rose, some from other London friends, some from Henry's family, an official-looking one from a London-based solicitor, a number from various members of the Arnott family, one that looked as if it might be from the Morgans and, most important of all, a total of six from Harriet. One for each week since

Sarah had last received any mail, and such slim pickings that last delivery had been, so soon was it after their arrival here.

Sarah put to one side all the correspondence apart from the letters from Harriet. She organised these by postmark so that she could read them chronologically. But the envelopes seemed so thin. She tore them open, one after the other. The letters were even shorter than usual, barely three or four pages each. She began to read. It didn't take her long to read the first letter. Disappointment started to gnaw at the edges of her happiness. Of course, it was wonderful to have even a note from Harriet but Sarah did wish she wouldn't write quite so much about painting. Or more particularly, about her disappointment with her own painting. Sarah read the second letter, and then the third and fourth. There was rather too much about politics in these letters too, she thought irritably. Of course, it was useful, if not edifying, to have Harriet's take on such affairs. She seemed to have absorbed an almost encyclopaedic knowledge of Australian Colonial political events. But it was as if she were writing letters to newspapers rather than to her sister. Sarah sighed deeply. Harriet's descriptions were always so logical, so clear. It was almost as if their father had written these letters. The personal side of Harriet, the side of Harriet that Sarah missed terribly, wasn't much in evidence. She felt tears pricking her eyes. Maybe Harriet was depressed and that's why the letters were so impersonal. Or perhaps Harriet was angry with her and Henry for not being there when she'd arrived in Sydney. Yet she'd decided so precipitously to leave London, without even thinking to telegraph ahead, and they couldn't possibly have guessed what was in her head. When she turned over the last page of Harriet's sixth letter, Sarah's heart started to flutter as she read:

I have today booked a passage with the Eastern and Australian Steamship Company and anticipate arriving at Port Darwin on July 5th or thereabouts. I have been in contact with Charles, who telegraphed his old friend Ramsey Richardson, the Government Resident at Port Darwin. Charles has arranged for me to stay at the Residency for a few days, after which I shall make my way south to join you at Dimbulah Downs Station. I understand that the train runs as far as Pine Creek. From there I can no doubt take a coach to your place, so I won't inconvenience you in any way by having to be met at Palmerston.

Dearest Sarah, I am really excited at the prospect of seeing you again – and Henry too, of course – for I have missed you so! I expect you are looking more beautiful than ever, but Aunt Charlotte would support me in hoping you are being careful in the sun and heat and always wearing a hat. I have to confess I often forget and have become quite an ugly, brown thing in this Sydney climate but I'm sure you will still recognise your loving sister,

Harriet.

PS Telegraph at once if not convenient and indicate what you would like me to bring.

Sarah's elation found immediate release in a few excited skips around the room and she even clapped her hands with joy. But then she paused: perhaps she had misunderstood. She reread Harriet's scrawled lines: yes, July 5th or thereabouts. Harriet at Dimbulah Downs, what an adventure that would be.

After running the length of the verandah, Sarah pressed her face against the fly screen of the enclosure. Frank was in mid-yarn, but she paid no heed and burst out, 'Harriet's coming! She'll be at Port Darwin in just over a month. Isn't that wonderful?'

Henry's expression was blank, as if he couldn't recall who Harriet was. He must have been miles away, Sarah thought, caught up in Frank's story. Or perhaps he was tired out after the day's muster; fatigue could slow his reactions terribly.

'Harriet's coming,' she repeated. 'She said she could make her own way here! She was so droll, she said she'll take a coach from Pine Creek. She has no idea of what it's like.'

'That's what I'm afraid of,' said Henry slowly. 'She has no idea of what it's like here. And of course, we'll have to go to Port Darwin to meet her.'

'I'm so excited! We'll have to telegraph back. She wants to know if we want her to bring anything.'

Now Henry was staring towards the billabong. He appeared to be deep in thought as he contemplated the dead gum tree adorned with white cockatoos.

'We must telegraph, Henry. Can one of the men be spared to take a message to the telegraph repeater station?'

Henry transferred his gaze from the cockatoos to Sarah. 'Perhaps Harriet could bring a Louis Lot flute,' he said. 'A silver one, not ebony. Ebony might crack out here, with the days so hot and the nights so cool.'

'Or the termites might make a meal of it,' Sarah said. 'Yes, Harriet must bring a silver flute with her.'

'A *Louis Lot* flute, Sarah. Write out a message and one of the boys can take it to the telegraph station tomorrow.'

'That telegraphic office's a grand thing,' Frank said. 'And Dimbulah Downs is barely a few days' ride away.'

'A very grand thing,' Sarah said, laughing now she saw that she had Henry on side. 'I'll tell Ah Soy next. He'll be so pleased.'

'He doesn't know Harriet.'

'I've told him all about Harriet.'

Ah Soy wasn't in the kitchen, but she could hear water

119

splashing in the kitchen garden behind. She looked out of the window and in the fading light saw him watering the neat rows of vegetables with one of the Aboriginal lads. She wouldn't disturb them; they looked so peaceful.

Glancing around, she tried to see things through Harriet's eyes. She would love the lush kitchen garden and the line of lemon trees flourishing along one side. The plumbing facilities would be a shock to her but she need never see the lavatory for the stockmen. A kerosene drum positioned over a pit, it was screened on three sides with hessian stretched between sapling posts. The lavatory for the main house was also some distance away, although in a different direction. It was of the same design, with the addition of the crude wooden seat that Henry had asked one of the men to fashion soon after they arrived. The stench there was so awful she'd have to issue Harriet with a clothes peg to wear on her nose, although the problem with that was the flies would get in her mouth. The enclosure had no door, just a hessian curtain that neither she nor Henry ever used; the throne had what he described as a quite splendid view of the bush. The shower room was located near the bore. It too had three hessian walls but possessed the added sophistication of a stone slab floor.

There were other hardships too. In the middle of the day, the temperature was in the low nineties Fahrenheit, and the light was blinding. You couldn't roll up your sleeves in the sunlight without getting burned. There were flies in the daytime and mosquitoes at night. And everywhere there was dust: remorseless dust that covered everything. Sarah could never get it out from under her fingernails: they were permanently bordered in red dirt.

Harriet would find the manager's residence a bit of a shock as well: two bedrooms with walls of unlined corrugated iron attached to bloodwood sapling supports, and separated by a large living room with roughly hewn doors that could be opened to let the breezes flow through. Living here was akin to camping, and at this point Sarah remembered the snakes. Harriet would have to learn how to shoot a snake. You never knew when one might come across a king brown, or that's what Henry said. She herself had never had to dispatch one, but she knew how to do it. She had seen how it was done.

Then there was the domestic staff. Harriet couldn't help but love Bella and Daisy once she'd accustomed herself to their ways. And Ah Soy too, who could grow vegetables under even the most unpromising conditions. What she would make of the stockmen was another matter. But the homestead was quiet in the dry season. Most of the men were out at the stock camps. Bob would probably wish himself there too once Harriet arrived.

Sarah glanced up at the sky, already darkening to indigo and with a scattering of stars faintly visible. Harriet couldn't fail to love it here. There was so much space, so much freedom. She would become obsessed by the light and do her best paintings here, paintings that would bring her happiness and not despair. Sarah smiled to herself and went inside to draft the telegram. The silver Louis Lot flute; Henry had been most particular about that. A piano wouldn't go amiss either, but you had to be realistic.

* * *

Once supper was over, Sarah persuaded Frank to pull out his fiddle. He'd made it himself and, while it lacked the resonance of the instruments that Sarah was used to hearing, she was delighted with the expressiveness of his playing. Soon a chorus of frogs from the billabong started up an accompaniment, followed not long after by the intermittent croak of a bullfrog that sounded so close it might almost be in the fly-screened enclosure with them.

When Frank tired of playing, Sarah took out the Hohner harmonica Henry had given her after his trip to Queensland all those months ago. It would be fun to play a duet with Henry once Harriet arrived with the Louis Lot flute, she thought as she put the harmonica to her lips. Now she would play some of the bush ballads she'd learned, beginning with the cheerful ones and then moving on to the saddest in her repertoire. Henry and Frank would be unable to resist singing very loudly about heartache and loss. Her own heart filled with joy. She had everything she could ever want here this evening, this moment.

Chapter 18

On the End of a Rope Was a Young Black Girl

Later that evening, Sarah went into the living room to retrieve Harriet's letters. The shutters, crude affairs of corrugated iron that were hinged at the top to the frame of the building, were still unfastened. Through the open window she heard the men's voices and saw, illuminated by the brilliant moon, Henry and Frank standing on the hard ground below the verandah. Frank was recounting a tale to which Henry was paying little attention. When Frank stopped talking, Henry said, 'A week ago, I saw something really odd at a station south-west of here.'

'What was that?' Frank leaned against the verandah rail as if preparing for a long conversation. He's used to isolated people yarning half the night, thought Sarah, just as Henry's about to do.

Henry kicked a number of pebbles to one side as if he had to clear a space before continuing. 'It was at Empty Creek Station,' he said. 'They've got a blacks camp there too, and three gins working in the homestead, and plenty of black fellows as well as whites working as station hands and stockmen.'

Henry paused, and Frank grunted as if to offer him encouragement to continue.

'So it seemed there was no need for them to try to get more blacks from elsewhere,' Henry said. 'But while I was there, and with no sign of shame, Bert Carruthers and his mates rode up – white fellows all of them, and they were all laughing.

Carruthers was trotting at a fair old pace and behind him, running on the end of a rope, was a young black girl, no more than twelve or thirteen. It looked as if he'd lassoed her; she had a rope around her neck. She'd have had her neck broken if she'd fallen over.'

Sickened, Sarah turned off the lamp and knelt next to the window.

'They chained her up near the house, like a dog. "Niggers aren't human," Carruthers said, and laughed again. He told me they were going to keep her chained for four or five days, until she was tamed, and then she'd work around the place. I had to leave not long afterwards, but it's been on my mind ever since.'

If it had been on his mind, why hadn't Henry mentioned it to her? Until this moment Sarah had thought that he told her everything – the anxieties as well as the joys. She understood Bella's fears now.

'Ever since then,' Henry went on, 'I've been agonising about whether I should have taken a stand. With men like Carruthers and his mates, persuasion doesn't work. I had no gun with me. Not even the revolver I usually carry, while Carruthers and his mates had a rifle and a revolver apiece. Mick had stopped off at the Empty Creek Aboriginal camp, so I was on my own.'

'What could you have done if you'd had a gun anyway?' Frank said. 'You were outnumbered.'

'I could have said more, I should have said more, rather than simply stating that I thought it was bally inhumane. Those were my precise words, *bally inhumane*. They sniggered at that. I know that some people see black versus white as the survival of the fittest. But the Aborigines I've met aren't savage, or at least not as I understand the word. Take Mick, for example. He's gentle and every bit as intelligent as I am. More so, in fact.'

'The Daly River massacre showed up the white fellow as pretty bloody savage,' Frank said.

Henry agreed. 'If I were a bit smarter I might be able to see a way out of this mess. But I'm not and I don't see how the two cultures can ever be reconciled. Life here isn't simple, I'm starting to realise. I thought being acting manager at Dimbulah Downs was going to be a straightforward adventure but it's not. I knew there were issues about black fellows before we decided to come up here, but I didn't expect they'd be this bad. Why aren't we paying the Aborigines, for instance? They're not paid, or only in food and clothing. And this is one of the better stations, isn't it?'

'It is indeed. And I know, I've seen them all.'

'Sometimes I think I'm on the wrong side. I'd rather be with Mick than people like Carruthers any day.'

'Now that's a thing I'd be after keeping quiet about,' Frank said. 'And there's no way I'll be repeating it, so don't you worry. These abductions happen, as you saw for yourself. Not as much now as they used to, but they happen. How do you think they got workers here to begin with once the leaseholds were granted? The blacks had to be pacificated. It's not so bad here at Dimbulah Downs. The boss here had a kindly attitude right from the start, but it doesn't work that way everywhere. Got to get their workers somehow or the place'll never get civilised. And they don't always care how.'

'If dragging women in on a rope is civilisation, it isn't what I understand by that term. It looks more like slavery to me. Carruthers is an animal.'

'They say a lot of the murders of whites by blackfellers are about the gins,' Frank said. 'They don't mind sharing their women but they draw the line at abduction.' He pulled out his tobacco pouch and rolled a cigarette. When he had lit it, he sucked hard before continuing, 'I've seen plenty of things at some of the cattle stations that would really shock you. Lubras belted over the head with hobble chains. Lubras forced to crouch on a hot tin roof in the heat until they were almost dead. And worse.'

Sarah shuddered and felt her stomach churn.

'The Territory's a beautiful place but it attracts all sorts,' Henry said.

'Folk who love the isolated life and the landscape. Though there can't be too many of those or the Territory wages for white fellers wouldn't be so high. Got to compensate them for the diet of beef and damper,' Frank said. 'Not to mention the infrequent mail.'

'Then there are people who are escaping from something. Or who think they can get away with doing what they like up here.'

'Until they get a spear in their backs, that is.'

The frog chorus stopped abruptly and the ensuing silence put an end to the conversation. When the chorus began again, Frank said, 'Time to turn in. I've got a long day tomorrow.'

'Sure you don't want to sleep under a roof tonight?'

'No, I like my roof star-studded and I've a grand place to lay my swag not far from the lagoon.'

* * *

Henry sat on the edge of the bed and yanked off his boots.

'I couldn't help overhearing your conversation with Frank.' Sarah pulled up the blankets to cover her shoulders. 'Why didn't you tell me about Carruthers and all that?' Her horror at what she'd learned was spilling over into hostility towards Henry, yet his crime of omission was by far the lesser. Although she should be supporting him not accusing him, she found it impossible to stop. She willed him to reach out his arms to her and hug her, but he didn't. Instead he sat staring at the wavering lamp, while letting her harsh words wash over him. 'Why didn't you tell me?' she repeated. 'Why did you keep it all bottled up until Frank O'Connor, a man you hardly know, came by? Why tell him everything but keep me in the dark? If I hadn't accidentally overheard the two of you talking when I went to collect Harriet's letters, I might still be oblivious of what's going on in front of our very noses.'

She paused, waiting for a response that didn't come. Eventually she said, 'You told Frank you knew things were bad between whites and blacks and yet you still wanted to come up here. Why did you do that?'

'You were keen enough.'

'But I knew nothing. I'd never been further north than the Hawkesbury River.'

'You read up about it. Leichhardt's journal and all of that.'

'That's history. And why not tell me what you told Frank? How can I trust you if you won't tell me what's happening? How can I feel safe here if I think you're hiding things from me? I've had a sheltered life, but I'm not completely stupid. You can tell me these things and I won't fall apart.'

'I'm sorry, Sarah,' Henry said at last. 'We were speaking too loudly. I didn't want to tell you because I didn't want to frighten you.'

'But I want to know. I don't want to be shielded. I'm not some silly girl who's easily frightened.'

Henry sighed. 'The trouble with the Territory is that too many white men think the black fellow is a lazy bastard and you have to push him hard to get him to work. Carruthers is like that and he isn't the only one, you can bet on it.'

'I heard what Frank said.' I've been sheltered all my life, Sarah thought, despite my education. Sheltered by Father, sheltered by Harriet, sheltered by Henry. Hiding behind my music. Escaping into my music. And blind to what's happening around me.

Henry took off his clothes and climbed into bed. She put her arms around him and, with her head resting against his chest, listened to the metronome of his heartbeat. In a few moments he was asleep, leaving her uncomforted.

For hours she lay awake, unable to push away the image of the tethered black girl running behind Carruthers' horse and the laughing faces of the white men, unconcerned at the fate that would have befallen her if she'd tripped. She felt a growing anger against Carruthers.

When Henry rolled over, presenting his back to her, she began to feel angry with him too, for falling asleep without talking through the issue. As soon as he began to snore, her hostility was replaced by irritation. She gave him a well-judged shove, sufficient to stop the noise but not to wake him. In his sleep he flung out an arm and pulled her to him. Slightly mollified, she began to think of Harriet's visit.

She wondered what her sister would make of the cattle stations and their practices when she arrived in the Territory. Harriet would be sniffing out injustices, reaching generalisations, writing articles. There was a lot that Harriet and Henry would disagree about. Henry already had enough to worry about managing Dimbulah Downs without dealing with lectures from Harriet.

Yet recording injustice and fighting against injustice were the right things to do. If Sarah had Harriet's talents she would do it herself. But she wasn't clever like Harriet. She'd had the same opportunities as Harriet, but she had none of her flair.

* * *

The next afternoon, after filling a number of large empty jam tins with water, Sarah found a thick rough-cut plank near the timber store. There were two trestles a short distance away, and with some effort she managed to lever the plank on to the trestles. On top of this sturdy base she arranged the jam tins, adjusting them so they were equally spaced. Only after she'd extricated several splinters from her hands did she remove her revolver from its holster.

The gun was silver-coloured, and so shiny she could see her likeness in it. Her pale reflection, distorted by the curvature of the metal, looked critically back. To avoid this appraisal, she examined the handle. It was of ivory like the keys of the beloved piano that she'd left behind in Gower Street. Small and elegant, the revolver was a recent gift from Henry. For the snakes, he'd said. But maybe he'd meant for more.

She hated it, although she'd kept that opinion to herself. Her palms were beginning to sweat at the thought of what the gun could do. She placed it on the plank while she wiped her hands on her skirt. A few seconds of deep breathing calmed her. Her fingers were now as steady as if she were about to play a favourite piano piece; Satie maybe, or Chopin. No, she should think of music a bit more savage than that, maybe the cannons from Tchaikovsky's *1812 Overture*. Carefully she loaded the revolver and stepped back a few paces. Don't think, do, she exhorted herself. You're becoming a woman of action. You know right from wrong. Do, do, do.

She pulled the trigger. Her hand jerked back with the impact at the same instant that the bullet bit into the top of the tin furthest to the left. It teetered for an instant and then toppled to the ground, leaking its contents on to the dusty red earth, darkening it like a stain of blood. I aimed slightly too high, she thought. The next tin went, the bullet biting into it slightly lower. Now I'm in control, she thought, each shot will be a quarter of an inch lower than the next. A perfect aim, a perfect shot, a perfect fall. And the next tin, and the next, until they all lay on the earth, rolling slightly, for the surface of the ground was not entirely even, until at last all was still.

I'm good at this, she thought, and I'll become even better. This round her hand had been steady, no trembling to spoil her aim, even her palms were no longer sweating.

'You have to keep practising,' Henry had said when he'd given her the revolver. And she would; there'd be no stopping her now she'd learned that she had a good eye.

Chapter 19

'You Have a Very Forgiving Nature'

Early afternoon, the sea smooth with a gentle swell. In the distance Harriet could distinguish a dark blur along the horizon, and rising above this were several plumes of smoke. It was Arnhem Land, the captain had said over lunch, and the *Guthrie* was making such excellent progress after leaving Thursday Island that they'd arrive at Port Darwin a couple of days earlier than scheduled.

Leaning on the ship's rail, Harriet thought she was alone until she heard a deep voice right next to her. It was Dan Brady, with his tanned face and long nose pointing this way and that, as if it had been broken a few times. A fighter or a footballer, or perhaps he'd been thrown a few times from a horse. Though he'd joined the ship at Moreton Bay and she'd spoken to him a couple of times, this had always been in a group of other passengers. She'd liked him; he'd seemed friendly without being pushy.

'I saw you sitting on deck this morning with your sketchbook,' he said. 'I stood right behind you and looked at what you were doing. You didn't even notice me.'

'Didn't I? You're too big to be easily overlooked,' she said, laughing. Big but lithe, she thought, with eyes the colour of the midday sky and a black beard so long it covered the top of his shirt front.

'I do cast a bit of shade, people tell me.'

'I'm sorry I didn't see you. I get rather absorbed once I start sketching.'

'Bit of an artist, eh?' He began to comb his beard with his fingers.

'Not a professional one.'

'Thought not.' He finished combing his beard and said, 'Good drawing, but.'

'Thank you.'

'Of the men playing cards.'

'It was just a quick sketch,' she said.

'None of the great artists have been women.'

His remark seemed so pat he could have been reciting something he'd been taught at school. She decided to treat it as a joke rather than an act of aggression. After forcing out a little tinkle of laughter – four notes of the scale were all she could manage – she said, 'Well, I do it because I'm driven to. I don't expect to make my living out of it. What do you do?'

'I'm a drover. You can tell by me hands.' He spread them out. Though strong and well-shaped, they were sunburnt and work-hardened too. He continued, 'Spent most of me time in western Queensland but I'm heading to the Territory to find work there. Thought of going overland but then decided to take a passage on this steamer. I've got some mates in the Territory. That's the thing about droving, you meet people on the road.'

'Not many, I suppose.'

'That's why you become mates with the few you meet.'

'Do you find it a lonely life?'

'Me wife left me a few months ago. Buggered off, excuse the language, when I was droving.' He began to chew at a wad of tobacco.

'That's tough.'

'Tough being rejected, is that what you mean?'

'I meant tough losing someone you love.'

'Yes. And I'll never forgive her.' He spat viciously into the ocean.

There was a moment's pause. She toyed with the notion of saying that until you forgive you can't move on, but dismissed that as patronising. Instead she said, 'I lost my father some months ago.'

'What about your mother?'

'My mother died when I was young.'

'I see. What's a good looker like you doing travelling on your own?'

'Not quite on my own,' she said, inwardly registering the rare compliment. 'I'm visiting family.'

'Going back home after?'

'Yes.

'You'll find yourself a good man up north. Not a bad place to look.'

'Is that so? But I'm not looking.'

He laughed. 'That's what they all say. Engaged, are you?'

'No.' When he edged closer, she wished she'd manufactured a fiancé. She could have told Brady that, like her new friend Annie McArthur, she was travelling to Port Darwin to meet up with him.

'You look a bit like me wife,' he said, 'but a bit younger.'

His chewing became more energetic and she wondered how she should respond to this remark. After a short pause she simply said, 'Do I?'

'She didn't draw, but. She worked as a housemaid.'

'I see. Do you have children?'

'No children. Me wife had a baby but it wasn't mine.'

The ringing of the lunch bell terminated their conversation.

* * *

Several afternoons later, Harriet sat on deck next to Annie McArthur. From the lower deck of the steamer came the raucous laughter of a group of men playing cards and drinking.

'Who's that man down there?' Annie had red hair and pallid skin that was better suited to the mists of the Scottish Highlands than the relentless sun of the tropics. 'The one with black hair dealing the cards.'

'That's Dan Brady.'

'I've noticed him following you around,' Annie said. 'Has he made a pass at you?'

'No. He's a bit lonely, that's all.' Although he stood too close to her each time they spoke, Harriet thought this meant nothing. Some people had no idea of social distance. They would either stand too far away, as if they couldn't trust themselves – or you – not to leap into an embrace, or too close, as Brady did. She added, 'He says I look like his wife.'

'He's married?' Annie said. 'What on earth is he doing trailing after you then?'

'He's not doing that. Anyway, his wife ran off.'

'*You* can't really run off, can you?' Annie said, smiling. 'There's nowhere much to run to, apart from our stuffy little cabins. By the way, I've been meaning to ask if you've been to Port Darwin before.'

'No, but I've read a bit about it.'

'It's hot, humid and horrid. The three H's. Well, my fiancé didn't actually write horrid, but that's what I'm expecting... It's a real hardship post, but the pay's much better than down south so that's why we're going to be spending at least two years up there. After that he'll be looking for promotion to a better job in Adelaide.'

'Maybe you'll stay on. Some people claim that there's something about the tropics that gets to you. The smells, the air, the light. The fact that it's so different to everything you've ever known before.'

Annie laughed. 'Maybe *you'll* be staying on then.'

'I don't think so. I've got rather fond of the Sydney light.' Harriet thought of the artists' camp at Balmoral, not far from Mosman where she'd stayed with the Morgans. She would love to be part of that group.

* * *

The next afternoon, Harriet developed a headache not long after lunch. It was her own fault, she thought, as she lay in her cabin, with a cold facecloth over her eyes. Too much standing out on deck without a hat, staring at the sparkling sea. Her temples were throbbing and she felt as if needles were piercing the back of her skull. The smallest movement made it worse.

When she surfaced again it was nearly ten o'clock at night. After almost eight hours' sleep she felt quite refreshed, although the cabin seemed claustrophobic, and her clothes were sweat-soaked. She washed and changed before going on deck. The sea was calm and the salty air heavy on her skin, but cooler now, a gentle breeze taking the heat out of it. The moonlight was so bright she thought she could distinguish the shoreline but perhaps it was simply a band of cloud.

Men's voices wafted up from the lower deck, with the occasional gust of laughter, as they continued with their everlasting card games. Harriet rested her hands on the ship's rail and watched the flickering ladder of reflected moonlight lying across the ocean's surface. Above her the stars seemed so close she might reach up and touch them.

For a brief moment she felt as if she was being squeezed between the immensity of the ocean and the weight of the heavens. Over two years had passed since she had last seen Sarah. Would she have changed much? And would Harriet like Henry any better? She would have to try. Apart from the fact that Henry had carried her sister off to a harsh and inhospitable world 9000 miles from London, there was nothing much else wrong with him, or at least not that she knew of. She grimaced at the thought that quite possibly Henry was dreading her arrival. The trouble with family being far away was that you couldn't just drop in on them for a day, a week, a month. Three months was what she had planned. That was a long time to stay.

Now she became aware that she was not alone. Footsteps sounded from the other side of the deck. She kept very still. Perhaps the person wouldn't come her way, or if they did, they mightn't see her; she didn't want to be noticed if it was one of those raucous men. The footsteps halted.

'Relax, it's only me.' The voice was unmistakably Dan Brady's. 'I hoped I'd catch you on deck. Have you been avoiding me?'

'No, I've been sleeping off a headache.' She felt pleased to see him; it had been half a day since she'd spoken to anyone.

'Don't want you running off on me as well.'

For an instant she wondered if there was something sinister in those words but dismissed that thought. He was simply a lonely man who was being friendly. Although she couldn't see his eyes, his collarless white shirt was a gleaming contrast to his black beard. It was good to think that someone was looking out for her.

'No one else but us around. The fellers are all on the lower deck.'

At this moment she felt her shoulders firmly gripped and Brady pulled her towards him. Pinning her against the railing, he bent and kissed her on the mouth, pushing his tongue that tasted of tobacco and whisky into her mouth. Pulling her head back, she tried to shove him away, but he had her pinioned against the railing. 'Don't,' she said, her voice catching. 'I don't want to kiss you.'

'Didn't look that way to me.'

She wriggled free and turned to face him. She stepped back a pace. He followed. He lifted one hand and put it over her face and with the other hand pushed her back, wedging her against the railing with his bent knee to her right and his free arm to her left. Heart racing, she gave him a hard heave, but she couldn't budge him. She wriggled her head against his hand and managed to bite one of his fingers. When he yelped and removed his hand, she began to shout. Though it was unlikely that anyone would hear her over the sounds of the engine, she carried on yelling until Brady gave her cheek a stinging slap. The shock of it stopped her scream and she saw the gleam of his teeth as he smiled. Then he was leaning against her, his hands cupping her face and bending down to kiss her.

'Let her go!' Annie stood a few yards away, her flaming hair blanched by the moonlight.

Brady let his hands slip from Harriet's face and turned to face Annie. It would be easy for him to tip her over the railing and into the ocean and blame it on a sudden swell. Heart thumping, Harriet hooked her arm through one of the life-rings hanging nearby and put out a foot. Brady stumbled on it.

'Stupid fucking bitch,' he said, his face contorted as he struggled to stay upright. 'You were asking for it.'

'Perhaps we're not as stupid as you think.' Harriet's voice was hoarse from shouting and her palms slippery with sweat as she gripped the life-ring with both hands.

'Doncha bet on it,' he said, stepping towards her with his hand raised.

She wondered if he would he hit her again. Tightening her grip on the life-ring, she turned her face to one side to avoid the blow. His image stayed with her: that gleaming white shirt and black spade-shaped beard, and above it all that searing look of hatred. Seconds passed. Raising one arm to protect her face, she stole a look. Brady had moved back a few paces. His hand lowered, he was turning away; he was shambling along the deck towards the staircase.

Annie put an arm around Harriet's shoulders and smoothed her hair. Harriet pulled out a handkerchief and rubbed her mouth with it. She had badly misjudged this man. Her legs began to tremble, and she sat down abruptly on the deck.

Annie knelt beside her. 'It's lucky I came along and heard you shout. We're going to have to report this to the captain.' Enfolding Harriet in her arms, she said, 'Was there a reason you were out on deck? You hadn't arranged to meet him, had you?'

'No, no. I just felt I needed a breath of fresh air before going to sleep.'

'So did I. The cabins are stifling. And Miss Foster's started having her meals brought into the cabin and, honestly Harriet, she hasn't had a wash for days. She's stuck in her bunk like a body in a coffin, and she says she's not getting up until we get into port, apart from to use the toilet. We'll go and see the captain once you've recovered. You don't want to feel you can't leave your cabin at night.'

'I don't want a fuss, Annie. Brady only kissed me.'

'But you know he was planning more.'

'I don't want to think about it.' Harriet couldn't prevent her voice trembling. The last thing she wanted was a fuss on arrival.

'Why not? He assaulted you.'

'I don't want everything spoilt when we get there.'

'You have a very forgiving nature.'

* * *

For the rest of the voyage, Harriet avoided Brady and he kept out of her way. During this time, she interrogated her actions, wondering if she had led him on. It was true that she was inexperienced, and yet searching for ambiguities in her behaviour towards him she could find none. Maybe he was unstable, or her physical resemblance to his wife made him think she was his for the asking. She hated the sense she'd had that he'd enjoyed pushing her around, had enjoyed slapping her. She hated that she didn't have the physical strength to fight him off. She hated the thought that this gave him power over her.

It was high tide when the ship arrived at Port Darwin. Harriet stood on deck with Annie as they steamed past the low mangrove-clad shoreline that gradually rose to cliffs perhaps sixty feet high, and then into a bay between two headlands. And there was the town of Palmerston, a smattering of white roofs amongst dense tropical foliage. How lovely it all was, and in a couple of days she would see Sarah and Henry.

As they were preparing to disembark, she felt a quick tap on her shoulder. Turning, she faced Dan Brady. 'You watch out for yourself, Miss Cameron,' he hissed. 'You bloody stuck-up bitch.'

'Take no notice,' Annie said, putting an arm around Harriet. 'The Territory's a big place. You won't see him again.'

Chapter 20

A Little Ingenuity and Some Scraps of Wood

The air was pressing down on Harriet like a heavy blanket. She couldn't imagine being here in the wet season. Even now, in July in the so-called dry season, she found the heat enervating. She surreptitiously wiped her sweating palms on her skirt and glanced at the harbour, visible below the lawns of the Government Residency. She hadn't been prepared for the startling rise and fall of the Port Darwin tides, a daily reminder of the volatility of the tropics. She loved to watch the tide turn: the water could rise five feet in a few seconds and if you were close enough you could hear a sucking sound followed by a roaring as the water pushed forward in a vast wave.

Then she looked at the other women seated in cane chairs on the Residency lawn. They were gazing at her expectantly. Suddenly she felt a little like a creature in a zoo whose sole purpose was to be inspected. In due course she might also be interrogated, although not by Mrs Richardson, wife of the Resident. Harriet had learned in the two days since the *Guthrie* had arrived early at Port Darwin that her hosts, the Richardsons, would never ask her questions of a personal nature.

'Well, I just don't know how you did it,' said Mrs Jacobs, putting her cup and saucer on an occasional table and settling herself more comfortably in her chair. A large woman in early middle-age, Mrs Jacobs' complexion had been made brighter by the indiscriminate application of rouge, or perhaps this was simply the after-effects of gulping down several scalding cups of tea. She added, 'Fancy travelling all the way from England to Sydney on your own and then coming up here barely two months later!'

To Harriet, Mrs Jacobs' words sounded like an accusation. She didn't feel able to offer Mrs Jacobs further justification for her presence here. She had already told the party that she was travelling to see her sister and brother-in-law, who would be arriving at the railway station the next day. She took a deep breath and looked down at the grass. Even if she were to try, she suspected vindication would be impossible.

'Plenty of women travel out here on their own,' Mrs Richardson said. 'Think of all those governesses and teachers emigrating to the colonies.'

'They have jobs to go to,' persisted Mrs Jacobs. 'Or they're engaged to be married.'

'I have relatives,' Harriet reminded the company.

'Miss Cameron is such a resourceful young woman,' said Mrs Richardson calmly. 'But perhaps you too would do the same if you were in her situation, Mrs Jacobs. Travel is so broadening, don't you think? I always tell my girls to seize the opportunity in the lifetime of the opportunity.' She paused, before adding, 'And of course necessity is the mother of invention.'

Harriet smiled at her hostess. Mrs Richardson was inclined to bring forth a proverb or two – usually but not invariably apposite – when she wished to guide the conversation from the personal to the general, or perhaps even to the metaphysical.

'Indeed that is precisely what you will discover when you begin your odyssey south,' Mrs Richardson continued, now addressing herself to Harriet. 'It's amazing what people can put together with a little ingenuity and some scraps of wood and metal. I'm always particularly impressed with the uses to which the simple kerosene tin can be put.'

Harriet laughed.

'It's true,' Mrs Jacobs said. 'People use them for cooking. They use them for their ablutions. They even make furniture out of them.'

'They possess a wonderful advantage that is vital in the Territory,' Mrs Richardson explained. 'They're unattractive to termites.'

The ladies now vied with one another in recounting examples they'd seen of the creative use of the kerosene tin. This competition was ultimately won by an account of a chest of drawers that one of the women had encountered at a cattle station in the Barkly Tablelands, where she'd been travelling with her stock and station agent husband. 'It was constructed out of a rough-sawn timber frame and runners,' she said. 'Into which were slotted kerosene tins on their sides with one face cut off. The handles were original, of course.' She turned to Harriet. 'Perhaps you haven't seen these cans? They're rectangular and come with handles attached to the top. So very useful! Of course, they can come in other shapes too, but the rectangular ones are particularly valuable for construction of the finest furniture.'

In this climate any effort, even of a verbal nature, generated additional heat and several of the ladies began to fan themselves. Another guest, an elderly woman whose name Harriet had not caught when they were introduced, now turned to Harriet. It seemed she had somehow found out about Henry's family – in particular about his father's baronetcy – and she took advantage of the general lassitude to ask Harriet if she and Sarah were presented at court. Harriet laughed, as did Mrs Richardson, who knew of James Cameron's background as well as his politics.

'My father was against all that stuff.' Harriet was pleased that, eighteen months after her father's death, she was able to talk of him with pleasure and pride and to conceal the grief she still felt. 'We had a very unusual upbringing. He brought us up to see all human beings as equal. And that everyone had the right to education.'

'A wonderful man,' said Mrs Richardson. Although she'd never met him, she greatly admired those whose principles coincided with her own. 'A strong supporter of sexual equality and the right to vote for all.' She smiled benevolently around at the other women, as if no one could possibly refute the logic of these opinions.

'Well, there's universal suffrage for the blacks in South Australia but the Aborigines don't all turn out for the elections.' Mrs Jacobs spoke almost triumphantly, as if this were an argument against giving everyone the right to vote.

'I think it's more that they don't know they're allowed to vote,' Harriet said.

'Whatever. My point remains. They don't know what to do with the vote once they have it.'

'Anyway, there's not quite universal suffrage,' Harriet added. 'I believe the Chinese don't have the right to vote. Not to mention women.'

The immediate drop in temperature could have been due to the slight onshore breeze that had sprung up rather than to the concerted intake of breath of most of the women present. Mrs Richardson, never at a loss for words, said quickly, 'And then there are the other Australian colonies. No votes for women there. Or the Celestials or the Aborigines. But I do think one needs to educate people before giving them the vote. That will come, but not for a long time I am afraid.'

'The blacks are savages, they'll never learn,' said Mrs Jacobs.

Harriet, about to respond, was pre-empted by Mrs Richardson. 'I don't think that's very Christian, dear,' she said. Her voice was as calm as ever, but a small pink spot had appeared on each of her pale cheeks. 'All men are equal in the eyes of our Lord.'

'But not in the eyes of our legal system,' said the woman who had travelled in the Barkly Tablelands. 'Just look at how those troopers managed to get acquitted in the Adelaide murder trial when it was as clear as daylight they'd massacred those blacks.'

'It's not what you know but who you know,' Mrs Richardson said. Her tone was slightly vague, her attention having been distracted by two housemaids who had embarked on some game on the Residency verandah rather than on the more important task of clearing away the tea-things.

This sight inspired some of the women to initiate a new subject, the perennial problem of obtaining good household help. Harriet let the conversation wash around her while she watched the harbour water turn a deeper blue. It had been high tide when her ship had steamed into Port Darwin and she'd thought she'd seen the last of Dan Brady.

But she'd been wrong. Only yesterday she'd gone out for a walk in the late afternoon, with two of the Richardson girls, when the air was a little cooler. They'd passed through the street known as Chinatown, a street that was lined with battered-looking buildings constructed from timber and corrugated iron, buildings housing laundries and tailors, a few stores, and a ramshackle edifice that was reputed, according to the Richardson girls, to be an opium den. Harriet loved the exotic scents of joss sticks and spices, and even the smells of dried fish and pungent tobacco appealed to her. A small Chinese child, dressed in a blue jacket and pink trousers, and with a shaven head apart from an almost perfect square in the centre, stumbled off the kerb in front of Harriet, and collapsed into a heap on the road. Harriet leaned forward to pick him up; he was more amused than shaken by his experience.

When she looked up again, she saw Brady not five yards away, lurching towards her. White collarless shirt, black hair and beard, face contorted with hatred: the image from that moonlit night on the *Guthrie* rose up before her again.

Hoping he was too far gone to notice her, she quickly averted her face. But when he was level with her, he turned and spat. A string of saliva, dark brown from the tobacco he had been chewing, landed on the skirt of her white muslin dress and dribbled down, leaving behind a dark, ugly stain. He gave a short laugh before walking on.

Involved in the antics of the little Chinese boy, the Richardson girls didn't notice. When Mrs Richardson remarked later on the soiled dress, she wondered if she should explain what had happened with Brady on board the steamer. Yet she didn't want to worry the Richardsons unnecessarily. She knew that if she told them, they'd become concerned about her welfare and start fussing if she decided to take one of her walks. Better by far to keep quiet about it. That way they wouldn't worry about her taking unnecessary risks. She wouldn't tell Sarah either. There was no need to. If people around her started to worry about her safety, Brady would have won. She was going to try to forget all about him. She could look after herself, and in a few days' time she'd be off with Sarah and Henry to the peace of Dimbulah Downs and the incident would be well and truly behind her.

Harriet would never wear that dress again. Despite her resolve to forget, she still felt violated and thought it would be impossible to remove the stain completely. Although Mrs Richardson had said that her Chinese laundry man could remove anything, how else could everyone wear so much white in the tropics, Harriet decided not to keep it. After having it laundered, she would give it to one of the housemaids.

Now one of the ladies at the tea table was asking her a question, was repeating a question; it seemed that she was inviting Harriet to attend, with Sarah and Henry, the little cricket match her husband was organising on Sunday. One side would consist of Aboriginal players and she might find that amusing.

'Is there an oval here?'

'Of course! It's one of the first things any self-respecting settlement creates. That and the racecourse, although in some places they're one and the same.'

'We'll be going,' said Mrs Richardson. 'It's such good fun to watch. You can come with us. Mr and Mrs Vincent too, of course, they'll be here by then.' At this moment she succeeded in attracting the attention of the maids and, with the removal of the tea-things, the tea party came to a conclusion.

After dinner that evening, Harriet wandered out into the garden through which moonlight poured, turning to shades of indigo and silver the foliage that by daylight had seemed green and gold. The air was heavy and scented with flowers that were unknown to her. Three pearling luggers, solid shapes in the shimmering water, were moored not far from the mangrove-edged shoreline. She sat on one of the chairs on the lawn and listened to the distant shouts from the crew of one of the luggers.

Presently she heard the haunting sound of a didgeridoo, which seemed to be coming from the direction of Mindil Beach, its reverberation so deep that she could almost feel its vibrations. The didgeridoo was joined by a rhythmic beating of what could be wooden sticks. After a time, a mournful voice started to chant, a chanting that continued for some minutes in a restricted range of a couple of notes, until it suddenly rose in a whooshing sound, almost like the cry of some startled animal, before settling back to its original narrow range of sounds, accompanied all the while by the didgeridoo and the beating sticks. The voice was articulating words in a language she could never hope to understand. The chant was almost hypnotic, for it made her want to tap her foot, and then to stand up and move, to stand up and dance.

So she did that after a while; she got up out of her chair and stamped around the lawn. As she danced, she moved out of herself and looked down on herself, a tiny figure on the lush lawn of the Government Residency in this tiny settlement next to the Arafura Sea, on an isolated continent on a planet spinning through space, for she had been well-educated in science and, by nature and nurture, was aware of the insignificance of man.

As she danced and contemplated the vastness of space and the unimportance of man, it didn't occur to her that she might ever find this frightening.

Chapter 21

'What on Earth's That Thing She's Got on Her Head?'

Leaning out of the carriage window as the little train inched to the end of the line, Henry was the first to spot Harriet. 'There she is, Sarah! My God, what on earth's that thing she's got on her head?'

'It's a hat, Henry,' Sarah said, leaning out a little further. 'Almost exactly the same as yours. Isn't she sensible? It's the perfect thing for Dimbulah Downs! Now don't you go spoiling things today, will you?' As Sarah spoke, she lightly touched his shoulder to take the sting out of her words. Then she called out, 'Harriet! Harriet! Oh, Henry, why is she looking in the other direction – has she gone blind?'

Henry opened the carriage door. Sarah was on the platform in an instant and reached Harriet just as she turned her way.

'Hattie, how glad I am to see you again!'

'Sarah, you look wonderful! I can't tell you how happy I am. Oh, my heaven, you're strangling me!'

'And you're squeezing my stays, Hattie, they're digging in terribly! You don't know your own strength!'

'You're not wearing them up here are you?' Harriet said, laughing and crying at the same time. 'It's far too hot for a corset!'

'But it's a very special *ventilated* corset. There are vertical tapes for the whalebone and horizontal bands to hold everything in place. The skin breathes through all the little gaps. Clever, isn't it?'

'Sounds like an instrument of torture,' Harriet said, running her hands down Sarah's back. 'But I understand the principle. It feels a bit like split cane!'

'I found a marvellous little place in Sydney that does them.' Sarah relinquished her hold of Harriet and watched her husband and sister confront one another. 'You can kiss your sister-in-law, Henry,' she said, smiling. 'Don't stand on ceremony.'

Although it was achieved slightly clumsily, Sarah decided it was because of the width of Harriet's hat rather than any residual awkwardness. Harriet had become, if not exactly beautiful, certainly rather striking-looking, with the bone structure of her sun-browned face more pronounced than Sarah had remembered. Although she seemed much thinner, her weight loss suited her and she'd become almost graceful in her movements.

But now Harriet's expression had become critical as she looked at Henry. Sarah wondered if she was appraising him as an artist might a model and might at any moment whip a sketchbook out of her bag to record her dishevelled brother-in-law, crumpled after a week's travel. Or perhaps more likely was that her sister was struggling to forget that she'd never really warmed to Henry.

* * *

Harriet thought that Sarah looked pale despite the heat, and even lovelier than she had remembered. Dressed in a beige riding skirt and high-necked white blouse, Sarah raised her hands to push back a curl that was escaping from her straw hat, and Harriet saw that her once-beautiful hands had become rough and dusted with freckles. They looked as if they belonged to a woman years older. Too much sun and harsh soap, Harriet thought. It was all Henry's doing, bringing her into such a cruel climate. And to make matters worse, there wasn't even the comfort of a piano at Dimbulah Downs. A harmonica was all very well, but it wasn't the same as a piano. But at least there was the Louis Lot flute, which Harriet had slipped into her handbag to bring with her to the station.

'I'm so glad to see you, Hattie,' Sarah was now saying. 'It's been nearly three years and I can't believe you're here at last.'

Harriet observed that there was a new serenity about Sarah's expression. Perhaps all her experiences since leaving home had been kind to her. Her letters had suggested so. Henry might have ruined her hands but maybe he'd brought her happiness.

Sarah continued, 'We're going to have such adventures and of course you must stay with us the whole time we are here. Mustn't she, Henry? We're not leaving until the build-up and we won't hear of you going before then.'

'The build-up?'

'Yes. To the wet. Dimbulah Downs gets cut off completely by all the rivers flooding their banks. But there's lots of warning before the rains start – storms and humidity – and the usual manager will be back in October anyway. I suppose it all seems very strange to you, Harriet? I do hope you will like it.'

'I shall, Sarah. I shall love it.'

'It's so exciting to have you here. Isn't it, Henry?'

Henry was nursing a sweat-stained felt hat in his hands. There was no sign yet of the baldness Harriet had predicted for him when they'd met years before. His fair curls were sun-bleached and worn long enough to cover his slightly protruding ears. Though he had obediently kissed her when instructed by Sarah, and had managed a smile, excitement was absent from his suntanned face; in fact, he appeared rather glum. He doesn't want me here, Harriet thought.

'Very good to see you, Harriet. Very good. You will excuse me for a moment, won't you? I have to find a couple of our stockmen who've come with us, to give them instructions before we head off.'

While Sarah struggled to put away her handkerchief in a pocket that was too small for the purpose, Harriet watched Henry thread his way around the edge of the crowd until he reached an athletic-looking Aboriginal man.

'That's Mick he's talking to,' Sarah said. 'He's going to purchase some more horses while we're here.'

Remembering the present she'd bought Sarah in Sydney, Harriet began to rummage in her bag. 'Here's the flute you wanted, Sarah,' she said, finding it at last at the very bottom although she'd put it in at the top before leaving the Residency.

'Thank you so much, Harriet. Henry will be so pleased.'

'Is it for Henry?'

'Yes.'

'I thought it was for you.'

'No, I have a harmonica. Henry wanted the flute.'

'I see.'

'Does it matter?'

'No, of course not.'

'I could only send a short telegram about it. Dimbulah Downs is several days' ride from the nearest telegraph station so we had to send one of the stockmen with the message. Otherwise you mightn't have heard from us at all before you'd left Sydney. Just as we didn't hear from you before you left London.'

'I did send you a telegram then, as I said in my letter.'

'We didn't get it, so there you are. I'm so sorry we weren't there in Sydney to meet you, but let's not go over all that again. We're here to meet you now, or rather you to meet us. What a surprise that the *Guthrie* got in a bit early! Oh Hattie, I'm so very, very happy you're here at last.'

151

At this moment Henry reappeared. At once he noticed the parcel that Harriet was holding, and his expression lightened. 'The flute?' he said.

'Yes, the Louis Lot flute.'

'Silver, not ebony?'

'Yes, silver.'

'That's so the white ants won't get it.'

Harriet laughed.

'It's true,' Henry said. 'Thank you very much, Harriet. You've made my day. It's really good to see you again.'

Chapter 22

'Rather Good at Cricket'

The Aboriginal batsman gave the ball a resounding thwack and drove it up into the air. Sarah clapped her hands as she watched it rise in an arc over Henry's head, far beyond his reach, before descending into the lake beyond the boundary of the Port Darwin cricket field.

'It's a six!' shouted one of the bystanders. 'There's no need to run!'

But the batsmen were already racing between the stumps as if their lives depended on it. Sarah laughed in sympathy. She'd been induced to learn the rules of cricket when she'd discovered that Henry played but she hadn't found them easy. She glanced at Harriet, seated on a tartan rug by her side. Harriet disliked team sports but even she was looking amused. The batsmen continued running. The crowd began to cheer, stimulating the batsmen on to further runs. Eventually the two umpires forcibly restrained the runners and appeared to be endeavouring to impress upon them the rules of the game once more.

'This is such fun,' Sarah said. 'I'm so glad the Richardsons brought us.' She surveyed the scene: the picnickers lounging on rugs or deckchairs in the shade of the trees that encircled the ground, the grass with its balding pitch bearing testimony to many games, and people still splashing about in the lake, although the cricket ball had long since been found and restored to the bowler.

'The Richardsons are very kind people,' said Harriet. 'Which is more than you can say of some of the others.'

'Oh Hattie, don't be so harsh.' Then Sarah thought of her own initial reception, both here and in Sydney. The welcome of some of the people she and Henry had met had been guarded. The more self-important ones had been suspicious of people from the place they called Home. She had guessed they were anxious that they might be judged as provincial. So they criticised the outsider first and in doing so felt the stronger for it. She tried not to think of that; she still wanted to believe that all people were good. Even now, even after all she'd learned of Carruthers and his ilk.

'Most of the people I've met at the Residency disapprove of me,' Harriet said. 'Not you, but me. I'm single and travelling on my own. They don't like that, especially people like Mrs Jacobs.'

'It's just some of the wives. No one else cares.'

'Maybe. But thank God you're here, Sarah! You and Henry have endowed me with some respectability!'

'You've never cared a fig for respectability,' Sarah said. 'And I hope respectability wasn't all you missed about us, Hattie.' She thought that Harriet seemed harder somehow and at the same time even more prickly, more inclined to take offence at the most harmless remarks. In the two days they'd spent together, Sarah had learned to think before opening her mouth, for sometimes an innocuous little comment would bring forth a strong reaction from Harriet.

As if she were a wounded animal, Henry had said last night, lashing out because she'd been hurt. Then he'd added that she was probably still grieving for their father. Sarah had felt slightly guilty at this. Though she'd mourned her father's death, she hadn't really missed him the way her sister did. While she often thought of him with affection and some amusement, she didn't miss him viscerally the way she'd missed Henry when he'd been away. Or even in the way she'd missed Harriet. She'd been so glad to see Harriet at the station, so glad to touch her, to envelop her in a huge hug. And afterwards she'd felt restored somehow. Not that Henry wasn't enough, but she'd known Harriet all her life; she was a part of her. Maybe that was why Harriet's heightened prickliness – or perhaps fragility was a better word – was so disturbing.

Mrs Richardson joined them and flopped down in the empty deckchair next to Harriet. She took off her hat and fanned herself with it. Hers was the sort of skin that went white in the heat. Or perhaps it was fatigue that was making her look so pale; she had spent all afternoon moving from group to group as she would at a Residency function. Sarah guessed that her mixing with the onlookers was not merely a part of the duties of the Government Resident's wife but also a careful monitoring of the whereabouts and behaviour of her three daughters and two sons, especially of the older daughters, Isobel and Alexandra. They were sitting – and flirting – with some of the young men who worked for the telegraphic office.

'See that man, the tall blonde good-looking one?' Mrs Richardson said, staring hard at the young men surrounding her daughters. 'I call him the Racehorse because he's so fast with the ladies. On no account can he be left alone with a female of any age, and certainly not with one of my girls.'

'My dear Mrs Richardson,' said Sarah, 'I'm afraid this is about to happen.' Isobel Richardson was now drifting away from Alexandra to join Mrs Jacobs and some other women; and at the same time some of the young men from the telegraphic office also wandered off, leaving Alexandra Richardson alone with the handsome blonde man.

'On with the game,' said Mrs Richardson, easing herself out of the deckchair. 'I simply cannot let Alexandra alone with the Racehorse. I'm getting more exercise than the batsmen and that's saying something. But a stitch in time saves nine, as they say.'

Sarah watched Mrs Richardson move with considerable speed to where Alexandra was sitting. She stood so close to the Racehorse that he had no alternative but to offer her his chair. This she graciously accepted, while waving the young man to a spot on the grass adjacent to her feet. Once he was seated, she engaged him in what appeared to be a lively conversation.

'A beautiful manoeuvre,' said Sarah.

'She could probably teach even Aunt Charlotte a thing or two,' Harriet said. Then she looked pointedly at Isobel Richardson, who was sitting on the grass next to Mrs Jacobs. 'I'm not sure if Alexandra needs protecting from the Racehorse more than Isobel needs shielding from Mrs Jacobs. If Aunt Charlotte were here, I wager she'd isolate Mrs Jacobs.'

Another example of Harriet's touchiness, Sarah thought. Not an hour earlier, she and Harriet had engaged in quite a lengthy conversation with Mrs Jacobs. During this, Harriet had taken offence when Mrs Jacobs described the Aboriginal players as savages. 'Savage is not the word I would use,' Harriet had announced, 'Especially in view of the occasional massacre of the savages by the supposed non-savages.'

There had been an awkward silence, broken by Sarah enquiring if the term Noble Savage would do instead. Everyone had laughed, including Harriet, who had perhaps felt she had been rude to one of Mrs Richardson's friends.

Afterwards Harriet had asked Sarah if she had been referring to the blacks or the whites when she mentioned the Noble Savage. At once Sarah knew she needed to be careful. She hesitated before replying, 'I think everyone, black or white, could be classified as a savage until proved otherwise. But what's the point of doing that? I believe that it is far better to behave as if everyone's inherently good unless proved bad. That way you bring out the best in people.' As soon as she'd finished speaking she began to wonder if she were right.

At this point Harriet inexplicably said, 'Sarah, you're so innocent but I wouldn't have you any other way.' Then she'd laughed again, and seemed sufficiently restored to her usual self as to pull out a book and begin to read, while the game of cricket proceeded on its flamboyant way.

Sarah said, 'Do you think I'm naïve, Hattie?'

'No,' Harriet said, looking up.

'I like to think the best of people until I learn otherwise. If you think well of people and they know it, surely they'll live up to your expectations rather than disappoint you.'

'You're a good person, Sarah.'

At this moment Sarah thought of Carruthers and how cruelly he treated Aborigines, and she wondered what had made him into such an ogre. Her father had often talked about the rule of law. People had the right to protection under the legal system and that surely included the Aborigines. She said, 'Are Aborigines protected under the rule of law?'

'Yes, they are,' Harriet said. 'At least in principle. They're the Queen's subjects and so they have the right to protection.'

'Has that been tested?'

'Yes, at the trials after the Myall Creek massacres. White men were hanged for murdering Aborigines.'

'When was that?'

'Back in 1838. There've been massacres since then that have had the opposite outcome in the courts but the basic right remains: Aborigines are *not* officially aliens in their own land. At least officially, they have the right to protection under the law.'

'They don't seem to have it on some of the cattle stations.'

'Don't they? That doesn't surprise me. This is still the frontier.'

'If that's the case, do you think people should take the law into their own hands and seek justice?'

Harriet put down her book. 'Are you referring to a particular incident?'

Sarah hesitated. She didn't feel ready to tell Harriet what was happening at places like Empty Creek. She'd let her see how well run Dimbulah Downs Station was first before telling her about Carruthers. She said, 'No, I'm simply looking for a general principle.'

'This is what I think.' Harriet's voice was clear and calm. 'If there's no rule of law, then individuals don't necessarily feel constrained to behave. Ethical people always will, because their actions are sanctioned by what they believe in. They won't ever break their own code of what is right and what is wrong. Empathetic people will too, because they can imagine what it would be like to be on the other side. But if people don't feel bound by any code of ethics, or any sense of empathy, they'll do what they please without ever caring for the consequences.'

Perhaps Carruthers was lacking in empathy, Sarah thought, and simply couldn't imagine what it would feel like to be beaten and brutalised. Yet surely he would carry an internal code of ethics. Or maybe he felt he was so superior to the rest of humanity that he was above such a code. 'Aborigines should be protected by the law, Harriet.'

'Of course they should be.'

'You sound so superior sometimes.'

'Do I? I'm sorry, Sarah. I don't mean to be.'

'Father sounded superior sometimes too. It was as if he couldn't believe other people were less intelligent than he was.'

'Do you think so? I never noticed that.'

'That's because you were his equal intellectually, Hattie.'

'That's nonsense.' Harriet looked embarrassed, her cheeks suddenly pink.

'No, it's just the truth.'

Harriet picked up her book again while Sarah looked around the oval. There were at least 200 spectators; Europeans of many varieties, Chinese, Hindus, Japanese. She wondered what they made of cricket, that most English of games. But cricket wasn't really the point; the carnival atmosphere was the point for most of the onlookers. She glanced at Harriet and then at the players. Englishmen playing Aborigines; what a unifying event this cricket match was! Without thinking, she said, 'Don't you think there's something encouraging about sitting here watching white men play black men at cricket? It's so truly English.'

'Don't you believe it,' Harriet said slowly, placing her finger on the page to mark her place. 'They're only allowing the Aborigines to play because they're desperate for a game and they need the numbers.'

'Do you always have to see the worst in people?'

'The truth in people.'

'But maybe you can alter them if you look for the best.' Sarah picked up a eucalyptus leaf and held it between herself and her sister, as if by so doing she could defend herself from Harriet's cynicism.

'You can alter them if you look for the worst, since then you know what needs improving. Thank God for Henry, I say. He can shield you from the white savages.' And Harriet laughed again.

The white savages like Carruthers, Sarah thought, and for the first time wondered if she were in need of protection. After a moment's reflection she decided she wasn't. It was young Aboriginal women like Bella and Daisy who needed protection. She shredded the leaf she was holding into small pieces, and tossed them into the air, and afterwards sniffed her fingertips that were scented with eucalyptus oil. Then she deliberately dismissed Carruthers from her mind and focused on the game.

When a few more sixes had been hit by the same irrepressible Aboriginal batsman, the game was halted. The two umpires conferred in the centre of the pitch before beckoning over the captain of each team. After a brief conversation they marched to the far-side boundary and tore off several sturdy branches from the trees. Sarah watched in perplexity as they stripped these of their leaves, and then ceremoniously presented them to the batsmen and removed their bats.

'What did I tell you? How truly English!' Harriet appeared to have absorbed this change without looking up from her book. 'They're too good, so the people in charge have to change the rules. Such an absurd game.'

The bowler now came lumbering down the pitch. He delivered a ball with so much spin that Sarah was convinced no one could possibly hit it, not even someone wielding a bat rather than a green stick. But the batsman made perfect contact with the ball and knocked it right over the heads of the fielders, way up into the vivid blue sky. There was a collective gasp of admiration from the onlookers as the ball soared beyond the boundary, and then a round of applause while the batsmen ran feverishly between the wickets. This time the umpires let them go, perhaps hoping to wear them out.

'They'll have to do more than take away their bats,' said Harriet, smiling. 'The so-called savages are rather good at cricket.' She shut her book and announced that she needed to stretch her legs. 'And on no account are you to give up watching the game, Sarah. I shall expect a ball by ball account when I return, and a handicap by handicap account too.'

'Where are you going?'

'To do some sketching by the harbour.'

'How long will you be away?'

'Not long. An hour or so. Don't worry about me, I know the way.'

Sarah watched Harriet pick her way carefully around the picnickers, stopping to talk to several of them, and to play with some small children. Like the cricketers, she was dressed in white, in the new muslin dress that she said she'd had run up at one of the Chinese tailoring establishments in Cavanagh Street. The dress was plain to the point of severity but Harriet didn't seem to care.

Sometimes Sarah feared for her sister, for her courage and her foolhardiness. She had no one to look out for her. Yet that never seemed to stop her in that determination to buck the card that she'd been dealt, her femininity in a man's world. For a moment Sarah wondered if she should go after her. But she knew Harriet would only become irritated. Sarah knew better than to try to curtail Harriet's independence.

* * *

Harriet sauntered along the dusty road leading from the cricket ground to the harbour. Putting her hands in the pockets of her new dress, she felt the reassuring shape of a small notebook in one pocket and pencils and an eraser in the other. The pockets in the side seams of the skirt had been an inspired idea on the part of the Chinese tailor. Perhaps she would have another dress like this one made before she and the Vincents left Port Darwin. Maybe a blue dress, more practical for the country than white. She would order a couple of pairs of lightweight men's trousers too. She could wear them at Dimbulah Downs, where no one would care what she did or how she dressed.

She began to whistle to herself. Although she'd become fond of the Richardsons, especially Mrs Richardson and her two older daughters, she wouldn't be sorry to move on from here. Sarah had told her that she mustn't get too excited about the impending trip, for nothing much happened at Dimbulah Downs Station, apart from a lot of hard work. Harriet should view it as a camping expedition, with all the hardships that entailed, rather than as a trip to the country. But at least there would be no cockroaches there, Mrs Richardson had informed her. Termites aplenty but no cockroaches to startle her in the evenings by scuttling out from behind the furniture or, worse, to lie about the floor like bloated pets, as they did in the Residency bathrooms.

Although the afternoon was hot, Harriet began to walk faster. Before the tide turned, she was keen to reach the path she'd walked with the Richardson girls a few days before, and which led down the side of the low cliff to the water's edge. She intended to sketch the mangroves whose twisting roots were exposed at low tide, together with new shoots emerging, indeed almost erupting, from the shining mud.

She passed a camp comprising several circles of huts. Made of bark, in egg-shaped sections, these were arranged five or six to a circle or segment, with the opening to each towards the centre. There was little sign of life. Harriet supposed that most people were at the game of cricket, though there were some elderly Aboriginal men sitting cross-legged in a circle in the shade of a tree. She nodded and smiled at them. Caught up in observing the scene, she almost tripped over an old man, who was lying on his side at the edge of the road. He had a shapeless felt hat pulled down low over shoulder-length grey hair and was dressed in something – clothes or perhaps rags would be a more accurate description. The two mongrel dogs lying next to him growled as Harriet walked past, but not loudly enough to disturb the slumber of the old man. Tired or drunk – or perhaps sick – she couldn't tell which.

She turned and noticed a younger well-dressed Aboriginal

man walking along the dusty track, perhaps a hundred yards behind her. After a moment she recognised the man she'd seen in the distance at the station: Henry's stockman, Mick.

She felt a stab of annoyance at seeing him here. She was probably being irrational, for there was no reason why he shouldn't be walking along this road at the same time as she was; the cricket was after all a big occasion here. On the other hand, her chagrin might not be irrational. Perhaps Henry had instructed his man to keep an eye on her, his recalcitrant sister-in-law.

She accelerated and after a few hundred yards, casually looked around again. The man was nowhere to be seen. I was mistaken, she thought. He hasn't been sent to follow me. She slowed down and resumed thinking about her mission for the next half-hour, the sketching of mangroves.

After her walk with the Richardson girls, she'd tried to draw these trees but had failed dismally. That was why she wanted to return. She remembered the dense, dark green foliage of the mangroves pressing down on her, like a tent roof strung too low, and perforated in one place by a shaft of brilliant sunlight that was almost apocalyptic as it illuminated its chosen patch. But this was the problem, this was what had escaped her, she couldn't grasp the meaning of this illumination, although she felt that if she could visit the place again, on her own, she might be able to comprehend its spiritual significance. And perhaps, if she were really lucky, to translate it later into paint.

Yet she was wrong about the tide; the water was now rising when she had expected it to be low. She strode up and down impatiently, until suddenly she became aware that she wasn't alone. Somehow Mick had managed to get ahead of her; he was leaning against a tree, not exactly watching her, for his eyes were fixed on the sea, but certainly near enough to be observing her movements.

'No good walkem there today,' he said, gesturing to the path down to the sea.

'Why not?' said Harriet. Although she thought the reason was fairly obvious, she wanted to hear what he had to say. She wanted an opportunity to challenge him for this intervention, or possibly she was seeking someone to blame for her miscalculation of the tides. She stopped a couple of yards away from him but he still didn't look at her. He had an attractive face, with a wide mouth and a deep furrow running from each side of the bridge of his nose down to the corners of his mouth.

'White feller followem. Him no good.'

This wasn't what Harriet had expected to hear and she looked around in surprise. There was no sign of anyone else. 'How do you know?'

'In trees back there. Him no good.'

'What did he look like?' Harriet said.

'White feller. Black hair, big black beard.'

Her palms started sweating as she recalled that night on the *Guthrie*: Brady's gleaming white shirt, the black spade-shaped beard, that look of hatred. Would spitting at her be sufficient revenge? Would staining her white dress settle the score for him? He had looked triumphant that afternoon in Chinatown, but that mightn't be enough.

She said as calmly as possible, 'White fellow, black hair. That could be anyone.'

'White fellers all lookem same to missus.' Mick smiled broadly, revealing all his teeth. Good teeth, she couldn't help noticing. She laughed. For the first time Mick looked at her, very briefly, before turning back to contemplate the view of the sea. 'Why you bin comen here?'

'To draw. I wanted to sketch the mangrove trees down there by the water's edge.' But it was impossible to complete that today and she would have to return another time. After

164

pulling out her little notebook and a pencil, she did a quick – and rather crude – drawing of the view from where they were standing: the curve of the land, the sea fringed by the mangroves, and the sampan with a dark sail heading towards the heads.

Mick didn't say anything but looked closely at the drawing and then the view. Harriet wondered what he was making of it. She was glad that he didn't do what many people did when confronted with a sketch: feel that they had to praise it – and sometimes to criticise it. This man was quite simply examining it and keeping his impressions to himself, and the silence lengthened to the point where Harriet became almost soothed.

'I keepem sketch,' he said at last.

'Why?' Nevertheless, Harriet tore off the page and handed it to him.

'Why not?' he said, smiling. There was no trace of rudeness in his tone. It appeared he simply didn't see any need to justify his request, or perhaps he was making fun of her earlier response.

'Back to the cricket pitch, I suppose.' Harriet shut her notebook and slipped it, and the pencil, back into her pockets.

'Good feller game.'

'Black fellow too good at it,' Harriet said, laughing. She again examined his face. His forehead was high and cut back sharply to his eye sockets, so that the eyebrows jutted out like a rocky overhang providing shelter to the eyes. His nose was straight, the upper lip long, and the jaw line firm. Perhaps she would paint him at Dimbulah Downs Station, if he would let her.

Without another word she began to trudge back along the road to the cricket ground. She scanned the bush on each side of the road to see if Brady were visible but there was no sign of him. The Aboriginal encampment was as it had been when she passed by earlier; the same ring of elders sitting in the shade, the same sleeping man and his dogs at the side of the road. The bush was silent, for it was too hot yet for the birds to start calling. Beads of moisture formed between her shoulder blades and under her arms, and trickled down into her waistband, but she didn't slacken her pace. She turned several times and saw Mick a couple of hundred yards behind her; he was making no pretence now about the fact that he was following her back to the cricket ground.

For once she was glad that someone had intervened on her behalf.

Chapter 23

The Mosquito Nets Looked Almost Like Ghostly Termite Mounds

The glowing campfire illuminated the pack-bags littering the campsite and cast shadows that danced like living things. Sarah helped Henry and Mick to suspend mosquito nets from the low-lying branches of trees. When they'd finished hanging the netting, she stood back to admire the effect: the mosquito nets looked almost like ghostly termite mounds leaning at strange angles. Although Harriet had offered to help, Sarah had refused her offer; she thought Harriet looked exhausted, with dark smudges under her eyes and a slight limp when she walked that was almost certainly caused by long hours on the saddle. Now she was sitting on a log on the other side of the clearing, with a sketchbook on her lap, even though there were just a few lanterns and the firelight for illumination.

'You've been unusually quiet this trip, Mick,' Henry said. 'That's not like you. And I've noticed that when Harriet's within earshot you only speak pidgin.'

'I talk to people in the language they expect.'

'What makes you think she only wants to hear pidgin? Your English is very good.'

'It's Mission-school English.'

'It's perfect English. And you can't carry on like this. Why did you start?'

'I thought Harriet was one of the Palmerston white ladies, so I spoke to her in pidgin.'

'But surely you knew she was my sister,' Sarah said. 'Didn't you see her at the railway station?'

'Boss kept me too busy.' Mick grinned. 'Found out after the cricket match. Too late then.'

'Didn't you tell him, Henry?'

'I guess I forgot.'

Sarah looked at Henry. Refusing to meet her eye, he said to Mick, 'But you've never spoken to me like that. Or Mrs Vincent.'

'That's different.'

'Why?'

'You're my mate, boss.'

Henry's expression softened. He cleared his throat before saying, 'Harriet will find out and she'll be annoyed. She'll think you're patronising her.'

'She won't,' Sarah said smoothly. 'I'll tell her tonight. She'll think it's a good joke. And tomorrow you'll be able to talk freely to us all, which will be a relief after your silence the last two days.'

Later that evening, after dinner was over, Sarah told Harriet. She seemed to think it amusing, or at least she laughed a lot.

'You're a Palmerston lady,' Sarah teased when they were preparing for sleep. This simply involved removing one's boots and pulling on a jersey before crawling into a swag laid out on a mattress of freshly cut grass, and unfurling the mosquito net suspended from a tree branch overhead.

'I suppose I am. We white women all look the same.' After a brief pause, she added, 'When I first met Mick he said, "White fellers all lookem same to missus." That was his little joke. The trouble is that most white fellers think the Abos are savages.'

'That's only the Jacobs and Gascoignes of this part of the world,' Sarah said, though she knew it was Carruthers and his ilk as well.

'And the Smiths and the Joneses and the Tom-Dick-and-Harrys,' Harriet said, struggling to remove a riding boot. 'Don't you think it's strange that Mick only reveals to a chosen few how clever he is?'

'I've never thought about it.'

'He's reinforcing the prejudices of the Palmerston middle classes. To them he's an ignorant Aborigine, so he retaliates by speaking to them in pidgin. It's like a type of revenge though it's not likely to be noticed. Maybe that's the point: the revenge brings satisfaction and amusement only to him.'

'Hattie, do you have to analyse everything?' Sarah said in mock exasperation. 'Why can't you just be?'

Harriet took no notice. 'Maybe he does it for self-protection. If he spoke really good English, people would ask how and where he learned it, and he might want to protect himself from questions.' She shrouded herself in mosquito netting before easing herself into her swag set up a few yards away from Sarah's.

'Good night, Hattie.'

'What would it be like being a black fellow in this country?' Harriet said.

Sarah pretended she hadn't heard, and lay on her side with her back to her sister.

* * *

Through the mosquito netting, Sarah could see densely packed stars swathing the dark sky with white. She rolled over in her swag and wondered if Harriet was enjoying the trip. She had certainly seemed as charmed as Sarah by the journey south to Pine Creek, the train meandering through jungle, beside rivers and billabongs covered with glowing waterlilies, purple and white flowers held erect on long stalks above the huge green pads. Occasionally the train stopped at one of the tiny settlements scattered along the line and the engine driver passed out mail, once placing letters into a kerosene tin nailed to a tree, and several times handing bags to stockmen waiting by the railway track.

Sarah now performed in her head the first few bars of the Fauré duet that she and Henry had played again at the Residency. She might have burst into song had she been alone. She rolled over in her swag, taking care not to dislodge the mosquito netting. Out here you could love humanity because it was but a part of the embracing whole. In a town you never thought that. You often couldn't see the embracing whole; you never saw even the stars in London, let alone the shape of the land.

Staring up at the sky webbed with stars, she felt herself rising up to meet them. Rising above the campsite, looking down on the rugged territory: the rivers, the plateaus and, a few miles east, the telegraph line snaking its way south. A two-chain-wide avenue kept clear by a line party that moved slowly up and down it, repairing the lines, hacking away at the encroaching grasses and shrubs and forests, maintaining the link between the South and Europe. That was humanity in balance with nature and not substituting for nature. Telegraph wires that hummed and vibrated with the lives of others, with the news from Home. She smiled at the thought of the vibrating wires, like the vibrating strings of a piano as the hammers struck them, playing out some melody at the whim of the pianist.

But she was getting carried away. Humanity was not in balance with nature. Out here people were jockeying for position, fighting for control over resources just as they were anywhere else. Harriet was right, she was naïve but she wasn't going to be like that any more.

'Are you awake, Sarah?' Henry was sitting bolt upright in his swag a few yards away.

'Yes. Can't you sleep either?'

After Henry crawled out of his mosquito net, he climbed in under hers and lay down next to her.

'You're not still worrying about Harriet, are you?'

'Not really,' he whispered.

But, of course, he was. She sighed. The peaceful spell of the evening was broken. She guessed he wanted to talk about the cricket match again. That afternoon had gone well until the tea break. Admittedly the Aboriginal batsmen were too good. Henry had said afterwards that the umpires were unsporting in making them play with sticks in place of bats. He should have remonstrated then; he might have remonstrated then had he not felt so carefree and happy.

Should have, should have, she thought. His conversation is becoming peppered with should haves. He should have known that Harriet would see this treatment as an insult and that she would write letters to the southern newspapers, which she posted before they left Palmerston. Witty, biting letters that were bound to get published, for there was no doubt that she wrote as brilliantly as Father, and considerably more comprehensibly. Sarah would never forget Harriet's letter to the *Northern Territory Times* that had been published the day before they left Palmerston, for Henry seemed to know it off by heart. He was forever spouting bits of it, whenever Harriet was out of earshot. It began by describing the cricket match in some detail, and ended up by stating that the replacement of the cricket bats with stout green sticks was a symbol of what was wrong with race relations, that those in control had one law for themselves and another for the blacks.

Sarah knew that Harriet was right about race relations but Henry needed to get on with their neighbours. He'd seen enough of life in the outback to know you might want your neighbours' assistance at any time. He thought Harriet should have had more tact than to snap at Mrs Jacobs for calling the Aborigines savages.

Sarah agreed that, although the comments of these women had been uncivil, there was no need for Harriet to be uncivil in return. 'Harriet sometimes lets her principles override her manners,' she said to Henry now, wriggling against him so she wouldn't be pushed out of her swag. 'But she's right.'

'Worst of all,' Henry continued, ignoring her comment, 'was Harriet walking away from the cricket match without telling anyone where she was going. If you hadn't told me and if I hadn't sent Mick to follow her, who knows what might have happened.'

'Shhh, not so loud, Henry. We don't want to wake the others. And anyway, nothing happened.' They had been over this incident many times since that day, but she thought another repetition might help him sleep.

'If I hadn't been worried about Harriet I might have thought it funny: Harriet being tracked by some white fellow who was being tracked by Mick. But she's irresponsible. Like a small child, she thinks she can do what she likes without thinking of the consequences.'

Exactly as he sometimes did, Sarah thought. She dismissed this thought as disloyal. To distract Henry from his catalogue of grievances, she said, 'She's certainly brave and fearless.'

'She's foolhardy. Do you remember how I remonstrated with her afterwards?'

'How could I forget?'

Although Harriet had laughed at Henry at first, when he told her she shouldn't have wandered off on her own at the cricket match, she'd apologised for worrying them both and had even thanked him for sending Mick. But Sarah suspected she thanked him for the wrong reasons. She and Mick had communicated about the mangroves and the harbour, or at least that was how Harriet described it. Henry had admitted that she did have an acute perception about people. That was often how he and Mick related to one another, he'd said: through silent communication rather than through words.

'I wonder who *was* following Harriet.'

'Who knows? Mick said it was a man he'd seen in a fight the day before and he didn't think much of him.' Henry now rolled over so energetically that Sarah's mosquito net became dislodged. 'Sorry, Sarah,' he said rather irritably. 'I'm never going to be able to sleep.' He sat up, yanking a portion of the net with him. 'I'll get up and fix your net. I might as well stroll around for a bit after that. No point keeping you awake.'

Poor Henry, as if you haven't already, she thought. After adjusting her net, he pulled on his boots. She watched him put another piece of wood on the fire and collect something from his saddlebag. The sickle moon and a swathe of stars illuminated him as he steered his way around the obstacles littering the campsite: the bags and rolls, the trees and bushes, and the occasional towering termite mound. When he was a few hundred yards away, she saw him squat down on the ground and started to play his flute: first a few scales and then a little Mozart. As he played a bush curlew joined in, interposing its wailing cry with the melody. After a while she began to feel peace descend on her once more and was soon asleep.

Chapter 24

How to Banish This Annoyance?

Harriet tried not to toss about too much in her swag. Each time she moved, the mosquito net became detached from its moorings and she had learned to her cost how miserable it could be to share a net with a persistent insect. Three mosquito bites on one ankle were itching and she had to fight the temptation to scratch. Her whole body ached from the previous day's riding, and her face was painfully sunburnt. It had been a mistake to leave off the hat, even though it had been for barely an hour. To add to her irritation, a twig seemed to have found its way into the swag and was digging into her back. By the time she'd located it, the mosquito net had become untucked and she had to start rearranging herself once more.

After pulling the cover up, leaving a narrow aperture for her nose, she inhaled the scent of eucalyptus leaves and wood smoke drifting across from the fire kept burning all night long. The gentle snoring of some of the sleepers was interspersed by distant clinking of the horses' hobble chains, and occasionally the light rustling of a small animal wandering about the camp. Earlier she'd thought she could hear a flute playing. But this must have been in a dream, for on the far side of the campsite she could see the veiled mound that was Henry asleep in his swag.

She tried to relax but she couldn't go back to sleep. Sarah had said that living at Dimbulah Downs was akin to camping.

Surely she was exaggerating. After all, there would be beds and showers and a toilet there. Harriet rolled over again and beneath her shoulder felt another twig, which she chose to ignore. She had to get some sleep before first light when she would be roused up again. Each day they were to travel in two stages, early morning until noon, when the sun glared down at you, with a break for a rest and a meal, and then another few hours' riding before setting up camp an hour before sundown. It seemed never-ending, though they'd been riding for just two days. With another five days to go, Harriet felt her body would never stand it.

Seeing Sarah again had brought their father's absence home to Harriet anew. When she'd last been with Sarah they were a family. Now they were only two – or three if you counted Henry. Every day since she'd been reunited with Sarah at Port Darwin she found herself thinking: Oh, I must tell Father about this. Oh, Father will find this so interesting. The void left by his death was growing not shrinking. But this was being irrational, she told herself. She missed him because this new land was so strange, the people so different, the creature comforts so few. Once they arrived at Dimbulah Downs, her anxieties would end.

Her thoughts turned to Charles. Like Father, he too had a rational enquiring mind. Maybe her affection for Charles was so tied up with her love for her father that she couldn't really tell if she missed Charles or her father. Briefly she wondered what she would have been doing right now if she'd accepted Charles' proposal. But her decision had been made and she had to look forward and not back. She reminded herself of the physical aversion she had felt at the sight of his hairy wrists. That seemed like a long time ago now.

Feeling more awake than ever, she sat up. The logs on the fire were glowing red. Buried under the ashes at the edge of the fireplace was the damper they would eat for breakfast in a few more hours. She remembered how closely Mick had examined her sketch – her caricature – of Port Darwin the day she'd wanted to sketch the mangroves, and felt embarrassed. She'd thought he was struggling to comprehend her representation of reality and now she realised how patronising that assumption had been. He must have seen many pictures at the mission; religious pictures, pictures in books.

A movement caught her eye and she held her breath: a wallaby was standing at the edge of the glade, its eyes shining as they reflected the firelight. Though she'd seen some in the distance at Port Darwin, she had never before been this close. She and the wallaby watched each other. Its large ears rotated to pick up sound from all directions, first one ear forward and the other back, then the reverse, almost like a little dance, the dance of the ears. At last the animal seemed to decide she was harmless and resumed eating grass.

For an instant she wondered why she cared about Mick's thoughts as he examined her drawing. She shouldn't care what anyone thought about her work. She drew for herself, she painted for herself, because in so doing she was seeking an interpretation of reality. Her interpretation and no one else's.

She lay down again and, holding up one hand to block out the firelight, stared up at the vast sky swathed with stars, an infinity of stars. As she was starting to wonder if there could be more than one infinity and, if so, should she try counting them, she fell into a profound sleep.

* * *

Harriet passed through the final day of the journey like an automaton, able to function solely because she was repeating what she'd done before. She still couldn't bear being too long in the saddle, although the soreness she'd experienced for the first few days of riding had almost gone. By mid-afternoon, when she felt at last as if she was starting to wake up, she and Sarah dismounted and walked for an hour or so, leading their horses, as they'd done every afternoon of this expedition. The glare was no longer intolerable; earlier she had felt that the harsh white light was so sharp it was piercing her eyes. The dust raised by some of the others, who were riding ahead, stuck to her damp skin. She looked covertly at Sarah, who somehow managed to look cool and beautiful even in this heat, even with a streak of red dust along one cheek where she had wiped a hand over her damp face.

Harriet's scalp felt itchy, her hair needed washing, and the mosquito bites on her ankles were being chafed by her boots. She would give anything for a bath, a deep cool bath with lavender soap, and fluffy white towels with which to dry herself afterwards. Yet she knew the reality would be a bush shower and perhaps later a swim in the rock pools that Sarah had told her about. She must forget about baths and clean towels.

She watched a couple of lonely looking white clouds that appeared to be following the sinking sun, until suddenly they glowed as if on fire. She looked away quickly and shut her eyes, while her feet kept mechanically marching forward. She saw a multiplicity of orange suns fading to blue and then to what she thought at first was no colour. But she was wrong; this deep red was the colour of the thin layer of flesh that could screen out all this light, all this space, and that could make her forget for a moment that here she was, an insignificant English woman, in the remoteness of northern Australia.

'How is Miss Harriet?' Opening her eyes, she saw that Mick had ridden up beside her. His white shirt was covered with a fine powdering of red dust.

She smiled. They hadn't talked much since she'd learned his pidgin was an affectation. Yet she had subsequently felt that this misunderstanding was a bond rather than a barrier. 'Apart from being hot and sweaty and in need of a shower, I'm fine.'

'It's a long ride when you're not used to it,' he said. 'But we're almost there. Look!'

Ahead lay the homestead, a glittering of white light off corrugated-iron roofs and walls. The building she guessed was the manager's residence was positioned on a slight rise. Harriet felt excitement mingled with apprehension. It would be hot but it was a shelter nonetheless, and a guarantor of privacy too. She longed to shut herself away and sleep for hours, for days. The residence was surrounded by some rangy-looking trees and an extensive collection of sheds and yards. Adjacent to the billabong to the north, perhaps a quarter of a mile from the homestead, was the Aboriginal encampment, and beyond that, dense bush. Plumes of smoke from campfires drifted lazily into the sky.

Harriet and Sarah mounted their horses again and broke into a canter. And so it was that Harriet entered the station, where awaiting them was a party comprising a crowd of Aborigines, a few white stockmen, and numerous small children and dogs weaving their way through adult legs.

At this moment a flock of sulphur-crested white cockatoos flew in from beyond the settlement and descended upon the bleached skeleton of a dead eucalyptus tree by the billabong. Their plump white bodies jostled for space on the branches, as if they too were spectators watching the arrival.

'Almost like coming home,' said Sarah. 'Welcome to Dimbulah Downs.'

PART V

Dimbulah Downs, July to October 1894

Chapter 25

A River of Shining Stars

Living in the outback there were never problems waking up in the morning. Ever since their arrival at Dimbulah Downs, Harriet had heard at first light a distant squabbling of cockatoos from the billabong. As the birds massed for their daily exodus it grew into a squawking so loud it almost drowned out Ah Soy's ringing of the bell for the stockmen's breakfast. Afterwards, when the men had gone, she heard children's voices from the camp by the billabong and the clattering of dishes from the kitchen as Ah Soy cleared up. Soon after came the creaking of the windmill pumping water, and then Sarah's laughter as she bathed with Bella and Daisy in the primitive shower room that was just a hessian screen around a shower head near the water tank.

Harriet had been so busy working with her sister that she hadn't the leisure to think in that first week. After the washing had been done, and then the cleaning that Sarah decided had been neglected during her absence, it had been a welcome relief to be on horseback again and spend some time riding to the nearer stock and muster camps.

One of the pleasures of mustering was discovery, Harriet had thought at first. Yet after the second of these trips she'd realised that her feelings about living at Dimbulah Downs were confused, if not contradictory. The immense emptiness here seemed sometimes like a tangible presence hemming her in. The blue dome of the sky looked so hard it felt confining.

The relentless sun pressed down upon her so that all she could do was to squint her eyes against the sharp white light and search for shade. It was almost as if she were being corralled, in ever-decreasing circles, like a rogue steer being fenced in by the ringers until the confined space induced it to accept its place in the muster.

She didn't belong here, even as a visitor. She no longer had any reference point against which to measure her own sense of worth. In London, her father's love had protected her. In London, and even in Sydney, she'd possessed an identity, as the daughter of the philosopher James Cameron, as well as a suffragist. But here she was nothing. Worse, she felt as if she were losing her old certainties. She didn't fit into this culture of hard riding and hard physical work. What she thought she was good at had no value out here.

Perhaps she should start painting once more. She'd given up after arriving. Yet it would be hard if not impossible to interpret the brilliant colours of the landscape sluiced by that unrelenting sunlight. Better not to try. It was all too harsh and confronting.

This morning she noticed as if for the first time the pile of books stacked on the chest of drawers and decided to read to the Aboriginal children. Reading to them in English would be an extension to the pidgin that was widely used and taught. In the afternoon, when it was too hot to do anything other than slump down in the shadiest spot, she asked Bella and Daisy to gather a small group of children. Initially she read to them the first few chapters of the battered copy of *Pickwick Papers* that Henry had brought with him but she quickly discovered this was inappropriate. Her audience had no conception of any of the references that made the book so entertaining. Although they laughed uproariously, she knew it was at her rather than at the story, so she might as well have been reading in Swahili.

Eventually she hit upon the notion of reading poetry to them. They listened, apparently captivated, and quickly learned whole stanzas off by heart. One girl, no more than eight or nine, was a particularly good mimic. She sat cross-legged opposite Harriet, and repeated with her accent, her gestures, her intonation, her rhythm, several stanzas of 'The Man from Snowy River' (it was first published in *The Bulletin*, an Australian news magazine, on 26th April 1890, and was published by Angus & Robertson in October 1895, with other poems by Paterson, in *The Man from Snowy River and Other Verses*), to the amusement of everyone, including Ah Soy. Sitting a short distance away, he chortled quietly to himself around the stem of his pipe.

* * *

'Are you reading again today, Hattie?' Sarah asked.

'Yes,' Harriet said, looking up from the clothes she was folding. 'Banjo Paterson was such a hit yesterday that I'm going to continue with him.'

'Don't you want to come out riding with me?'

'Where are you going?'

'To one the stock camps. Henry's offered to take us both.'

'No, I'd rather stay here. Bella's going to tell me some of her stories too.'

'Do you mind if I go?'

'No, of course not.'

Later, sitting in the shade, Harriet listened, transfixed, while Bella told the tale of how the stars had formed, her elegant hands with their long, slender fingers gesturing as she spoke. Once the sky had been dark, darker than anything they could imagine, dark until two ancestors had sailed up the river into the sky, and there they'd transformed themselves into a star to shine down on their people. And thereafter the spirit of the earth mob after death went up into the sky and made a river of shining stars, big mob star.

So began a new phase in Harriet's days at Dimbulah Downs. Bella and Daisy would take it in turns to tell stories, and asked Harriet to help them with their English. There were some words that she couldn't bear to change, for they were like poetry themselves. English was a hybrid language, she told herself, a developing language, and now she would always think of the Milky Way as a shining river, a big mob star.

Soon she realised that the emptiness surrounding her was not emptiness at all but was peopled with a rich and beautiful mythology and history. It seemed that every aspect of the physical world had a spiritual meaning; every place had some relation to the Aborigines' ancestors. Although the relationship was with their ancestors and not hers, she began to feel as if the landscape were no longer alien, and thus she began to lose her fear of it.

Chapter 26

'Cleaning Country'

A moth battering itself against the glass shade of the kerosene lamp distracted Harriet from her mail that had arrived with Frank O'Connor that afternoon, some weeks after her arrival at Dimbulah Downs. After crawling out from the mosquito net, she guided the insect out of the window with Aunt Charlotte's letter, and fastened the shutter. On the counterpane lay a pile of unopened correspondence.

In elegant prose, Aunt Charlotte's letter expressed the fervent hope that female enfranchisement would soon be enacted in England, although she wasn't optimistic about the likelihood of this occurring. 'And Harriet, dear, do please send me more information about the activities of the South Australian Women's Suffrage League,' she wrote. 'How blessed is the colony of South Australia in being founded by social idealists.' But ruled by pragmatists, Harriet thought, who needed to be re-elected. Strategy might yet win the day: there were more urban voters for Labor than rural, and enfranchisement would work in that party's favour.

Next Harriet opened an envelope from the Morgans. Mrs Morgan had enclosed newspaper clippings of Harriet's two letters about the Territory that had been published by Sydney newspapers. She saw that Professor Morgan had scribbled on the top of one clipping: 'You are your father's daughter!'

Although part of her was pleased by this, she also felt a twinge of irritation. Professor Morgan meant well but Father had never visited Australia and her opinions were her own. And she was her mother's daughter too. She thought of those yellow silk slippers left in storage in London. Her last memory of Mother was of laughter. Laughter, and her slippers lying under the bed, in a room rinsed with sunlight. Pale yellow sunlight that was nothing like the merciless glare experienced here.

Now she slit open Charles' letter. It was better than a newspaper, full of politics and news from both London and Australia. How generous of Charles to devote such care to selecting material that would interest her. When she reached the last page, she read:

I understand that you are still grieving for the loss of your beloved father. He was an exceptional man: a loving father, a loyal friend, and a fine scholar whose works will live on for many years to come.

I trust that your time with Sarah and Henry is bringing you comfort, and that the experience of 'living at the frontier' is in every way meeting your expectations. I hope that there you will find the space and the peace to work out what you want from the next phase of your life.

My offer of marriage is still open, my dear. Do not feel you need to reply to this, as I know it is far too soon for you to reconsider your earlier decision. However, if you ever change your mind, do let me know. I wish that one day you might agree to share your life with me, whether in Australia – there are always jobs for men of my experience in the colonies – or at Home.

She felt deeply moved by his concern, touched by his willingness to consider changing country for her. He was a fine man:

clever, loyal, rational, supportive, kind. Everything one could wish for in a lifelong partnership. Marriage to Charles would in a sense emancipate her. She could gain influence as well as companionship in her role as his wife.

She wondered what he would gain from such an alliance. It would be impossible for her to give him what he deserved. Marriage to him was a compromise that she was not ready for. Maybe later she would change her mind – but not yet. Her dreams were still evolving, her ambitions still not clear.

Of course, Charles' offer wouldn't stay open for ever. If she didn't want him, she should give him the chance to find someone else. He would easily find another woman to marry, one who could provide him with companionship and love. But the thought of losing the option of marriage to Charles filled her with unease. Apart from her father, she had never come across a man with qualities as fine as his. Nor had she met a man who would be as willing to give his wife independence. Yet it was Father she was missing rather than Charles. After folding up his letter, she put it away in the envelope, retrieved her travelling desk and set it up on her lap. Writing to Violet would clarify her views and she would welcome Violet's advice. As usual Violet would be forthright and decisive; she would provide a sounding board, although it would be months before the reply echoed back.

'My dear Violet,' she began to write. After imparting the news that a suffrage bill might soon be introduced in South Australia, she got to the real point of the letter.

I'm still feeling a bit lost without Father. Here in the outback I'm trying to decide what to do with the rest of my life. I love both political economy and painting. I'm good at political economy but I cannot carve out a career for myself in this field because I'm a woman. I'm competent at painting and sketching, activities deemed suitable for young women of my class, as you know! On the principle of comparative advantage, I should be like Father, working at a university, and I should buy my paintings from someone else. If I were a man, perhaps that is what I would do. Once women are emancipated this will become possible. But I fear this will never happen in England in my lifetime.

She stopped writing and read what she had written. Though she'd intended the paragraph to be humorous, its content left her confused and angry. She had been brought up to think that anything was possible. There had been no barriers put in the path of her education and she was glad of that. But with her father gone, she was simply a single woman battling along on her own, with no identity apart from the few people who knew her as James Cameron's daughter. This was hardly her father's fault. He had always said that it was imperative that women were given the vote, that the situation had to change. She began to write again.

I can almost hear you say that I could become a Poor Law Guardian like you. But that isn't what I want nor is it what I'd be good at, despite what you've told me. The best I can hope for is to be an unpaid but full-time agitator. Don't laugh at me, Violet, for I believe I have become rather good at this. All my letters to the newspapers get published and they may even bring forth controversy and lively discussion!

I should stop complaining and be thankful that I have the means to support myself and to be free to choose between agitating and painting. But I know that my painting will never make the world a better place. It will never bring joy to anyone, and especially not to myself. In fact, I have more or less given up since I arrived in the Territory.

That wasn't quite right. Nibbling the end of her pen, she thought of the sketch of the mangroves she had dashed off at Port Darwin, and of the few drawings she had produced as they travelled to Dimbulah Downs. The truth was that she had only given up drawing and painting since arriving here. She dipped her nib in the inkwell and continued to write.

Perhaps you will be advising, why not do both, agitate and paint? I don't think this is feasible. Amateurs do several activities and none of them really well. My father was never an amateur. He was so successful because he was brilliant and because he devoted all of his time to his work.

The truth of the matter is that he didn't view artworks as worthwhile. I have realised this now, this minute, as I sit scribbling to you here in the outback.

She stopped writing and put down her pen. The shock of this new discovery took her breath away. Father was a scientist, and to him art and music were luxuries. How strange that she hadn't seen this before. She wiped her inky fingers on a pocket handkerchief she kept in the travelling desk for this purpose, and continued writing, more slowly now.

This is probably partly why I've felt guilty spending time improving my painting techniques. This is probably also why I felt guilty when Father was alive when I was not helping him with his work. Being his 'unpaid secretary' was what you once told me.

Perhaps you will also be thinking as you read this that your old friend is engaging in self-pity. You would be right to think this and I trust you will forgive me. Although writing to you can never be as good as sitting talking to you face to face, I find that explaining my dilemma about my future does help me to look more dispassionately at the options that lie before me.

She put the pen in the slot in her travelling desk. For too long she had been evaluating her painting with her father's eyes rather than her own. She'd always thought of herself as objective, but only now had she become detached enough to see that she'd internalised her father's prejudices, which conflicted with her own. No wonder she'd felt so ambivalent about her work. This letter was not for Violet, it was a letter to herself. After she screwed the lid on the inkwell, she picked up the letter and scrunched it into a ball.

I'll write to Violet later, she thought. I'll describe the Aboriginal customs of the Dimbulah Downs tribe, or as much as I've been able to work out. The complex clan system. The spirituality. The way the camp is arranged, in circles of wurleys. The way the dogs devour the bones and others refuse from a meal. The raised scars worn by men and women. Violet will be much more interested in this than in my endless introspection. But first I must write to Charles.

She pulled out a clean sheet of writing paper and picked up her pen. She began to write very fast, not thinking in advance what she would say, simply letting the words pour out.

My dear Charles,

Thank you for your letter. It is so kind of you to write with the news that you know will interest me. I shall try my best to reciprocate.

The Aborigines' belief in a spiritual existence may intrigue you. There are many layers of meaning in their lives and much of it remains inaccessible to Europeans, and maybe always will. The Aborigines believe in the immortality of human souls. Children are born out of a spiritual world and spend a lifetime journeying back to it. Elders are close to their ancestors, to their Dreaming, and for this reason are to be respected. Yet it isn't only the spirits of men and women that exist timelessly but the whole of creation. The Dreaming place is important because it gives an identity and a sense of belonging. This is as much as I have been able to find out so far from my conversations with the women.

Yesterday afternoon there were fires near here, on the far side of the billabong. I felt frightened and asked Bella, who is a housemaid here, if we should worry. She said no. It seems that the Aborigines use these fires to manage the land, and the usual Dimbulah Downs manager has encouraged this. They call it 'cleaning country', Bella said, and they do it from early to mid dry season to avoid the potential for larger more destructive fires later in the dry season. They light a number of small fires on damp ground, typically not all at once, and they create a semicircle of these, with each end joining up to the creek. This way they create a firebreak around an area.

Yesterday I watched the dense plumes of black smoke rising into the still air. There were a dozen or so black kites circling around the burning area, waiting to swoop on any escaping small marsupials or reptiles.

Not long before dark I could see a wall of flame where they had lit the nearest fire. Later, after nightfall, the clouds were red tinged and occasionally I heard the sound of what I took to be a burnt tree crashing to the ground. Anxious the fires might get out of control, I had a bad night's sleep, thinking all night I could smell smoke in the air. In bed, I heard the sound of the corrugated-iron roof creaking against its constraints as the temperature dropped from ninety degrees Fahrenheit to the high fifties. That seems very chilly in a building that leaks cold air. Periodically I imagined the smell of smoke was stronger and got up to look out for fires. There was nothing: the Aborigines had it all under control. Eventually, I fell asleep to a lullaby of chirping geckos, interspersed with the distant sound of the inevitable bush curlews.

After breakfast this morning, I went for a walk around the far side of the billabong. The dry leaves on the path crunched underfoot. The fire remains were still smoking; the pandanus palms and gum trees burnt but not completely, the black kites still circling, and a three-quarter moon floating in an already harsh blue sky.

Then I thought that I too need to 'clean my country'. I carry with me so much baggage from the past. To what extent are my views my own, formed by careful thought? Or have they instead been moulded by Father, and my lifelong desire to see him happy?

I don't yet know the answers to these questions. But here, in this savagely beautiful country, I intend to find them. Can I carry on in a new sphere away from past influences? Can I clean country like the Aborigines and discover what to do with my life?

Thank you again for your letter, Charles. Hearing from you always means a great deal to me, and it always will.

I have kept the most important matter to the end of this letter. In asking me to become your wife you have again done me a great honour, and I must ask your forgiveness when I say that I don't know yet if I can marry you. I'm changing too much to make any immediate commitments. I hope you're not hurt by this, and I take some comfort from the words that you wrote, that you don't expect an immediate decision.

Yours very affectionately,

Harriet

She waved the last page until she was quite sure the ink was dry, before folding the letter and placing it in an envelope. Perhaps, she thought, by the time Charles receives this letter I will know who I am and where I'm going. And then I'll write again to Charles.

Chapter 27

They Give Me Civilised Name

Harriet was strolling past the storeroom when she heard a loud male voice that she didn't recognise. Coming from the direction of the kitchen, the voice sounded authoritative, although she couldn't distinguish the words. After an interval, she heard the gentle murmur that was Ah Soy's reply.

She was almost at the kitchen when a big white fellow stepped through the doorway. He looked to be in his late forties, after allowing for the fact that white men aged early here, dried up by the cruel sun. She smiled and held out her hand. It would be good to have some company. Perhaps this man would have something else to talk about apart from station life. 'Welcome to Dimbulah Downs Station. I'm Harriet Cameron.'

The man touched his broad-brimmed hat in a gesture that struck her as a parody, or possibly it was too tightly jammed on to his head to be easily removed. 'Welcome to Dimbulah Downs Station yourself, Miss Cameron. I'm Bert Carruthers from Empty Creek Station. Empty by name and empty by nature.' As he gripped her hand in a firm handshake, he laughed uproariously at a joke that she guessed was well-worn. His palm was calloused and the sun-hardened skin on the back of his hands was as knobbly as a lizard's skin. 'I was just passing by with some of my stockmen and thought I'd call in to welcome you to the Territory.'

'Thank you.' Harriet looked around for the stockmen.

'Blacks all of them. They're down at the billabong.' He gestured towards the camp.

'You'll stay for supper?'

'We'll stay the night,' he said. 'But you don't need to worry, we'll be camping a few miles away.'

'Henry and the others will be back soon. I hope you can stay until then at least.' After asking Ah Soy to make them some tea, she led Carruthers into the shade of the fly-screened enclosure on the verandah of the main house.

'I heard about you from my new ringer.' Carruthers sat down opposite her at the table, while Ah Soy distributed the tea-things. With some difficulty he pulled off his hat. It left a red welt around his tonsured head.

'I don't think I've met any of your men. I've ridden out to the stock camps a number of times but the men I met were all from Dimbulah Downs.'

'My new ringer came here by way of Port Darwin, on the same steamer as you. Dan Brady's his name.'

'Brady? You've got Brady at Empty Creek?' With startling clarity, Brady's angry and distorted face appeared before her like an apparition. Aware that Carruthers was watching her closely, an amused expression on his face, she blinked quickly, and the vision was gone.

'He's working for me. You can come over and see him if you like, though it would take you the better part of a week to get there.'

Harriet smiled at the joke she thought Caruthers had made. She doubted she would ever see Brady again and was glad of it.

Ah Soy brought out a tray loaded with the teapot, biscuits and a cake. His usually smiling face was a scowling mask, possibly because Carruthers referred to him frequently and to his face as the Chink. Tell the Chink my tea's too weak. Tell the Chink my cake's a bit short on raisins. Tell the Chink my plate's a bit dirty. At the third repetition, Harriet was moved to tell him what she should have done at the second: that he was a guest and shouldn't abuse her hospitality or Ah Soy.

Carruthers found this enormously diverting. He slapped his hands on his beefy thighs and threw back his bovine head to let forth a roar of laughter not unlike a bull bellowing. Evidently he'd been hoping for a reaction and she resolved not to rise to the bait again. Soon he recovered himself enough to splutter, 'By Jove, you're a card! Give you a few more months up here and we'll see what happens to your manners!'

'That's all, thank you, Ah Soy,' Harriet said. 'We won't need anything else till the others get back.' Glancing at Carruthers, she saw that one of the raisins from the allegedly raisin-free cake was nestling in his moustache. Ah Soy appeared to have noticed this too: he grinned at her over Carruthers' head as he padded back to the kitchen block.

Now Carruthers began a monologue designed to convince her that, if something was in short supply but demand was buoyant, prices were bound to rise. Although she didn't feel comfortable with this man, allowing him to dominate the conversation was one way of filling in the time before the others returned.

But perhaps she'd missed something. Carruthers was actually talking about specifics: stock prices rather than a political economy treatise. Yes, he was talking of cattle; she'd been distracted by his treatment of Ah Soy and she wasn't being a good hostess. Maybe he owed thousands to the South Australian government for his leasehold, she thought while watching him more attentively. Probably he was plagued by worries about the health of his cattle and the economic depression affecting all the colonies. She began to feel sorry for him. He might be affected by one of the bank failures they'd read about in the last batch of newspapers that had come with Frank O'Connor.

Yet when he finished summarising for her what he termed the labour problem, she decided unequivocally that she didn't like him. 'There're only two sorts of black fellers,' he said. 'The blighters who fawn all over you and the blighters who'd put a spear through you if you didn't get them first. We've got too many of those murderous blighters and not enough of the fawning sort.'

She looked at his eyes, as relentlessly blue as the sky. 'There are no problems like that here,' she said. Beyond him, she saw plumes of smoke from the campfires by the billabong drifting slowly through the pandanus palms and paper bark trees and diffusing into the still air.

'Don't you believe it. At Empty Creek we're getting our cattle speared all the time and it's getting worse. The only way to stop the wild blacks spearing the cattle is to put the fear of the devil into them. Take a few pot shots at their campsites, for example. We pay big rentals to the South Australian government for this land and it's time the government troopers looked after us a bit so we don't have to take the law into our own hands. I reckon there should be a bounty on the blacks, a pound for every curly black head. At my reckoning I'd have myself thirty quid by now.'

When Harriet gasped, he seemed gratified by her reaction. But those days of massacres of blacks had ended over a decade ago, she'd heard. He was the type of man who would boast about something in order to shock you, and she wondered how much truth lay behind it. 'No wonder you're short of workers,' she said.

'Keep the lubras for that,' he said, laughing. 'They're good workers day and night.'

Perhaps I've become an honorary man, Harriet thought, and that's why he mentions this. Or conceivably he was simply baiting her again.

'More use than the white women,' he added, hard eyes gauging her reaction. 'God's police all of them, yourself excepted.'

She wondered whether to argue with this man or to tread more warily. She hadn't been cautious with Brady and she'd made an enemy there. It would be a good idea to avoid making any more.

At that moment Bella appeared with a pot of hot water. She looked uncomfortable, and Harriet watched Carruthers overtly scrutinise her, looking her up and down as if she were livestock at a country fair. He was almost licking his lips, Harriet thought; thick lips under a greying moustache. But he wasn't appreciating Bella's beauty as something to admire; he was viewing her as something to possess. 'You can go now,' she told Bella.

'They're good workers night and day,' Carruthers said once more, as if she might have missed his meaning. 'If you know how to treat them, that is.'

'I heard you the first time, Mr Carruthers.' She turned away as a black cockatoo flew overhead, screeching. Should she point out that if the settlers killed the men and fornicated with the women the black race would soon die out? No, this was precisely what men like Carruthers wanted. Doomed to extinction, that's what the white settlers often said about the blacks. Doomed to extinction so it wouldn't matter if they hastened it on a bit. Whiten the blacks who were left by miscegenation and then whitewash this with inevitability, for they all knew that God's chosen race was white.

The sinking sun now sliced so sharply into the horizon that the sky appeared to be bathed in blood. With relief she observed the column of dust along the track to the homestead that signalled the return of the others.

Presently Henry and two of the white stockmen joined

them on the verandah. Sarah, looking pale and tired, stopped long enough to say a brief hello. Bending low over Harriet, she whispered, 'Where's Bella?'

'In the kitchen, I think.'

Sarah hurried across the bare ground to the kitchen, small flurries of dust eddying behind her. After a few moments Harriet heard footsteps in the homestead. The shutters over the windows to Sarah and Henry's bedroom were closed so gently that you would only notice if looking that way. Afterwards Harriet could hear a murmured conversation that she guessed was Sarah talking to Bella.

With Henry and Carruthers engaged in a discussion about branding and ear-marks, Harriet seized the opportunity to withdraw. She knocked on Sarah's door. When her sister opened it, her fair hair streaming over her shoulders, Harriet saw Bella sitting on the bed with a hairbrush in her hand. 'Bella will stay with me until Carruthers has gone,' Sarah said quietly, shutting the bedroom door behind her and leading Harriet over to the door on the other side of the living room. 'However long that takes.'

'Carruthers is a dreadful man. Why didn't you tell me about him?'

'I didn't think he'd come this way. I've met him just once before, at one of our muster camps, a long way south-east of here. Bella's told me about him though and I want to keep her away from him.'

'I'm not surprised. I didn't like the way he looked at her.'

'Like horseflesh, I expect.'

'Yes. I can't bear to go back out there again.'

'Don't. You could go for one of your walks.'

* * *

199

Harriet wandered across to the far boundary fence of the home paddock, away from the sheds of the homestead and the shanties of the encampment. Resting her elbows on the railing, she watched the bleeding sky fade slowly to bands of orange and gold and thought of Carruthers. He treated Aborigines like animals or slaves. He would treat white women like that too, she thought, if he had the chance. He was a man in Brady's mould.

As soon as the sun sank below the horizon, a sprinkling of stars became visible; a creek of stars rather than a river. Small mob of stars. A few years more and the sky would be white with stars as the ancestors crowded the heavens.

'Evenin' missus.' The soft voice made her start with surprise. 'Boss' missus asked me to bring you this.'

Mick was standing several paces behind her, holding out a shawl. As she took it and thanked him, she realised that this was the first time they'd been alone together since they met near the mangroves at Palmerston. He nodded and grinned and was about to walk away when she said quickly, 'Don't go. I'd like to talk to you.'

Yet now he'd stopped, now that he was leaning on the fence railing not three yards away, she realised that she could think of nothing to say. Or perhaps it was more that she didn't know how to begin. The evening was far from silent though. The eerie cry of a bush curlew from somewhere near the billabong overlaid the deep hum of a didgeridoo, and soon this was accompanied by clattering clap sticks and the rhythmic chanting of a corroboree.

Eventually she said, 'That new man Carruthers has taken on. Do you know who he is?'

'Yes, missus.'

'Was he the man you saw following me at Palmerston?'

'Yes, missus. Bent nose white feller. He's working as a

ringer at Empty Creek. He and Carruthers are good mates. Met droving in Queensland years ago.'

'How long is he here for?'

'Dunno, missus.'

'One should try to forgive, I suppose,' Harriet said, more to herself than to Mick.

'Not that one. Or Carruthers. Got to avoid fellers like that.'

'You're not from around here, are you?'

'I'm from a long way away. The Coorong, south-east of Adelaide. I was educated at a mission school.'

'But you speak the language from around here?'

'Yes. And Yaraldi and Pitjantjatjara too.'

'What's your other name?'

'Spencer.'

'That's not your Yaraldi name, is it?'

'No. White fellers can't say my name. Too many syllables. They give me civilised name.'

'I hope you don't mind me asking these questions.'

'No, missus.'

'May I ask why you came here?'

'There wasn't any work on the mission for an educated blackfeller like me. I worked for a while as a storeman in Adelaide but then I got fed up with the city and headed north. Got a job as a ringer at a station near Alice Springs, then I met the Dimbulah Downs manager. After he saw me riding, he offered me a job as a stockman here.'

Harriet looked at Mick but he was staring ahead. Although the fading light made it impossible to make out his expression, it reduced his strong head to its essentials. For the first time in some weeks, for she'd neither sketched nor painted since arriving at Dimbulah Downs, she felt the urge to find a pencil and paper. She would like to draw his profile: the high forehead and the sharp angle at which this cut back to his eye sockets. Briefly she wondered if he would think she was viewing him as a curiosity but dismissed that notion. He'd noticed her sketching all manner of things on the trip south from Palmerston, and he'd certainly observed her drawing of Port Darwin. She wondered what he'd done with that; probably consigned it to the rubbish where it belonged.

As if sensing the direction of her thoughts, he said, 'There's a beautiful gorge down river from here that I could take you to one day, you and boss' missus. You might like to sketch it.'

'I would love that. Thank you, Mick.' To her surprise, she found that, by accepting this gift he was offering, she was now able to talk of her painting. She told him how she'd been unable to draw or paint since she'd arrived at Dimbulah Downs, so overwhelmed had she been by this landscape. She talked continuously, as if the dam wall had burst that had been holding back any expression of her feelings. Mick didn't interrupt, but simply interspersed the occasional sound, no more than a grunt really, that indicated he was listening. Then she told him that, while she missed her own country – so small and green with its cities dirty and crowded – she now feared that, wherever she travelled, there would be no place she could truly call home.

'I know where my country is,' he said. 'It's the Coorong.' He chiselled at a loose piece of wood on the eroded railing of the fence, until it splintered off and fell to the ground. After a few moments he said, 'Soon I'll take you and boss' missus to the gorge. And you'll need to bring your paints as well as your pencils, because when you see it you'll want to paint again.'

The dinner bell rang, putting an end to their conversation. Harriet began to stroll towards the homestead, aware of Mick by her side. As they got closer, the dinner bell rang a second time. By the time it had stopped, and she turned to speak to him, she discovered that he'd already gone. There was no sign of him anywhere; it was almost as if he'd never been by her side.

Of all the people she'd met since leaving London, she thought as she reached the kitchen block, it was Mick she felt most comfortable with.

Chapter 28

You Must Be Vigilant at All Times

'The revolvers are for the snakes,' Henry explained to Harriet again.

Sarah avoided looking at her sister, who was not taking gun practice with the seriousness it deserved.

'Yes, Henry,' Harriet replied. 'You've told me that before.'

'You have to keep practising.'

'I practised yesterday and when I aimed at the fence post I shot the eucalyptus tree, so I'm getting better. That was only one yard away from the target.'

'Anyone can hit the target if they concentrate and work at it.'

'Yes, Henry. I shall do that. Though Mick says snakes are timid and will mostly slither off.'

'Mostly, Harriet. You know what *mostly* means.'

'Yes, I do.' Harriet grinned at Sarah who looked away. She didn't want Henry to think they were making fun of him.

'You must carry the revolvers everywhere.'

'We will, I promise,' Sarah said.

'You never know when you'll come across a poisonous snake,' Henry continued. His brow was furrowed again. 'The taipans are the worst. I wish I had time before the cattle drive to give you more instruction but…'

'There are simply not enough hours in the day,' Harriet concluded, laughing.

For the past week, Henry had given Harriet daily training

sessions in the far corner of the home paddock. Speed and accuracy, he'd exhorted both sisters during these sessions. Indeed, so often had he repeated this mantra that Harriet had started saying 'Speed and accuracy' whenever she saw him. 'Speed and accuracy,' she now repeated.

'It's no joke,' Henry said with dignity. 'You must be vigilant at all times while I'm away.'

A month before, when Henry had first mentioned the cattle drive, Sarah had wanted to accompany him. But she had been easily dissuaded. Harriet had said – and Sarah suspected this was at Henry's behest – that she needed Sarah's company, and that there was no way she herself could bear to travel again to Palmerston so soon after the last trip. Even if she felt strong enough to face the matrons of Palmerston, she'd only recently recovered from her saddle sores. However, what had really deterred Sarah was her suspicion that she would hold up progress. Henry had to get 500 head of cattle to Port Darwin quickly to fulfil their part of the Goldsborough Mort contract with Java. While the Dimbulah Downs cattle were free of tick fever, he wanted to move them fast; he wanted to be without the worry that they might end up worthless and that he would be held responsible.

She looked at his anxious expression as he spoke to Harriet, and said, 'We will be vigilant at all times, Henry.' The last thing she wanted was for him to fret about what might happen at the homestead as well as about the cattle.

'At all times,' Harriet repeated.

Apparently mollified, Henry strode off to find Smithy and Mick. Harriet fired another round in the direction of the target. Once Henry was out of sight, she put down the revolver and began to laugh. 'Your husband will never make a markswoman out of me.'

'I think he knows that,' Sarah said. 'But you really must try harder, Hattie. Here, let me show you how to hold the revolver again.'

'Forget it, Sarah. You spend too much time firing the blasted thing.' After putting the gun on the ground by her feet, Harriet shook her hands vigorously before massaging her right wrist.

'Do I?' Sarah said. 'I find it quite satisfying. It must be the hand-eye coordination.'

'Good god, is that what excites you?'

'And the popping. It's a bit like playing an instrument,' Sarah said, laughing.

Harriet raised an eyebrow. 'What on earth are you doing with your life out here?'

'It's just for six months. Such an interesting experience.'

'So I see. And do you plan to stay in Australia?'

'Henry does.'

'And you?'

'What is this, the Spanish Inquisition?' For a moment Sarah wished Harriet was going on the cattle drive with Henry. She could do with some peace. The truth was that she had no idea of what she wanted for the future; sometimes she felt it was a farm in Suffolk, sometimes a house in London, once or twice she'd even thought of how pleasant it might be to farm on the south coast of New South Wales. She and Henry hadn't talked about their prospects since arriving at Dimbulah Downs. He'd been kept too busy and she'd wanted to delay the conflict between them that she suspected was inevitable.

'I'm your sister. Don't I have a right to ask if you want to remain in Australia?'

'I don't know. Henry and I do love this country, and he said months ago he would like to stay.'

'It's always what Henry wants to do.'

'Is it? He's the one who can get the work. He's the one who inherited the money.'

'Do you resent that? That Father didn't leave you much? You could always come back with me. I'll share it all with you.'

Sarah hesitated, surprised by the question. Did she mind that Father hadn't shared his estate equally with both his daughters? This had never occurred to her before. Since her marriage she'd generally felt cared for and comfortably off. In contrast, she viewed Harriet as being uncomfortably off, with her fierce desire for independence uneasily allied with her goal to improve the world, and both of these warring with her need for love. No, of course Sarah didn't mind the terms of the will. It was a relief to know that Harriet was well-provided for. In all probability her conflicting ambitions would never be reconciled. But if ever the skirmish were to end, Sarah felt that independence would be the victor, and Harriet's desire for love would be left wounded on the battlefield.

She became aware of Harriet scrutinising her and realised that her hesitation would give a misleading impression. At once she said, 'Of course I didn't mind, Hattie. But thank you for thinking of it. And I don't want to leave Henry. I love him and I married him for better or for worse.'

'But if you ever did want to leave, Sarah, you only have to say the word.'

Sarah decided to turn the questioning around. She said, 'You don't like it here, Hattie, do you?'

'I'm not saying that. I love it here in some ways. But is it really the life for a well-educated music lover like you?'

'It's an experience. I told you that before. I've learned a lot about all sorts of things.'

'Well, remember it's your life to live, your dreams to follow, not just Henry's. Where do you want to be eventually?'

'When I settle down, is that what you mean?' Sarah couldn't keep the sharpness out of her voice. 'I don't know yet.

I'm barely twenty-one. But I do love the light in Australia.'

'Is that a reason to stay?'

'You'd understand that surely, Hattie. You're the artist of the family.'

'I've given up since arriving at Dimbulah Downs.'

'Oh dear, have we done that to you? I hope not.' Sarah picked up the revolver from the ground. After releasing the safety catch she fired one shot at the can on the top of the fence post. The can clattered to the ground. 'Not bad,' she said.

'I'd call it perfect,' Harriet said.

'Thank you. For your compliment and for your offer.'

'It annoyed you, didn't it? I'm sorry if I upset you.'

'You didn't.' Sarah spoke as lightly as she could, although she was still irritated with Harriet for suggesting that she could abandon Henry to Australia. 'Let's go inside,' she said. 'This is enough of serious things for one afternoon.'

Yet what she wanted was some time to absorb what Harriet had said. Would she really consider leaving Henry if things got bad? It was reassuring to know that there was an outside option if they did. She was immensely grateful to Harriet for providing that, and yet she didn't want Harriet to see the extent of her relief. If she did, she might get the wrong idea about her marriage to Henry.

Nor did she understand quite why her gratitude was so great. Her subconscious self might have been agitating about how she might survive if she were to leave Henry. Yes, that must have been the case, and she found this deeply unsettling.

* * *

Sarah struggled to sit up in bed. She had woken earlier, when Henry had arisen, well before first light. Yet despite her intention to have breakfast with him before he left, here he was, fully dressed and ready to go. He put a mug of tea on the bedside table – a crude affair, roughly hewn from termite-resistant bloodwood – and sat on the edge of the bed.

She rubbed her eyes. These past few weeks she'd felt so tired, going to bed early and even once falling asleep over dinner, with her chin cupped in her hands and her elbows resting on the table, and her meal untasted on the plate in front of her.

She felt Henry gently touch her lips. Harriet's words of the previous afternoon had spun themselves into a fine veil that hid his features. She blinked and the veil was gone. Why should she take any notice of Harriet's opinions? She was living her own life and not her sister's. Smiling, she raised her arms to pull his face down to her own.

'I've got to leave,' he said at last. 'I've told Mick to stay behind, and of course Bob.'

'But don't you need them both?'

'Bob's not crucial and his leg still hasn't fully healed. And there are some odd-jobs he can do around the homestead.'

'But Mick's crucial.'

'We've got Smithy and plenty of other good stockmen,' he said. 'They're nearly as competent. I want Mick to keep an eye on things here.'

'Why?'

Henry opened and shut his mouth without any words coming out.

'Why, Henry?'

'I've just heard some bad news.' He hesitated, making that mouth like a goldfish's again.

'What news? Say it quickly, Henry. I'm thinking the worst.'

'Carruthers shot an Aborigine. One of the wild blacks west of Empty Creek.'

'But why?'

'He claimed they'd been stealing his cattle. They probably had, but you can't really blame them. They've got to eat. You've got to be prepared for some losses of cattle. And he treats the black fellows so badly.'

'Are you quite sure he did it? It's one thing to treat them badly, quite another to murder one of them.'

'I'm afraid it's true, Sarah. I heard it from Tommy who got back late last night. He saw it happen. Things could get bad at Empty Creek if the blacks retaliate. I've sent a man to the telegraph repeater station to report it.'

The police would do nothing, she knew. She began to feel an anger so cold it made her shiver. She buried her face in Henry's chest.

'I'll leave it to you to tell Harriet and Ah Soy,' Henry said.

'Won't Ah Soy have already heard?'

'No. Just Tommy and Mick know so far. Mick will tell Bob. Are you sure you're happy about being left behind? Remember you once said you wanted to accompany me everywhere?'

She might have thought he was joking had she not seen the seriousness of his expression. She said, 'Only last week we spoke of this again, and we agreed it was best for me to stay here with Harriet.' The truth was that she no longer had the smallest desire to go on the cattle drive. She didn't especially like Palmerston, and she was tired, oh so tired. The presence of Bob and Mick would surely keep Carruthers in line if he decided to make a visit to Dimbulah Downs.

'Mick will keep an eye on Harriet,' Henry said. 'She needs to be watched. She's inclined to wander about a bit and there are all sorts of people passing through here now the boom's over. You never know what sort of trouble she'll get into; you've said as much yourself. And she trusts Mick.' He looked at her intently before adding, 'Promise me you won't forget to take your revolver with you whenever you go out. Harriet must too.'

Of course,' Sarah said. 'I promised you that yesterday, and you know I always keep a promise.'

After Henry left, Sarah unfastened the shutters. The early morning air felt cool and she pulled a shawl around her shoulders. Although the mob of cattle was already some way north of the homestead, she could hear their bellowing overlaid by the staccato calls of the stockmen, and occasionally the crack of a stockwhip. She watched Henry gallop along the track to catch up, until eventually he became a small speck, one of the dots of men and horses encircling the dust-shrouded mob.

Carruthers killing a wild black; she couldn't get the thought out of her mind. She felt suddenly faint, and an instant later nauseous. After lurching outside, she leaned over the edge of the verandah and vomited on to the hard ground. Again and again she retched, until all that remained in her mouth was the bitter taste of bile.

When she felt slightly better, she took the water pitcher from her bedroom. After rinsing her mouth, she poured the remaining water on to the ground and retrieved one of the buckets of sand standing by the verandah. Quickly she tipped this over the earth. Back in her bedroom, she ran her hands lightly over her breasts. They were swollen and slightly tender to the touch. She was definitely putting on weight and she was almost certainly pregnant.

She felt a twinge of guilt that she hadn't told Henry before he left. He would have been delighted but she feared he would have insisted on her going with him to Port Darwin and leaving her there for the duration of the pregnancy. She didn't want to leave Dimbulah Downs yet. She was feeling well and healthy, if a little tired. There was no need to leave until just before the wet season started.

Although it was time to get dressed, she felt so exhausted

that she crawled back into bed and pulled the covers up around her chin. A moment later she fell into a deep sleep.

When she woke, it was to the sound of Harriet and Ah Soy talking on the verandah. She felt exhausted still, and her usual good spirits were sorely absent. Absent like Henry: she began to count up all the days and the weeks to be endured without him. She rolled on to her face and pulled the pillow over her head. Still she could hear Harriet and Ah Soy, so distinctly they might almost be in the room with her. Later she would have to share with Harriet the news about Carruthers, but for the moment she wished her sister and Ah Soy a long way away so she could continue sleeping.

'Very big,' Ah Soy said.

'The biggest I've ever seen,' Harriet said. 'We could eat it now, I suppose. It does look delicious.'

'Good flavour,' Ah Soy agreed. But his voice was not enthusiastic.

'They lose their flavour when they get too big.'

'Missie know best.'

'But it does seem rather a shame to think of picking it,' Harriet said. 'It's quite tempting to leave it for a while longer. I've never seen such a big one and it would be nice to see how large it might grow, by way of an experiment. We could measure it daily.'

'Water daily too.'

'I've seen you do it twice daily,' Harriet said, laughing.

'Best ever seen. Best you ever see, Missie?'

'It's by far and away the best I've ever seen. We don't grow them like this in England.'

At last Harriet's being positive, Sarah thought, and her anxiety dissipated slightly. It was Ah Soy's cabbage, of course, the one that he'd been talking about for weeks. The notion of Harriet becoming animated about a Northern Territory vegetable greatly pleased her.

'I think we might defer the picking of the cabbage in the interests of science, Ah Soy,' Harriet was now saying.

'Pick later,' Ah Soy agreed.

Sarah removed the pillow from her head and sat up. After struggling out of bed, she gathered up Henry's pyjamas that he'd left in a bundle on the covers. She sniffed them: how was it that Henry's sweat smelt so delicious and the stockmen's so awful? She would make sure they weren't washed until he returned. For a moment she wondered if he were already missing her; but no, he wouldn't be thinking of her yet, he had far too much to do.

She put Henry's pyjamas into a drawer so that Daisy wouldn't scoop them up to be washed. Obsessed by washing, Daisy immediately removed any garment left lying around and carried it off to be sorted into one of the laundry bags hanging on pegs in the outhouse next to the coppers. Every second day she would enquire, 'Today washem clothes, missus?' It was because of the swimming afterwards; the final rinsing of some of the garments in the waterhole. 'Washing day is on Monday,' Sarah would reply, but Daisy always lived in hope that she might one day change her mind.

Sarah pulled on her dressing gown, collected a towel and her sponge bag, and went out on to the verandah. The morning air was fresh and the dust from the departure of the cattle had long settled. Half a dozen small children were kicking something around beyond the windmill. Bella and Daisy were showering in the hessian-screened enclosure, enjoying it as they always did, as they enjoyed everything. She wondered if they'd heard the news of what Carruthers had done. She wondered what changes Carruthers' crime might bring to their lives and to the lives of people living on other cattle stations.

After plucking one of Henry's old hats from a peg on the verandah, she jammed it on her head. Before slipping her feet into her riding boots, she checked that no insects or reptiles had chosen to settle in them overnight. Henry would be away for six weeks at least. She'd have to take one day at a time. It would be a struggle but she would try to take pleasure in small things: the beauty of the morning light, the long shadows cast by the trees, the honking of a flock of pied geese rising from the billabong. The laughter of Bella and Daisy, and the measured conversation of Harriet and Ah Soy working amongst the vegetables.

Chapter 29

Sarah's Shooting Practice

How wonderfully quiet the homestead seemed, Harriet thought, once the mob had left and the bulldust had settled at last. Sitting in the kitchen she watched Ah Soy busying himself at the range; he seemed in holiday spirits too at the departure of the mob and the success of his cabbage.

'Two egg, Missie?' His question was redundant, for as he spoke he slid the plate in front of her and stood back, hands clasped in front of his chest, to watch her reaction.

'Delicious,' she said around her first mouthful.

'Cake this afternoon. Plenty egg.'

From somewhere about the homestead buildings she could hear Daisy and Bella singing, and was amused when she recognised the melody as the Fauré duet that once she had hated so much: all that endless practising in Gower Street when Sarah and Henry were getting to know one another through music. How long ago that now seemed and how far the music had travelled.

When Sarah appeared, she looked dishevelled: her hair wet and uncombed, and she was still in her dressing gown. Her expression was anxious, Harriet thought. More anxious than she'd expected even allowing for Henry's departure. Once Sarah had seated herself at the kitchen table, Harriet strode across to the doorway and stood there, her back turned to the room. Squinting against the harsh light, she waited for the reaction. When she heard Sarah's barely suppressed laughter, she turned.

'What's the matter, Sarah?'

'Nothing, Hattie. It's simply that you look ever so slightly different.'

'Do I?' Pleased, Harriet smoothed down her trousers. This was the first time she'd worn them, and it would take her a while to become used to their freedom. Perhaps they were a little baggy, for she seemed to have lost weight since she'd had them made, but on the other hand this was an advantage, for it meant that the contents of the numerous pockets wouldn't press in upon her.

'You look so funny,' Sarah said, grinning. 'Not that they don't suit you. They do. It's just a bit of a surprise.'

'Good.' Harriet had chosen today for their first appearance to distract Sarah and it was certainly having the desired effect. 'I feel like a new woman.'

'Or a new man?'

'No, a new woman. Don't you know that women are wearing trousers for cycling now? I thought you were a keen follower of fashion.'

'I saw those pictures in the *Illustrated London News* but they were a bit different to yours. They were more baggy bloomers than trousers.'

'I had these made by the Chinese tailor in Cavanagh Street to my own specifications.'

Sarah smiled. 'I love you, Hattie. You're like a tonic.'

'One that does you good but tastes horrid?'

'Your medicine never tastes horrid. Well, hardly ever. When it does, I hold my nose and swallow.'

'Without a protest?' Harriet said, laughing. 'I'm glad you don't do that, Sarah.'

Ah Soy poured more hot water in the teapot. Sipping her tea, Harriet decided to take advantage of her new trousers and the stockmen's absence to try riding astride. It would be such

216

liberation compared with perching on a side saddle. 'Would you like to try riding astride this morning?' she asked Sarah. 'You could wear a pair of Henry's trousers.'

'No,' said Sarah. 'I don't want to get saddle sores in different spots. Anyway, I don't want to ride today. Let's go for a walk along the river.'

Harriet shrugged her shoulders. She'd seen the way the Aboriginal stock women rode, as fast and as carefree as the men, and she wanted to experience this for herself. Then she noticed that Sarah's forehead had creased and she was drumming with her fingers on the tabletop. 'A walk by the river would be lovely,' she said, placing her hand on Sarah's shoulder. 'Let's go as soon as you're dressed.'

* * *

Strolling with Sarah across the home paddock, Harriet watched the red dust swirl around her ankles and settle on the tops of her boots. Sarah seemed distracted; she stumbled on a tussock and might have fallen if Harriet hadn't taken her arm and guided her towards the track that followed the course of the river. Her face looked slightly feverish, a bright pink spot on each cheek. Lightly Harriet touched her sister's forehead: her temperature seemed normal. The fever's emotional not physical, she thought, perhaps Sarah should have gone with Henry.

For an instant, Harriet felt a sharp pang of envy at their intimacy. Yet why should she? There was no one she wished to be close to. Mostly that was a blessing: no one to tell her what to do, no one to disapprove of her. But no one to approve of her either; no one to support her the way Father always had.

When they reached the first in the sequence of rock pools, bordered by casuarina trees, Sarah stopped. 'Let's sit,' she said, plonking herself on to a wide leaf-littered rock at the edge of the track. As she raised her arm to wipe her forehead on her sleeve, Harriet saw that her hand was shaking.

'What's the matter?'

'There's something I need to tell you.' Sarah scowled at the green, slow-flowing water in the river below the path.

At that moment Harriet was distracted by a movement in the pool that was furthest away. Someone was swimming, cutting gracefully through the water in an energetic overarm. Though the figure was too far distant to identify, she thought it looked a bit like Mick. Yet it couldn't have been Mick, she knew he'd gone with the mob that morning. Averting her eyes, she said, 'What is it, Sarah?'

'Something that Henry mentioned just before he left this morning.'

They've had an argument, Harriet thought. Perhaps it had been a mistake to mention Father's will yesterday, not long before Henry left on the cattle drive. She should have had the tact to wait a bit. After plucking a small branch from a shrub, she used it to flick a layer of dead leaves off a section of rock. 'What is it?'

'It's about Carruthers.'

'Carruthers?' Harriet sat down next to Sarah and sighed. She'd hoped to hear no more of this man.

'Yes. Tommy, one of the ringers, got back late last night with some news. That's why Mick isn't going with the mob.'

'Mick's staying?' She glanced at the furthest pool but the swimmer had gone. 'You'd better tell me what's happened.'

'It's something horrible.' Sarah hesitated for a few seconds, before blurting out, 'Carruthers shot an Aborigine, Harriet. One of the wild blacks west of Empty Creek. They'd been spearing his cattle.'

'Does Tommy know that for sure? Carruthers told me he'd

shot dozens of Aborigines when I met him but I didn't believe him. He seemed like the sort who'd boast about something in order to shock you.'

'You didn't believe him, Harriet?' Sarah's voice sounded loud and far too high. 'But you told me at the cricket match about all those massacres. They'd be by men just like Carruthers.'

'I know that's how the cattle runs were first established ten or twenty years ago but I thought it was confined to the Kimberley these days.'

'*Confined to the Kimberley these days!* Who's being innocent now? It might be over at places like Dimbulah Downs but not at Empty Creek.'

'But there's a Territory police commissioner and police.'

'You said at the cricket match there was one law for the whites and one for the blacks, and you were right. Henry's arranged for the murder to be reported at the telegraph station but you can bet the police will do nothing.' Sarah picked up a twig from the ground next to her scuffed boots and began to break it methodically into small pieces, though her hands were still shaking. 'The wild blacks might do something in retaliation though.'

'The wild blacks?'

'Yes, the ones south-west of Empty Creek. The ones that haven't been pacificated. I'm really worried.'

'They won't do anything to us, Sarah.'

'You think so?'

'Yes, I'm sure so. Why should they? And anyway, what can we do? There's no point worrying about it.' Yet, despite her calm words, she heard her own heartbeats, too loud and too fast.

'But they might do something to Carruthers, don't you see? Then there'll be reprisals. That might affect our people.' Sarah threw away the last fragment of twig and waved an arm in the direction of Dimbulah Downs homestead. 'Or Carruthers might come back for Bella. And if he does, the locals will retaliate, I know.'

'He won't.'

'You told me how he'd been making eyes at her. And she's afraid of him.'

'He wouldn't dare take her.'

'But Henry's away with most of the men.'

'You said Mick's staying here, and there's Bob and Ah Soy too.'

'But...' Sarah hesitated, and Harriet observed near her collarbone a pulsing vein that was surely beating too fast. 'Do you ever think we should take the law into our own hands, Hattie?'

'No, I don't. I think we should change the way it's implemented but not administer it ourselves.'

'The Aborigines have their own system of law. Bella's told me about it.'

'Yes, I know.'

'And you don't think that should be stopped?'

'No.'

'You're confusing me. How can we have two systems of law?' Sarah stood up, the better to aim a kick at a small stone on the pathway. She winced as it turned out to be embedded in the path.

'But they're both aiming at the same thing. Justice. If a black man spears Carruthers now, he's acting justly.'

'By their law, not ours,' Sarah said.

'Does it matter?'

'I'm getting even more puzzled,' Sarah said irritably. 'This is all far too much for one day, Harriet. Do let's talk of something else.' She raised her hands in front of her, fingers splayed as if she might be about to play the piano. They were steady now; how quickly Sarah could control herself.

* * *

Late afternoon sunlight filtered through the eucalypts; Harriet, on a chair on the verandah, buried herself in a book, until she was distracted by a movement down by the stockyard. Peering through the glare, she saw Sarah talking animatedly to Mick. A few moments later, Mick hauled a plank of wood on to a couple of trestles. Once this was positioned to Sarah's evident satisfaction, the two of them fetched a wheelbarrow from near the woodpile and loaded it with short lengths of wood. Mick trundled the barrow off to the trestles, and he and Sarah lined the blocks upright along the length of the plank. Soon after, Mick walked towards the men's quarters, apparently dismissed from further involvement in whatever activity Sarah had in mind.

For a few moments Sarah stood and sized up the line of blocks. Arranged in order of height, they might be a musical instrument, Harriet thought, although they were not hollow. At any moment Sarah might pull out a drumstick and start beating.

Sarah stepped back half a dozen paces. Now Harriet saw that she was holding in her right hand something shiny, something that reflected the late afternoon sunlight. She raised her hand and directed it towards the line of blocks.

Bang-bang-bang. The blocks went down like skittles. Sarah picked up those that were still intact and restored them to the plank. Over and over again. *Bang-bang-bang.* The sound was driving Harriet loopy. She shut her book and went inside, closing the shutters in her room. This made little difference. *Bang-bang-bang.* It was as if Sarah and her dratted revolver were only a few yards away.

Harriet rummaged in the bottom drawer of the chest next to the bed. She pulled out a notebook and the tin containing sticks of charcoal. Sitting on the edge of the bed, she executed a sketch, quickly, unthinkingly. A man lying on the ground next to a horseman with a rifle. With her forefinger she smudged the charcoal over the prone figure. A black man lay in a pool of blood.

Though starting to feel queasy, she flicked over the page and embarked on another sketch. Autonomous drawing, she thought; I know not what I do. A few more quick lines and it was complete. A white man lying face down next to the blackfeller.

A white man with a spear in his back.

Bang-bang-bang from the stockyard still. Sarah was becoming as focused on shooting as she had once been on her music.

Harriet flung the book and charcoal stick on to the bed. After finding her hat and boots, she headed off towards the men's quarters. Mick wasn't there but she found him a few minutes later down by the horse paddock.

'I'm sorry about this, Mick.' Her words were, of course, inadequate but even so they were better than leaving unacknowledged what had happened. 'It was a truly terrible thing that Carruthers did. He's not like other men.'

'But that's the trouble, missus. Carruthers *is* like other men.'

She puzzled over this remark. 'Do you mean like other white men?' she said.

'No. Like all men.' The words were indistinct; he didn't turn his head as he spoke.

'That's why we have laws. To stop men killing one another.'

'Yes, missus.'

She felt this response was both mocking and final. He was

giving her the last word because she was white and she felt hurt at his unwillingness to continue the discussion. The sound of the breeze rattling the eucalyptus leaves filled the silence. Mick didn't move and she waited to see if he would say more.

'You know the gorge I told you about?' he said at last, his eyes on the horses in the paddock.

'Yes.'

'Would you and boss' missus like to go there? In three, four days? Pick good weather day.'

'They're all good weather days at this time of the year,' she said. 'That's what Henry says.'

'Boss knows a thing or two.' He smiled at the horses not at her.

'Thank you, Mick. We'd love to go.' Though she too directed her smile at the horses, she knew Mick had seen her pleasure at the invitation.

Chapter 30

Spears of Light

Harriet had slept for less than five hours but she was finding it impossible to go back to sleep. She lay in bed listening to the creaking of the walls and the chirping of geckos and the curlew that seemed so close it might almost have been in the room with her. Soon, bored with inaction, she got up and checked the satchel she'd packed the night before. Everything was in order: paints, mixing tray, rag, sketchbook and pencils, and a few sticks of charcoal at the bottom, wrapped in a cardboard tube for protection.

The sky was tinged with gold to the east when she knocked on Sarah's door. She found her sister was already dressed, even down to the holster and revolver. She looked happier than she'd been for days, and unusually alert for an hour that was not yet six.

In the kitchen Ah Soy had a pot of fresh tea on the table and there were eggs sizzling in the frying pan.

'We must pack a billycan and some mugs,' Harriet said.

'Mick already gottem,' Ah Soy said.

'And food?'

'Yes. Him ready to go. See, down at the stockyard. Horses saddled and Bella there too.'

'Mick's thought of everything,' Sarah said, around her last mouthful of toast. 'Grab your hat, Hattie! We're off.'

Mick didn't meet Harriet's eye: he appeared interested solely in establishing whether or not Harriet had brought her painting materials. Only after she showed him did he manage a smile, one that was directed at the stockyard rail rather than at her. She thought it unlikely the contents of her satchel would be used. All she had drawn since arriving at Dimbulah Downs was the pair of charcoal sketches of a few days ago, and she had destroyed those.

'How do we get to the gorge?' Sarah said. 'Do we follow the river?'

'No, we can't get in that way, it's too steep,' Mick said. 'It's quickest to go over the top of the plateau and down into the next valley. Then we wind back to join the river at the bottom of the gorge.'

As Harriet and Mick rode side by side along the track, she said, 'Any more news from Empty Creek Station?'

'Carruthers is saying he's taught the black feller a lesson and there'll be no more troubles.'

'No more murders?'

'No more cattle spearing.'

'And what do you think?'

Mick's expression became like a mask. 'I don't think about it,' he said.

Around them, the spidery orange flowers of grevillea glowed in the sunlight; she registered them but was today indifferent to their beauty. She wondered if Mick thought she sounded superior, as Sarah had claimed the day of the cricket match. Feeling a pang of self-doubt, she reminded herself that the trip to the gorge was a gift that Mick had offered her. She would do her best to make it a day that they would all remember.

By ten o'clock the morning was starting to feel hot. Harriet became anxious about Sarah, who was starting to sway a little on her horse. On the banks of the slow-flowing river, they halted in a small clearing surrounded by dense foliage: ti trees, corkscrew palms and stately fan palms, some of which must have been sixty feet tall.

225

Harriet spread out a rug on the sandy ground and Sarah lay down and fanned herself with the branch of a palm. Mick busied himself some yards distant, lighting a fire to boil the billycan for tea.

'Are you all right, Sarah?' Harriet asked. Her sister looked pale and there were dark circles under her eyes.

'I'm fine,' said Sarah. 'Don't fuss.'

Bella sat cross-legged next to Sarah. She gently relieved her of the palm branch and waved it so enthusiastically over Sarah that she started giggling and complaining of the cold.

'Missus catchem newfellow piccaninny,' Bella suggested.

'Yes,' Sarah said.

'That's wonderful news!' Harriet, squatting on the ground next to Sarah, felt delighted though not very surprised at the news. 'How pregnant, do you think?'

Sarah didn't reply immediately. It occurred to Harriet that perhaps she didn't know. At once she began thinking of the logistics of Sarah's confinement; she couldn't be more than three months pregnant or else it would be showing, but perhaps they should take her to Palmerston where there was a doctor.

Sarah said, 'Probably four months.'

Harriet caught her breath. 'That's wonderful!' It was almost as if Sarah had been in the bush for twenty years and had lost the art of communication! She couldn't prevent herself from feeling irritated for an instant that she'd been excluded from this secret. 'But you look so slim!' she exclaimed. 'And how secretive you've been!'

'Don't be acerbic, Hattie. I'm sorry I didn't tell you before. Anyway, I've got on a loose dress and I've started wearing stays again so I can fit in.'

'I don't think that's a good idea. Have you got them on now?'

'Yes.'

'Well, take them off. They're too hot, even your fancy ventilated ones, and anyway, I don't want my niece or nephew getting confined by your confinement.'

'Me squashem newfellow piccaninny,' Sarah said, laughing with Bella. 'I'll do it in a minute. Just let me rest for a bit.'

'You shouldn't have come.' Harriet regretted these words as soon as they slipped out. It was as if she were punishing her sister for telling her the good news.

'But I wanted to. And you couldn't have come on your own.'

'I don't see why not. Who cares out here? But I didn't mean that you shouldn't have come today. It's only that it's all a bit of a surprise. A wonderful surprise.' A niece or a nephew, how marvellous that would be. A niece first; she would like to have a niece. A girl who would grow up able to vote. A girl who would inherit her grandmother's pearls, how odd that this thought should spring at once into Harriet's head. 'Does Henry know you're expecting?' She glanced across the clearing. Mick, apparently oblivious to their conversation, was crouching next to the fire and blowing so that the flames leapt up around the blackened billycan.

'No. I'll tell him when he gets back. I thought he'd make me go to Palmerston with him and I'd slow him down so much he'd miss the Java deadline.'

'That's probably true.' Harriet wondered if Henry would appreciate the irony of the situation. They had worked hard to convince Sarah not to accompany the cattle drive yet she hadn't wanted to join it in the first place. The trouble with empathy was that, while it had you projecting yourself into someone else's position, you still carried with you your own perceptions. She tried imagining she was Henry: disappointed his wife hadn't shared the news of the pregnancy with him; pleased he hadn't had to take her with him to Port Darwin;

delighted he was to be a father and not caring whether she was three or five months pregnant as long as she was well. Yes, empathy had her thinking of many possibilities. All of them – or none of them – could coexist in Henry's mind.

She picked up the palm branch that Bella had placed on the ground and gently fanned her sister.

Sarah smiled though she kept her eyes shut. 'That's lovely, Hattie.'

'Henry will be overjoyed when he hears that you're pregnant,' Harriet said, smiling.

'Of course. Do keep fanning, won't you. I so love being spoilt!'

Once tea was over, Harriet led Sarah behind some pandanus palms and helped her out of her corset. 'You might be well-ventilated in this thing,' she said, laughing. 'But now you look like a piece of basket-weaving. Red marks where the bands have been digging in and white everywhere else. Are you sure you're pregnant?'

'Quite sure. All the expected signs.'

'Are you feeling well enough to continue?'

'Yes, I feel wonderful now. Nothing like a cup of tea to revive you.'

* * *

Harriet rode behind Mick, who had been quiet all morning. Occasionally he turned to check on the others' progress. With the sun directly overhead, his large felt hat so shadowed his face that it was impossible to gauge the expression in his eyes. Harriet interpreted his silence not as a withdrawal but as a measure of the seriousness of this expedition. She might have asked him if he'd taken other white fellows along this route if she hadn't felt this could be interpreted as intrusive.

For the last half-hour of the journey, as she rode behind

him, she was infused with an increasing sense of anticipation, indeed almost of trepidation. Behind her rode Sarah and Bella, and she periodically turned to watch them. Sarah, looking refreshed after their break, was chatting to Bella, their voices interweaving like a pair of doves, or like two schoolgirls on holiday, forgetting life's complications, laughing at everything as if being alive was an enormous joke.

She noticed that Mick was now sitting unnaturally upright. His posture seemed to express anxiety at what he might be setting in train, but it was possible that she was misrepresenting the significance of this trip to the gorge.

The valley began to narrow rapidly. Soon they were riding between perpendicular cliffs, in whose fissures trees had managed to find a toehold. A bird whistled in the dense undergrowth, a melodious call that started low and rose quickly on half a dozen distinct half-notes. The ground had become very rough, so that their progress was slowed as the horses stepped delicately around boulders. After a time, the sound of falling water could be heard. As they rounded a large rock that must have fallen from the cliff top, the gorge widened into a semicircle containing a pool of green water into which a white waterfall plunged from a hundred or so feet above.

The fall was beautiful but what startled Harriet was the light. The sun threw into the chasm luminous spears that struck bright sparks from the quartz in the rock face, so that the whole gorge was ablaze with a brilliant pink glow. It was the coruscation that would be the challenge, she thought. That and the sharpness of the spears hurled down by the sun. Perhaps she should simply try to draw the canyon; the shapes of the rocks would surely not elude her. She became aware that Mick was watching her. He had relaxed; he was smiling for the first time that day, his white teeth almost luminous. She smiled back, and he nodded before looking away.

'It's a very special place.'

'Yes, missus.' It seemed that Mick was making up for a morning of not smiling.

'We'll make a fire,' said Sarah. 'Bella, do come and help me. We'll boil the billy and then maybe you can show me how to catch a fish without a line. This is such fun!' She began to collect kindling assisted by an equally enthusiastic Bella.

Harriet and Mick remained side by side at the edge of the pool, contemplating the pink cliffs.

'Paint now,' Mick said. 'This will only last an hour. Paint now and paint fast.'

He spoke like an artist and not a stockman, Harriet thought, glancing at him curiously. He had removed his hat, which he was holding close to his chest as if he were in a church. His wavy black hair partially obscured his profile.

She had a sudden flash of intuition: Mick wanted to paint too. 'Would you like to use the paints?' she said. She wondered if this was the reason for his preoccupation all morning.

He turned to look at her. 'Yes, missus.'

'Was that why you brought me here, so you could use my paints?' She could bite off her tongue, for this had sounded almost like an accusation. She kicked viciously at a stone with the toe of her boot, as if she could kick away what she'd said.

He replied with dignity, 'No, missus. I brought you here because I thought it might make you want to draw again.' His face was inscrutable. He was perhaps used to such allegations, even from those who exposed their souls to him as she had the evening of Carruthers' visit, when he'd offered to take her to the gorge.

'Thank you,' she said carefully. 'And I do want to draw again.' Even if she didn't, she would have to try, after what had happened between them. 'I'll draw and you will paint. Now and fast.'

230

When Mick laughed, his face was transformed, the lines at either side of his mouth so deep they could be gorges themselves, and the skin around his eyes creased into myriad tiny gullies. From her satchel she pulled out the sketchbook and some pencils, tore off some sheets of paper, and handed Mick the sketchbook and the canvas bag of paints and brushes. 'Have you painted before?'

'At the mission. I had a tin box with little squares of colour.'

'Try these paints.' Harriet burrowed in her satchel that Mick was now holding and pulled out one of Ah Soy's smaller cake tins, with its indentations for cupcakes. 'You squeeze a little bit of paint from the tube into this recess. You mix it with water, just a little. Do you know how to mix colours to make other colours?'

'Yes, missus.'

'Blue and yellow make green. Blue and red make purple. And there are other colours here too, so you might not have to mix.'

'Yes, missus.'

'I'm going to sit on that boulder over there and I'll leave you with the paints.' She observed his hands, which were almost quivering in his eagerness to begin.

She took off her revolver and holster before climbing to the top of the rock. Deliberately positioning herself so that she couldn't see him, she studied the fragmented nature of the cliff face, whose component rocks took up many geometric forms. After a time scrutinising the play of light on the cliff, she started to analyse its structure and, when she felt she had understood it, to sketch out the shapes that made up the gorge. And then she became so absorbed that she no longer thought of Mick, she was unaware of Sarah and Bella playing like children as they constructed their fire. She thought only of conveying the essence of what she was seeing, in a few pencil strokes on paper, on sheet after sheet of paper, and scribbling notes at the side of each sheet about colours.

Suddenly the pinkness vanished from the gorge as if an electric light had been switched off. The cliffs were now in full shadow and the shapes of the rocks were no longer revealed. She put down her sheets of paper and slipped the pencils into her trouser pocket, while a peace descended on her.

Eventually she turned and saw Mick at the edge of the pool, washing the paint brushes and cleaning the makeshift palette. She clambered down from the rock, curious to see how he'd interpreted what they'd witnessed.

'Those are good paints,' he said, laughing. He was holding her sketchbook in one hand but at an angle, so that its surface was concealed from her.

'Will you show me the painting?' said Harriet.

'Shut your eyes, missus.'

She held out her hands and shut her eyes until she felt the weight of the sketchbook on her uplifted palms. Then she looked down. He had covered the page with blocks of colour representing different planes of rock – pinks and rose madder and the palest mauve; it was almost as if he were using oil paints. The transient moment had become a scene of solidity and, to Harriet's critical eye, his interpretation seemed exactly right, exactly as the gorge had appeared in that short hour in which the light had streamed into it. She opened her mouth to speak but barely a croak came out. Mick was a born artist. For an instant she felt envy but she repressed this quickly. 'Brilliant painting,' she said at last. 'You're a natural artist.'

'No, missus. I learned at the mission.'

'With squares of paint in a tin box? I'm going to give you my water colours, Mick.' Now she wondered if there had been something patronising in her attitude to him, the way she'd found white men patronising her.

'No, missus. We'll go painting together until the boss comes back. You keep them.'

'It's a deal,' she said, smiling. And perhaps later, after she had left this place, she would be able to work out her own way of representing the pink light flickering from quartz crystals in the rock face.

On the ride back to the homestead, Mick began to talk to her. He's been liberated by this trip, she thought, as have I. He'd given to her the trip to the gorge and she'd lent him her paints, and together they'd created an experience that neither would ever forget. Yet the sharing was not to stop there, for now – his face more animated than she'd ever before seen – he was telling her about his earlier years. His time at the mission school, what he'd learned there and how much he missed his country when he first went to Adelaide for work.

She didn't interrupt him but simply interspersed the occasional comment to encourage his unburdening, in the way he listened to her that evening when she had confided to him her feelings of being overwhelmed by the Territory and her realisation that she belonged nowhere. Then she'd felt comfortable with him. Now she realised that she was beginning to feel close to him.

Chapter 31

She Felt Like Giving Him a Good Shove

On her way back from the shower, Sarah saw Mick with Aidan, one of the white stockmen from a muster camp several days' ride away. Aidan had arrived at the homestead that morning to exchange some horses and collect more stores. Standing on the far side of the stockmen's quarters, neither man noticed her walking by.

'How are you, you black bugger?' Aidan was a short chunky man, with bandy legs and no neck. His egg-shaped head looked as if it might roll off his shoulders at any moment if you gave it a push.

'Better than you, you skinny white feller,' Mick said, grinning. 'You look like you need a good feed.'

'When are you coming back to work, you lazy bastard? Looks like you're getting fat lounging round here.'

'What do you think I'm doing here? It's work, same as you're doing when you're not riding around admiring the anthills.'

'Don't look like work to me. Hanging around with a couple of sheilas, a Chinaman and a gammy-leg bastard. Regular tucker you don't have to cook yourself. Don't look like a hard life to me.'

Mick laughed. 'Better get Ah Soy give you a feed. That might sweeten you up a bit.'

When Sarah returned from the shower, Mick was nowhere to be seen. As she passed the kitchen, she heard Aidan talking to Ah Soy inside. Looking through the doorway, she saw the cook at the range stirring the contents of a large pot. Aidan was sitting at the long table, eating as he talked.

When she heard what he was saying, she blushed and hurried on to the residence.

* * *

Once lunch was over and the plates cleared away, Sarah said, 'Are you riding again this afternoon, Hattie?'

'Yes.' Harriet pulled on her riding boots and rapidly laced them up.

'Where are you off to?'

'Just to that spot below the rock pools.' After plucking her hat from one of the pegs on the verandah, Harriet looped the tie around her wrist.

'I'm too tired to go with you today, Hattie.'

'That's fine. You have a good rest.' Harriet smiled as she twirled her hat. 'Mick's coming with me.'

'Again?'

'Yes, of course. Henry did say that Mick and Bob should keep an eye on us. Bob will stay here; Mick will come with me.'

'You've been out with him every afternoon since the gorge,' Sarah said. 'That's fourteen days in a row. And you haven't read to the children for a while.'

'No. There'll be plenty of time to do that when Henry gets back.'

'I see.'

'Sarah, you've been with us every day until today.'

'Yes, I know. But I need a rest from all that and I want Bella to stay with me.'

'You mustn't feel you have to accompany me everywhere. Why shouldn't I go out, though? Is there anything wrong with that?'

235

'Well, you wouldn't do it in London.'

Harriet laughed. 'I hardly ever rode in London. And anyway, who's there to see me here?'

'Sometimes people come through. Stockmen from other stations. Men looking for work. Ah Soy feeds them, they have a bit of a gossip, and carry on spreading the word after they've gone. And the Aborigines are coming and going all the time. It's not like this place is an island.'

'Why would anyone care about us?'

'People talk,' Sarah said, frowning.

'So you said. But surely you're not serious. Who cares what anyone says? I'm only sketching.'

'Mick's black, Harriet.' Sarah saw Ah Soy appear at the doorway into the kitchen. He seemed puzzled. After a quick look he withdrew, and a second later she saw him hurrying towards the vegetable patch, well beyond earshot.

'You think I haven't noticed, Sarah?'

'White women and black men don't mix.' Sarah felt her face flush and she began to drum her fingers on the tabletop.

'But white men and black women are allowed to, is that what you're pointing out?'

'Think rationally, Hattie. We have to fit in here. We can't go upsetting people.'

'But we haven't upset anyone.'

'Aidan said something this morning. I overheard him talking to Ah Soy.'

'And what did he say, this fine upstanding pillar of Territory society who has an Aboriginal mistress, did you know?'

'No need to be sarcastic. He said you and Mick were becoming very friendly.' His words had been cruder than that but Sarah wasn't planning to repeat them.

'And is there something wrong with that?' Harriet shook her head so vigorously that her hairpins became dislodged and

236

her hair cascaded over her shoulders. Irritably she twisted her hair around the fingers of one hand, swept it on to the top of her head and secured the knot firmly with hairpins.

'No, there's nothing wrong with that in principle. It was the way he said it. The innuendo.'

'To Ah Soy? That man never gossips.'

'That's true. You can tell Ah Soy anything and he won't repeat it. But the point is, if Aidan is talking about you to anyone he meets, there'll be some who'll listen.'

'What was he saying?'

'I don't want to repeat it. Black velvet, that sort of thing.'

Harriet laughed in a sarcastic sort of way. 'Have you become so conventional, Sarah, that you care what people say?'

'I'm the wife of the acting manager and I have responsibilities while Henry's away.' Sarah wondered if she should mention what else Aidan had told Ah Soy, that Brady had become obsessed by Harriet and talked about her all the time. She looked just like Brady's missus, Aidan had said, and his missus had walked out on him with a baby that wasn't his.

'I see,' Harriet said. 'You have responsibilities. Is this what Henry has done to you? Made you so hidebound?'

'How dare you say that about my husband.' Sarah's voice shifted half an octave higher and her neck and face began to feel even hotter. 'Henry's liberated me not shackled me.'

'Liberated you, is that what you call it? You traipsed off to the colonies because that's what Henry wanted, but not where you wanted to go. Don't think I didn't notice that, Sarah. Then, as if New South Wales wasn't far enough, he dragged you up here to this godforsaken place. Call that liberty? What have you ever chosen for yourself?'

'I chose my husband.' Sarah coughed, and with a shaking hand poured some water from the jug on the table into her glass. She took a sip before continuing, 'And I chose to come to Dimbulah Downs. Henry would never have taken this position if I hadn't more or less insisted on it.' She didn't care that she was exaggerating; she had to protect herself somehow.

'But is this really what you want? To be pregnant here, miles away from anywhere remotely civilised, and with Henry away? There's not even a piano to bring you some comfort. You can do better than this, Sarah.' Harriet unhooked her riding crop from the peg and impatiently tapped her leg with the handle.

'But you've said to me several times that the Aborigines have their own civilisation. We're learning from Bella, learning from Mick, that's what you've said.'

'I was thinking of doctors and midwives, Sarah. That's what you're missing.'

'How do you think the Aboriginal women manage to have their babies? And are you really so blind to the beauty of this place? You of all people, the artist of the family. Or do you only want to paint tame little paintings of London streets?'

At this moment Sarah saw Mick leading horses from the stables. There were just two and they were already saddled.

Harriet said, 'Did you tell Mick that you and Bella aren't riding today?'

'Yes.'

'I see. So you knew I'd be going out anyway.'

'I'd hoped to get you to change your mind.'

'You know how stubborn I am.' Harriet's voice was sharp. 'There's no point trying to get me to do something merely because Aidan and his ilk might disapprove. I have to be true to myself and I'm *choosing* friendship with Mick.' There was a moment's silence before Harriet continued, her voice softer now. 'Dear Sarah, I'm so sorry we quarrelled. But I have to be free to make up my own mind, don't you see? I can't live out my days constrained by silly customs.'

'At least take your revolver. To please Henry and me.'

'What on earth for?' Harriet said. 'Mick will have his.' She bent to kiss Sarah before picking up her painting satchel.

* * *

Observing Harriet's nonchalance as she walked across the home paddock, Sarah envied her independence. Her own heart was racing still, and she had yet to see Aidan before she could have a rest. After retrieving the store keys from the drawer at the back of Henry's desk, she hurried past the kitchen block. Almost certainly Aidan would have seen Harriet riding off with Mick. Sarah braced her shoulders as she hurried to the storeroom.

Aidan had tethered his team of horses close by. She unlocked the door and he followed her in. Methodically they worked through Aidan's list and she registered what was taken out in the accounts book. Flour, sugar, tins of jam, canned vegetables, Worcester sauce, tea, tobacco. While she was locking the door again, Aidan began loading the horses. With his back turned to her, he said, 'Glad you're stayin' up here, missus.'

'We're not.'

'No? Maybe it's just the boss stayin' then. You goin' down south again then?'

She felt cornered; she needed to get some information without giving anything away. She said, her voice quavering slightly, 'We're still discussing our future.'

'Is that so? Heard somethin' different.'

'Fancy that. From whom, may I ask?'

'One of them new ringers.'

She had no idea who he meant and didn't want to probe

further. He was a troublemaker and she would tell him nothing. But his words had got into her head like bacteria into a wound that would soon begin to fester. 'We'll let you know when we've made a decision.'

When he turned to face her, she saw that he was grinning and wondered what he found so funny. Perhaps it was the deliberately remote way in which she'd spoken, or maybe he was pleased that she'd risen to his taunt. She felt like giving his egg-shaped head a good shove to see if it might roll off his shoulders but instead said, 'Good day, Aidan. I do hope you have a pleasant ride back to your camp.'

She sat in one of the planter's chairs on the verandah and watched the drifting plumes of dust thrown up by Aidan's train of horses as he rode south. Surely Henry wouldn't have tricked her, promising they'd come up north for only six months but planning to stay for ever. He knew she didn't want to stay. He knew she was far from the people and things she loved, the music that she was missing. She had to have faith in him.

Yet maybe Aidan was right, and Henry had decided to stay here without telling her. She had little idea of what to do if that were the case. She'd have to get away but she didn't really want to go back to England. With Father gone and Harriet out here, it wouldn't be the same place that she'd left three years ago. And Harriet might not even go back to England. At present she felt she couldn't predict what Harriet might do from one minute to the next.

She began to wish she'd told Henry about her pregnancy. The news would surely have made him see sense. Or maybe instead he'd have some hare-brained scheme about sending the baby off to be educated at a boarding school, just as he had been. Never was any child of hers going to be raised like that. Never, never, never.

Her thoughts in a turmoil, she went into her bedroom.

The sun had moved off the roof and a light breeze had arisen, cooling the room. She stretched out on the bed and picked up a book. Usually Dickens enthralled her but today she couldn't concentrate. She shut her eyes and in a few minutes was asleep.

Chapter 32

'From the Land They Came, and to It They Returned'

Harriet wondered if she had been too harsh on Sarah. Almost certainly she had been, but she'd been so shocked by her sister's comments – her accusation – that she'd lashed out without thinking. *Black velvet*, that was how men like Aidan summarised sexual arrangements between white men and black women. *Black velvet*, said with a snicker and a wink or a nudge.

Anyway, she didn't care what people thought. There were so few folk around that those who were here had to make up fantasies about one another, that was all. She would try to forget what had been said.

She walked towards the waiting horses and Mick. He removed his hat as she approached and smiled. Above him, the great dome of sky looked almost solid. She was lucky not just to be alive, but to be alive here and now, this very instant, under an enamelled blue sky.

Mick was changing the way she viewed the landscape, she thought later as they rode side by side alongside the river. Hot and inhospitable it might sometimes seem, but occasionally she felt a glimmering of understanding of how the Aborigines viewed their country.

Yesterday Mick had said it should be left as each generation found it. From the land they came, and to it they returned. They had a duty of care for the country.

She liked that philosophy. She had much more to learn from Mick.

* * *

'I'd like to draw you, Mick,' Harriet said late that afternoon when they were sitting by a waterfall. 'Do you mind?'

Judging from his broad smile and the alacrity with which he removed his hat, she guessed he was delighted with this suggestion. Her desire to sketch him was merely an artistic impulse, she told herself, something she'd thought of doing many times. His head was noble, the black skin was luminous. But perhaps she was also looking for an excuse to stare at him. If she didn't understand his character, even a little bit, she wouldn't be able to do justice to that fine head. Did she need to stare at him to understand him? Probably not, she thought, and reddened.

'Keep very still,' she said quickly, not wanting her blushes to be noticed. 'Don't look my way, look at the river.' He was more than a friend: the impossible was happening.

Quickly she began to sketch his head. He sat so still that he seemed almost a part of the landscape. She would need to make a number of studies, in smudged charcoal, of the way the light reflected from his dark skin. Later, if they were good, she would work these up into a painting.

When she'd finished, she showed him the sketches. He made no comment unless you counted that approving nod of the head.

Her regard for Mick was confusing her, she thought, turning away to pack her materials in the satchel. After drawing his face, she knew its every plane but that didn't prevent her from wanting to look at him again and again. She wondered how long she had successfully repressed her true feelings. Perhaps not long. She guessed that was because Mick was not of her kind. She had let conformity dominate emotion. Although she'd accused Sarah of being conventional, she hadn't applied the same standard to herself. Now she found it astonishing that the daughter of James Cameron could be so easily influenced by society's opinions about the roles of white women and black men.

Aidan was the embodiment of those views. White men like Aidan had no trouble befriending black women: people simply looked the other way. The reverse was not the case. Now she better understood her own feelings, she could decide whether or not she cared what society thought.

And she cared nothing.

Yet she doubted if she would ever be able to make a choice beyond this, and she had no idea of what Mick's feelings for her were. He had a duty of care for her because Henry was away, and perhaps that was all. Then she remembered their conversations in the evenings by the stock rail. He was fond of her, that was clear, but probably he too would be confused if he felt any more than that.

Riding back towards the homestead, she saw a cloud of white cockatoos in the distance, advancing fast, as if blown by the wind. Once the birds were overhead, their squawking drowned out even the sound of the river. Their bodies looked bloated, she thought dispassionately as if she were seeing this for the first time, and far too heavy for their wings. It was a miracle they stayed aloft. Wheeling over the billabong, they seemed at first to be making for the dead tree, before veering sharply to the right and descending on the ghost gum adjacent to the camp. As of one mind, they methodically began to strip the tree of leaves and small branches, and to discard these on to the ground, so that in the space of just a few minutes it was littered with debris.

She and Mick reined in their horses and watched the cockatoos attack the eucalypt. At last, as if bored by their own destructiveness, the birds moved to the dead tree that was their usual perch and began their evening ritual of jockeying for position.

White people are like that, Harriet thought; we might destroy this country.

Chapter 33

'Something Comin', Missus'

Several days later, Sarah, who had been collecting eggs with Ah Soy, gave up the search to watch as Bella walked towards them carrying something. It looked like a small canoe, no more than two feet long, with curved sides.

'Carryem newfellow piccaninny,' Bella said when she was a few yards away.

'It's beautiful.' The coolamon was decorated on the outside in an intricate design in yellow, white and ochre.

Bella smiled, displaying all of her teeth. 'For missus.'

Taking the coolamon, Sarah found she was laughing and crying at the same time. From nowhere Bella produced a ring made out of twisted grass and white feathers and placed it on Sarah's head. After stepping back to admire the effect, she gently appropriated the canoe and placed it on the ring. It felt to Sarah surprisingly light. She wiped her face with the back of her hand and tottered a few steps with the cradle balanced precariously on top of her head. Bella began to giggle.

'My crowning glory,' said Sarah, laughing again. 'Clearly I need more practice. Thank you, Bella, I really love this and my baby will love it too. You couldn't have given me a nicer present.' When she saw Bella's puzzlement she understood that the canoe was not a gift. Rather it was an affirmation of kinship. Kinship obligations tied her to Bella and Bella to her, in ways that she still didn't fully understand.

* * *

Sarah thought that only in Bella's company could she laugh. Away from Bella, her general anxiety expanded as she grew more and more tired. Getting through the chores, and the day, required a disproportionate amount of effort, leaving her exhausted.

She watched her sister, lounging in a battered planter's chair on the verandah. Harriet seemed oblivious to Sarah's inspection. She read fast, the pages of her novel flipping over to the accompaniment of Bob's tuneless humming as he plaited thin strips of wallaby hide to form a stockwhip handle. Mick, his back supported by a verandah post, was reading one of the Adelaide newspapers that had arrived in the last mail delivery.

'Did you read that article about the Adult Suffrage Bill?' Harriet said to Mick, looking up from her book.

'It passed the Legislative Council,' Mick said.

'Now it's got to get through the House of Assembly,' Harriet said. 'Hello, Sarah, I didn't see you there, you came up so quietly. There are so many articles in the South Australian newspapers about the suffragists, but hardly any in the *Northern Territory Times*.'

'You know how slow that steamship journey is,' Sarah said feeling slightly irritated with her sister.

'Someone comin', missus.' Mick pointed to the track leading into the home paddock.

Sarah stood abruptly. A slight swirl of red dust was all that she could see. It was too soon for the mailman but it might be Henry. Squinting against the glare, she felt infused with hope.

'It's Aidan back again,' Mick said. 'Must have run out of stores real quick.' He stepped off the verandah and strode across the yard to meet him.

Aidan slid off his horse and conferred briefly with Mick.

Grim-faced, the two of them walked through the dust towards the homestead. 'What's the trouble, Aidan?' Sarah called.

'Bad news, missus.'

'What is it?' Please not Henry, she thought. Let it be anyone else but Henry.

'It's Carruthers.'

'Carruthers?'

'Yes.'

'What's he done?'

Aidan gulped and tried to speak but only managed a croak. He was ashen-faced, his clothes drenched with sweat, his beard unshaven. He took off his hat and fanned himself with it.

'Spit it out, mate,' Bob said.

'Let me get you some water.' Harriet removed the canvas water bag kept hanging from one of the rafters, unscrewed the cap and poured some water into it.

After Aidan had drained the cap, he began to talk. 'We was ridin' south, me and Curly, on the track of some cleanskins that needed brandin'. We didn't want the Empty Creek mob to run them off. You know how hard it is to track them down, no fences, no nothin'. Hard to know who owns what if they're not branded. We saw in the distance some black fellers camped. I said to Curly we'd better check up on them, maybe they knows somethin' we don't, about who's been roundin' up our calves. They was havin' a right good feed. Looked like one of our bullocks they was tuckin' into, but we didn't say nothin'. That's what the boss tells us to do. Don't want no war, he says. Let them have the odd bullock or two if it keeps the peace.'

Aidan's voice cracked, and Harriet poured some more water for him. After a few seconds, he continued, 'The blacks hadn't seen no duffers, so we went on our way. Camped out overnight, after we found a few unmarked bullocks. We was takin' them back the way we come when who should we see but Carruthers and some of his men.

'"G'day, Aid," Carruthers says, cool as can be, though it looked like he had a few of our steers in his muster. "Seen any black fellers around?" "Yes," I says, "we got some workin' back at the camp." "Seen any other black fellers?" he says, crackin' his stockwhip. "The bastards have taken one of my bullocks." "Can't say I have," I says, annoyed like, because them black fellers weren't eatin' no Empty Creek stock. It was a Dimbulah Downs steer they butchered, I'd swear, and we was on Dimbulah Downs land too. But I didn't want no trouble.

'So off Carruthers trots with his mob, takin' no more notice of us. "Don't go that way," I says quickly. I didn't like the mean look on his face and I seen that he'd pulled out a pistol. "No one along there," I says. But he kept right on goin', towards where we saw the black fellers the day before. Then I heard a yell that made me hair stand on end. I twisted round and there was Carruthers with a ruddy big spear stickin' out of his back. He slid off his saddle slow like, and fell to the ground. And you know, there wasn't a black feller in sight, not a single one.'

'So you didn't see who did it?' Sarah said.

'No, they was invisible like. No way me and Curly can say who did it because we didn't see nothin'. Then all hell broke loose, with Carruthers' blokes firin' in all directions. Me and Curly lay low for a bit, hopin' we wasn't going to get a spear in our backs or a bullet in our heads. After things had quietened down, we came out of the bushes and saw Carruthers still lyin' on the ground. In a pool of blood, all black it looked against the red earth, with Dan Brady bent over him. That daft cove was tryin' to pull out the spear and there was tears on his cheeks. But Carruthers was already dead.'

'Then what happened?'

'Brady and one of the ringers managed to pull the spear out, and they slung the body over the back of a horse. Tied it on with a bit of rope. Their mob was takin' it back to Empty Creek Station. Brady didn't go, though. He sent a young feller to the telegraph repeater station, and said he was goin' to look around for a bit. He was angrier than a mad bull by then. Said them murderin' black fellers had put him out of a friend and a job.' He paused for another swig of water.

'What did you do then?' Bob said.

'Me and Curly boiled the billy and tried to calm him down. Told him our boss would be back soon and he'd know what to do. That made him go all quiet, like he was thinkin'. After a bit, he left and we mustered our bullocks again, they'd stampeded with all the shootin' and shoutin'. When we found as many as we could we drove them back to the stock camp. I changed my horse and rode straight here. Rode all night. Lucky there was a full moon.'

'You've done well,' Sarah said. 'I'm sure Henry will think so.'

'What's going to happen now?' Harriet said.

'I think we know how it will be,' Bob said. 'The troopers will come from Palmerston. They'll bring black trackers from somewhere else to find the Empty Creek mob. They'll promise the trackers a pardon for whatever they were in gaol for, and then they'll pick out some black fellows – any black fellows – from Empty Creek and take them to Fannie Bay Gaol. That's how it will go.'

Sarah sat down abruptly. For the first time she felt her baby move, the tiniest little flutter. This flicker of hope was instantly overwhelmed by fear. The frontier war was still being fought, and it had taken her months to realise it.

* * *

Sarah wished Harriet would say something, instead of sitting staring at the salt cellar, as if it held the answer to everything. Harriet might as well be in another country for all the notice she was taking of Sarah's attempts to start a conversation. Not about Carruthers, she didn't want to talk about that, but there were a hundred and one other things they could discuss as a distraction.

When at last the meal was over, Harriet stood up and stretched.

'You're not going walking this evening, are you Hattie? Not after what's happened.'

'Why shouldn't I?'

'But after Carruthers getting speared, aren't you worried?'

'Of course I'm upset about what happened and I'm worried about the troopers coming.'

'But aren't you concerned about your own safety?'

'No, why should I be? We get on well with the Dimbulah Downs Aborigines. I doubt if I'm going to get a spear in my back. Bella certainly wouldn't do it, and her clan wouldn't do it either.'

'It's no joking matter, Harriet.'

'What else do you expect me to do? Hang around the homestead waiting for Henry to come back?'

'Is that what you think I'm doing, hanging around the homestead waiting for Henry to come back?'

'Well, you are, aren't you? You're expecting him to come galloping in any moment now. There's nothing wrong with that. And the sooner the better.'

'I'm glad it meets with your approval.'

'Sarah, we've got nothing to fear at Dimbulah Downs. The trouble lies elsewhere. Carruthers is dead and I reckon none of us here is sorry.'

'No, none of us is sorry.' For barely an instant Sarah

251

wondered if she should feel guilty at this. Carruthers was a human being, after all, and someone's son. 'Please stay, Harriet.'

'No, Sarah. I'm not going to change anything I do.' Harriet plucked her hat from the hook by the door, although the homestead paddock was largely in shadow. 'I always go for a walk at this time of day,' she said. 'And I intend to go out painting tomorrow too, and the day after, and the day after that. I see no reason to change my habits because of Carruthers' fate.'

Sarah watched her wander across the grass. You still sound like Father sometimes, she thought bitterly. Ever so slightly pompous. There's no reason to change your habits because Mick is already waiting for you. At the usual spot, as he always is. And tomorrow the two of you will be off painting again, leaving me to wait for Henry's return.

Chapter 34

We None of Us Can Win

The trees, glowing in the early morning light, seemed unusually still. Harriet, perched on a flat boulder at the edge of the hollow, listened to the silence and felt uneasy. Not a bird was calling, not a leaf was moving. The bush seemed to be waiting for something to happen.

Yet her disquiet could be a part of the anxiety she'd been feeling for the past few days, ever since Aidan had told them of Carruthers' death. Wanting to conceal her apprehension from Sarah, she'd tried to carry on as usual. Sarah was already worrying too much and that couldn't be good for the baby.

Maybe the bush had been expectant like this for thousands of years. All that occurred were the changes of season, year after year. The rising then falling of the water, the dropping of leaves and nuts, the shedding of long strips of bark, and occasionally – a major event this – the crashing of a gum tree as it fell to the ground.

The dry depression in front of her was littered with rocks and other debris. In the wet season it would be a lush green pool connected to the creek through the small eroded gully. The light defining the disorder of this place fascinated her. You never saw this sort of a view in England.

The landscape as untidiness, she'd told Mick ten minutes earlier. He'd laughed, and she guessed he found her perspective strange. But this was what she aimed to draw, and why she hadn't gone with him further down the creek to paint the ghost gums that they'd sketched the day before. Creating an impression of the hollow would be a challenge because of the apparent randomness of the debris lying here. If she stared at it hard enough perhaps she would find meaning in it.

Between her shoulder blades she felt a tiny trickle of sweat and wished she'd worn a looser blouse. After pulling a handkerchief out of her trouser pocket, she wiped her damp brow and the palms of her hands. In a moment she would put pencil to paper and try to convey this sense of a slow accumulation of litter that would eventually smother the hollow in which she sat.

When she was about to make the first mark on her sketchpad, she felt that something wasn't right. Everything was as still as before but something had changed. But glancing around, she saw that nothing had altered. It was only her imagination: the heightened awareness that she always developed when she was about to start drawing. Yet this awareness was more pronounced than usual. It was verging on discomfort.

Presently she heard a twig break. Nothing to see. It might have been a wallaby, or even a snake; not visible now but keeping still to avoid detection.

'Mick!' she called. 'Is that you?'

There was no reply. Perhaps she should have gone with him after all. He hadn't wanted to leave her alone but she'd insisted on it. Knowing how much he wanted to finish his study of the white gums, she'd more or less pushed him away.

Several minutes passed before she looked again at her blank sketchbook. She'd barely made two marks with her pencil before she heard again the snapping of a twig. A light breeze had arisen and the noise she heard could have been a rattling together of dry branches. The leaves of the eucalyptus trees caught the sunlight as they twisted and the entire bush seemed to glow with a silvery green light. She shifted her position on the boulder slightly, so that she was completely in the shade, and glanced at her sketchbook. The lines she'd drawn were wrong. Moving had destroyed the composition and she'd have to start again. She turned over the page and looked up at the view that she would draw.

So startled was she at the sight of a still figure leaning on a tree-trunk, barely ten yards away, that she almost dropped her sketchbook. Wearing dark clothes and with a felt hat pulled down low, the man was well camouflaged. Although she couldn't see the man's face, she didn't think he was from Dimbulah Downs, but it was hard to be certain when he was standing in deep shadow. Once he'd observed her surprise, he took a couple of steps towards her.

'All alone, I see.' At once she recognised the voice. He moved into the sunlight. Her stomach turned at the sight of Dan Brady and the animosity in his eyes.

'I'm not all alone,' she said, her voice breaking slightly. 'My friend isn't far away.' Putting her hand to the waistband of her trousers, she cursed herself for leaving behind her revolver and cartridge belt and wondered what Brady was doing at Dimbulah Downs. It wasn't the most direct route to Port Darwin. 'I'm sorry to hear about Carruthers,' she added.

'You're not the only one. That's the end of my job. Those murdering black bastards would spear you in the back soon as look at you. Can't ever trust a blackfeller.'

Her mouth felt devoid of all saliva and she tried to wet her dry lips with her tongue. 'Treat them with kindness and they'll treat you with kindness.'

'That's how you treat the blackie Mick,' Brady said, combing his unkempt beard with his fingers. 'I saw him when I came up the creek. You're a bit of a nigger lover, eh? That's what I've heard.'

Her face flushed with anger. She opened her mouth to speak

but her throat was too dry. After swallowing she tried again. 'Mick's a fine man. I'd trust him anywhere.'

'I've heard you've been riding all over with him. And I see you're wearing the trousers now.' Brady was grinning, pleased at her discomfort.

Harriet took a deep breath. His goal was to humiliate her; she had to stay cool. 'Do you have business here today?' Her voice sounded remarkably calm now. She thought of starting to draw, to show her bravado, but her hand was shaking too much and the pencil fell to the ground.

'Just passing through. Saw a tasty sight here and thought I'd take a look. Give us a kiss then, why don't you,' he said, taking a few more steps towards her. 'Like you were trying to do on the *Guthrie*. Remember that? Led me on a bit then, didn't you? Like my missus used to. What about that kiss now, eh?'

'Let me draw you instead. I could do a good likeness.' Pretending to look for her pencil, she stood and stepped back a few paces. Mick couldn't be more than a quarter of a mile downstream. If she could keep Brady talking while edging back a little, she could try to make a dash for it.

But Brady jumped across the gully separating them and grabbed hold of her arm. Her heart turned over when she saw the hatred in his eyes. She'd seen the same expression on his face that night on the *Guthrie*: his features twisted, the eyes dark pools, the beard black against the gleaming white shirt. She'd seen the same expression on his face again when he'd spat on her in Chinatown, and afterwards the dark brown tobacco juice dribbling down her white skirt.

In an attempt to loosen his grip, she shook her arm and the sketchbook fell to the ground. The smell of his sweat was overpowering. His face was so close she could see the orange-peel texture of his skin with a scattering of blackheads around his nose. He put one hand on the small of her back and the other on one of her breasts, squeezing so hard it hurt. 'Only little titties but little titties are better than no titties,' he said roughly. 'Just as black dicks are better than no dicks, wouldn't you say? But I've got something better than that for you. Something that won't let you forget your old friend Dan Brady in a hurry.'

Harriet broke out in a cold sweat and tried to struggle free.

Brady almost spat at her, 'A dead black dick's no good to you now, is it?'

When she flinched at this, Brady again tightened his pressure on her breast. There was a tearing sound as he ripped the fine cotton of her blouse. 'It's your lucky day for I'll soon be giving you a glimpse of a white dick that won't be forgotten in a hurry. And then you can see what you've been missing.'

Struggling to loosen Brady's grip, Harriet tripped on a stone and fell to the ground. Brady landed sprawled on top of her. His weight pressed down on her, pinning her to the ground. There was no way she'd ever be able to wriggle free of him.

* * *

Bella shaking Sarah's shoulder, the room spinning, Bella panting so much that her words were slurred, no way of knowing what the trouble was. Pull yourself out of this nap, Sarah. Make the walls stop rotating. Speak slowly, Bella. Speak slowly and clearly.

Later it would seem to Sarah that she'd metamorphosed into someone else that morning. Someone else who'd dashed out of the house after Bella had woken her by bellowing about *no-good Brady* whom she'd seen barely minutes before down by the creek. Later it would seem to Sarah as if it were someone else who'd loaded her revolver, put on the safety catch and fastened her holster before saddling her horse. Someone else who'd galloped in the direction Bella indicated, stopping only when she saw a chestnut roan tied to a sapling, a roan that she knew wasn't from Dimbulah Downs.

Her clothes were saturated with sweat by the time she tethered her foam-whitened horse to a tree a few yards upstream. Stealing through the brush, avoiding piles of leaves and twigs that might crackle underfoot, she prayed she would find Harriet. Carolling birds concealing her footfall but not the pounding of blood in her ears.

But where on earth was the hollow Bella had described? Harriet might be anywhere and she could be stumbling around for hours trying to track her down. She heard a horse whinny. Not her own. Something – or someone – must have disturbed the chestnut roan. She hesitated, undecided as to whether to go back or carry on. At that moment she heard voices. Harriet's, unusually high and tense, was punctuated by a deeper growl.

'Brady,' Bella had said. 'No good Carruthers feller from Empty Creek.'

An instant later Sarah heard a piercing scream. Her revolver was in her hand before she'd realised it. No one would be allowed to hurt her sister, no one.

Even though she'd prepared for a moment like this, her hand was wavering as she raised the gun. It felt heavy, too heavy. Her palms were sweating and the grip slippery. Six rounds were all she had. She had to get this right.

Carefully she crept forward until she could see the clearing. Could see Harriet lying on the ground, with a big man sprawled on top of her.

Sarah raised the revolver in her right hand, its grip supported in the centre of her palm, her left hand underneath to steady it, safety catch off. She squeezed the trigger. The shot rang out.

* * *

Brady lurched as the shot sounded, and then lay still. Unable to move, Harriet felt her heartbeat pulsing at a faster tempo than his. His body was becoming heavier. Fleetingly she noticed that sharp stones were digging into her shoulder blades. Chest-to-chest she lay with Brady. As if he were her lover, and her stomach clenched at this thought.

If only she could see who had fired the gun. There might be more shots. It was an effort to expand her lungs against the weight of Brady's body pressing down on her. A sudden rush of anger gave her the strength to twist her torso slightly, and now she could see around his shoulders. If she hadn't been so furious at Brady, she might have wept with joy at the sight of Sarah. Barely three yards away, silhouetted against the brilliant sky, she was pointing her revolver at Brady's legs, the sole part of his anatomy well clear of her.

'Get up, you.' Sarah's voice was cold and her cheeks were flushed but she held the revolver steady.

Brady used his arms to lever himself off Harriet, who took a deep breath and felt a cooling draught of air as her diaphragm expanded.

Moving a few paces closer, Sarah said, 'Get up, you, or I'll blast your leg off.'

If the man hadn't been lying on top of Harriet when she'd raised her gun, she would have shot him in the heart instead of aiming over him. If he'd been nothing more than a block of wood on a plank, he'd be lying shattered on the ground. He'd had a brief reprieve and now she had to decide what to do with him.

She kept the gun trained on him while Harriet stood unsteadily. Sarah's peripheral vision registered the ripped blouse and torn trousers. She began again to feel that curious dissociation, as if she were an outsider looking down at the scene. It is shock, she thought, nothing more than shock.

A sudden movement from the other side of the clearing distracted her. Mick couldn't have been here long for he was panting still. But she wouldn't relax her concentration just because Mick had turned up. 'Keep your hands raised, Mr Brady.' Aiming the revolver at his heart, she said to Harriet, 'Did he... you know, did he...?'

'No.' Harriet's face was ashen. 'You got here in time. He didn't rape me.' She pulled the sides of her torn blouse together, passing each corner around her waist and knotting them together at the back.

'Dirty black bastard,' Brady yelled at Mick. 'I'll get you, boy. I saw you kill Carruthers, that's what I'll tell the troopers when they come.'

'Keep quiet, Mr Brady,' Sarah said, her voice calm, though she wondered why Brady was shouting at Mick when she was the one holding the gun. Probably he thought she was a poor shot because she'd fired over his head. She sized him up as he stood before her, arms raised and legs wide apart.

'Carruthers speared in the back by one of your niggers, that's what I'll say. Don't pretend you didn't know, you fucken bitch.'

'Keep your mouth shut, Mr Brady, I'm a crack shot.'

'I'll tell the troopers I saw Mick spearing Carruthers in cold blood. You haven't got a chance, boy. I'll see you hang or shoot you myself. White fellows are never hanged for shooting a black.'

'Keep still, Mr Brady. Stay exactly where you are.' Sarah lowered the gun slightly and squeezed the trigger. The bullet went between Brady's legs and hit the target rock a few yards behind him. A perfect shot.

Brady started and dropped his arms with the surprise, or perhaps he was reaching for a gun hidden somewhere that she couldn't see. She shouted out, her words hard like bullets, 'Hands in the air!' When he raised his arms, she saw that he was shaking visibly. 'You must go away, Mr Brady,' she said. 'You must go a long way away and never come back. Go back to Empty Creek, you're not wanted here. But before you go, I'll give you something to remember me by. Keep very still. If you don't, I might get your heart if you have one.'

It was another person who coldly squeezed the trigger. It was another person who heard with satisfaction his yelp of pain. It was another person who watched the blood-red flower blooming on his right arm that was now hanging limply by his side. Payback, she thought. He won't do this to my sister again.

'A little graze on your wrist, that's all,' she said. 'It won't hurt much, you'll see. Or at least not for the first hour. That's long enough for you to find your horse and head out of here.'

* * *

Once Brady was out of sight, Harriet began to shiver. Although she was still in a state of shock, angry thoughts churned through her mind. The man was completely unhinged if he'd ridden from Empty Creek Station to Dimbulah Downs to seek revenge. Perhaps he'd been passing by, brooding about Carruthers, and had seen a chance of getting even with someone on the other side. Whichever way you looked at it though, his goal had been her degradation.

Anger was soon replaced by horror that Brady had so nearly humiliated her. How brave Sarah was and how foolish she'd been to be dismissive of her marksmanship.

261

'It was a minor wound,' Sarah said. 'I barely grazed his arm. Carefully judged.'

She seemed so calm, Harriet thought as she wiped her trembling hands on her trousers and longed for a shower. She felt filthy after rolling on the ground, filthy after what had happened.

'What on earth was he doing here, Hattie?'

'Something happened on the *Guthrie*. He thinks I humiliated him.'

'How?'

'He thought a few conversations we had were an invitation.'

'An invitation to what?'

'To make advances. He thought I was leading him on.'

'So this has happened before?' Sarah said, putting an arm around Harriet's shoulders.

'Not really. Well, perhaps it might almost have. His wife left him and I looked like her, he said. So I think he turned all that anger against me.'

'But to come all this way…?'

'Perhaps he blames me for Carruthers' death too. The man's unbalanced.'

'Clearly,' Sarah said. 'And now he's going to try to get Mick blamed for that. But let's take you back to the homestead. It's been a frightful day. And we'll have to get someone tracking where Brady's gone. We don't want him bobbing up here again later.'

'How did you know I'd be here?'

'Bella told me where she'd seen Brady.'

Harriet thought of Sarah's careful marking of the target, her perfect shots. She had metamorphosed into a calm and competent young woman who had dealt with danger as if she'd been trained to do so all her life. She was the strong active sister, when Harriet had always thought it was she.

'Brady will head back to Empty Creek,' Mick said. 'That will give us some time.'

'But he could be hanging around Dimbulah Downs waiting to take revenge,' Harriet said. 'That wound's superficial. Just a graze, didn't you see?'

'He can't do much harm while he's blundering about on foot wondering if a black feller's going to put a spear through him,' Mick said.

Sarah said, 'I take it that no one from here is going to spear Brady.'

'Who knows about there, though.' Mick stared into the distance as he spoke. 'Different language group. Can't tell what happens there. At least not yet. We'll check later where Brady's got to. They'll know in the camp.'

Those smoke signals, Harriet thought. A flip, a flap, and news could be conveyed in a language she could never hope to understand.

Mick took Harriet's arm as if it was the most natural thing in the world and guided her out of the hollow. At the top, he brushed some leaves and twigs from her clothes before taking her arm again. Harriet continued holding on to him tightly as they walked over the rough ground, and after five minutes, they reached the spot where they'd left their horses. It was hard to believe that was barely an hour ago. 'Good job Brady didn't find the horses,' Mick said. 'I thought he might have and let them loose.'

'The troopers will be coming soon,' Harriet said. 'Someone would have telegraphed them.'

'That won't be good for black fellers like me once Brady starts telling lies.'

Sarah said, her voice indignant, 'Brady can't pin Carruthers' death on you, because you've been here with us all that time.'

'Brady will try to get Mick accused of murdering

263

Carruthers,' Harriet said. 'It'll be his way of retaliating for another humiliation. Brady isn't a man to forget a grudge.'

'He'll probably head back to Empty Creek and wait for the troopers to arrive,' Mick said.

'But you've got an alibi, Mick,' Sarah said.

'Alibis don't matter for me,' Mick said. 'White fellers' law won't protect me. I'm going to have to go walkabout for a bit. Go where they won't be able to find me.'

'But you've done no wrong,' Sarah said. 'And anyway, why should they believe Brady?'

They would believe Brady because he was a witness to Carruthers' murder, Harriet thought angrily. They would believe Brady because he was white.

'I'll be all right,' Mick said. 'I'll find somewhere to hide.'

'The troopers will have trackers,' Sarah said.

'Of course they'll have trackers,' Harriet said. 'They'll have them as long as they have blackfellers in the lock-up they can blackmail to do the tracking.'

'Anyway, they won't find me,' Mick said. 'I'll go when the boss gets back. Soon I reckon. Tomorrow or the day after. Maybe I'll go further west. Or south.'

He seemed too confident, Harriet thought, worried. 'If you go, won't your absence be taken as guilt?'

'My presence would be as well. Can't win.'

'We none of us can win,' Harriet said, so overwhelmed with sadness that her voice emerged as a whisper.

* * *

Sleep wouldn't come easily to Harriet that night. No matter what position she adopted, her body ached. Falling flat on her back with Brady on top of her had bruised and jarred her all over, though she'd barely registered this at the time. Far worse than these aches and pains was the consuming anger that now surged through her, followed by waves of fear and a sense of powerlessness.

She tried to focus on the deep gratitude she felt to Sarah for her quick-witted actions and her care of her once they'd returned to the homestead. Sarah had taken away her torn blouse and given it to Ah Soy to dispose of in the kitchen range, and she'd taken away Harriet's other clothes too. 'Here, wear my silk dressing gown,' she'd said. 'Go and have a shower. Take this new cake of lavender soap.'

That afternoon Mick had conferred with some of the camp elders and afterwards he and Bob had ridden out again. They hadn't found any trace of Brady, although Harriet knew Mick hadn't wanted to go too far from the homestead. Some of the Aborigines from the camp would track him at first light, Mick had said. They would soon find out if he was on his way back to Empty Creek Station.

Though Harriet had lathered herself all over in the shower, and shampooed her hair and scrubbed her fingernails, there remained a circle of red dust embedded around the nail cuticles, and at moments she thought she could still smell Brady: his sweat, and her own, mingled together. After the shower, her fury with him had remained; that was impossible to wash away. So too was that memory of his face, twisted with hatred. And for what? Because she'd humiliated him on the *Guthrie*. Because she looked like his wife who'd run out on him.

Now she sat up in bed and fumbled for the matches to light the candle on the bedside table. Her clock showed eleven o'clock; it would be seven hours before the sun rose. There was something else simmering at the edges of her consciousness and refusing to be pushed away. With Mick's departure from Dimbulah Downs – tomorrow, the day after, the one after that – she would lose the friendship of the person who had given

265

her peace. But this wasn't his only gift: he'd also brought her back to painting.

Of course there was more, she could freely admit that to herself now that he was going. She punched the kapok pillow into a more accommodating shape before lying down again. Never could she countenance marriage to Charles. Not after she'd grown to love someone else.

With that decision made, she fell into a fitful sleep.

Chapter 35

Sarah Makes a Decision

Sarah woke, rigid with terror. Her body was soaked in sweat, her mouth felt parched, and she had no idea where she was. Surrounded by darkness, her arms were fastened to her sides as if she were in a straitjacket. She opened her mouth to scream but no sound came out. Several deep breaths later the nightmare began to recede: she was in her bed at Dimbulah Downs.

After untangling the bed covers, in which she was wound like a grub in a chrysalis, she swung her legs over the side of the bed. No lamp on the bedside table. No candlestick and matches either. Shivering, she felt her way around the unlined corrugated-iron walls to the washstand on the other side of the room. Immediately above her head, a gecko chirruped, followed by a faint scrabbling as it scuttled along a timber support. She ran her hand over the surface of the dresser and found the matches and the candlestick. Only back in bed, lit candle on the bedside table, was she ready to confront her nightmare.

She'd dreamed that someone had speared Henry. It hadn't been an Aborigine though. Brady had speared Henry, knocking him to the ground, where he lay motionless, the spear poking out of his back like a darning needle in a pin cushion. In his hand he held the Louis Lot flute that glinted in the sunlight.

Briefly she wondered if this was an omen. Of course it wasn't, she told herself sternly. Of course it hadn't happened, it wouldn't happen. It was anxiety expressing itself, anxiety induced by yesterday's events.

She'd fired at Brady's arm. It was a minor wound, she'd barely grazed him. She would have aimed for his heart if that wouldn't have threatened her sister's safety. With Brady sprawled on top of Harriet, she couldn't possibly have taken that risk. Yet she would have succeeded if that had been her goal. All that practice had made her an excellent markswoman. Speed and accuracy had been Henry's mantra when he'd taught her to fire a revolver. Though he'd never mentioned that you had to decide whether to shoot to harm or to kill, making that decision had been easy for her.

If she'd shot Brady through the heart, she would now be a killer. But, of course, that had been impossible; the risk to Harriet was too great. Anyway, Brady was responsible for his wound. By inflicting it, she'd simply chosen the lesser of two evils: it was clearly far worse to let Harriet be raped – and probably afterwards murdered – than it was to injure the man intent on assaulting her. The choice had been straightforward. Sarah would suffer no remorse over Brady's fate.

She guessed that Carruthers' death would have frightened Brady and probably maddened him too. Perhaps then Aidan had said something to Brady about Harriet and Mick that could have set him off. For an unstable man like Brady, humiliation could be hard to take from a woman like Harriet. A woman who subsequently fraternised with a black fellow.

So shocked had Sarah been at the sight of Harriet collapsed under Brady, and an instant later at her own cool calculation in marking where to aim, she'd barely noticed Brady's words to Mick. She wondered which would be the greater mortification for Brady: being wounded by a white woman or by a black fellow.

I too fraternise with the blacks, she thought. Brady

might want to punish her as well, and her unborn child. She remembered all the times she'd swum with the station's Aboriginal women. She thought of Bella, whom she loved like a sister. She thought of the humiliation she'd inflicted on Brady. Her fear returned and with it came that hateful image from her dream: Henry lying face down on the ground with a spear poking out of his back.

It would be impossible to sleep again. The dream was still too close, too real. After donning her dressing gown and a thick shawl, she picked up her revolver and stepped out on to the veranda. The thin crescent moon and a vast swathe of stars faintly illuminated the homestead grounds. A horse whinnied and was then quiet. Outside the stockmen's quarters she could discern the glowing end of a cigarette and a figure hunched in a chair.

'Is that you, Bob?' she called. The grunted reply was unmistakably his. He was keeping watch, as he and Mick had agreed.

The air was cool and she could distinguish a faint sweetish scent, perhaps from the vine that Ah Soy was training along the verandah to the kitchen. A distant wailing could have been a bush curlew, or one of the children from the Aboriginal encampment. The crying stopped. The night became so silent that she became aware of the sound of her blood pulsing near her eardrums. It was beating too fast. She had to stay calm, she had to keep alert. It wasn't right to leave all the station security to Mick and to Bob.

She imagined Henry sitting in a campsite a day or two away, perhaps awake and thinking of her. There was safety in numbers: surrounded by stockmen, no harm would come to him. Her spirits lifted at this thought, and her blood stopped thudding in her ears.

She put the revolver on the trestle table in the screened-off corner of the verandah. Resting her hand lightly on her belly, she thought of how surprised Henry would be when he learned about her pregnancy. He would be surprised too once he discovered how decisive she had become. When she'd been faced with the dilemma of how to save Harriet she'd felt it was someone else who was acting in her place. But it wasn't someone else. It was she. She'd always had the potential to be strong, she thought. And today she'd realised it.

Henry would be even more surprised when he learned that she – always so affable, always so agreeable – was going to lay down an ultimatum about what they would do in the future. The Carruthers and Brady incidents – and her nightmare too – had enabled her to reach a clear decision. There would be no more thoughts of leaving Henry. She loved him; there was no doubt in her mind about that. But the outback was too savage for her. She didn't want to be confronted by choices like those she'd faced today. The Territory had made her into a potential killer, and she had to get away.

Consequently Henry would have to get away too, as soon as his contract ended. She had made up her mind at last and she would stick to it. *They* would stick to it.

They would go to Port Darwin when the manager returned before the dry season ended. After that they would sail south and begin to look for a property south of Sydney. She agreed with Henry now – even after all that had happened – that they shouldn't go back to England. She had grown to love Australia too much.

Perhaps they would buy a place near Braidwood, in the High Country. Or maybe somewhere on the south coast, just north of Eden. A place with proper seasons, all four of them. Although Eden was a long way south, the steamship service was good and she liked the idea of being near the sea. On their property they would construct a large and solid house, with walls made out of bricks and not corrugated iron, and she would have a grand piano. And there they would bring up their family and Henry would farm the land. She flexed her fingers. She was so out of practice that she would find playing the piano again difficult but how her soul yearned for it, how her body yearned for it.

Now that she'd decided, she couldn't wait to get away. She would miss Bella and Daisy and the others but she wanted a home of her own. She didn't want to live in a place where she had to worry about Henry getting a spear in his back or Harriet being attacked. Picking up her revolver, she went back inside. The candle on the bedside table was burning low. For a moment she thought of putting the gun under Henry's pillow but that was too dangerous. She placed it on the bedside table. With Henry's pyjamas cradled against her, she fell into a dreamless sleep.

Later she woke again with a start. Though a thin band of moonlight filtered around the edges of the shuttered window, the room was in darkness. She stayed quite still and listened. There was a change in the atmosphere. Perhaps a storm was on its way. She couldn't hear the wind blowing or the rattling of leaves or shutters, so that hadn't woken her. Perhaps it was the snick of the catch to the outside door. Brady might somehow have managed to get back to Dimbulah Downs undetected. What an idiot she'd been not to leave the revolver under Henry's pillow. Maybe Brady was already inside the room with her and waiting to pounce. She held her breath. Carefully she put out a hand to reach for the revolver.

Instead of metal she felt something soft and warm, and she gave a little yelp.

'It's me,' Henry said. 'I thought you were asleep. Sorry I frightened you.' He struck a match and lit the candle.

'Thank God you're back!' She held up a hand against the

glare of the flame and his shining eyes. Her tension drained away as he took her hand and raised it to his lips. They were dry and cracked, and his face was sunburnt, apart from a strip of white forehead that still bore the welt of his hat. Six weeks on the hoof. Six weeks in the sun. Six weeks in which she'd changed too, though in ways that were perhaps less visible.

'I've heard all about what happened from Mick. Dearest Sarah, what an awful time you've had of it.'

'Harriet's the one who had the awful time. Henry, I'm so very glad you're back!'

'Mick's heard that Brady's riding back to Empty Creek.'

'So he can't be all that badly wounded.'

'Apparently not. Or not so wounded he can't sit on a horse. Mick's going away, Sarah.'

'I know. He has to. Harriet will be sad.'

'Harriet?'

'Yes, Harriet,' Sarah said firmly. 'They've become good friends.' Mick would go away, perhaps a long way away, and Harriet would never see him again. She might find that hard to cope with, for Mick had brought about what Sarah described to herself as Harriet's recovery. He had been instrumental in restoring to Harriet her desire to draw and paint, but there was more to it than that. Sarah had seen the way they looked at each other when they thought no one would notice.

'The stockman and the suffragist? Seems an unlikely friendship.'

If Sarah hadn't been so pleased to have Henry back, she might have been irritated by his grin. 'He's encouraged her to paint again,' she said.

'I see.' She knew from his struggle to keep a straight face that he didn't believe her.

'A lot has happened while you've been away, Henry. I've changed, for a start.'

272

'I hope not, Sarah.'

Suddenly it seemed droll to her that in the six weeks he'd been away she'd grown up. In that time she'd learned to formulate her own opinions. In that time she'd learned a lot about human nature, including her own. She'd learned what she was capable of. That she should discover this in the remote outback, rather than in Gower Street in London, seemed to her intensely comical, and she began to laugh. Her laughter was slightly hysterical, but she really didn't care.

Henry joined in. Although they were laughing at different things, it didn't matter. As soon as she was able to speak, she said, 'Henry, I want to leave soon too.'

'Yes, yes, my dear. Of course. That's what we agreed. As soon as the manager gets back we'll be on our way. That's in just four weeks.'

'But Aidan told me you were planning on staying.'

'Aidan? What would he know?'

'He said he'd got it from one of the ringers.'

'How could he have when they were on Dimbulah Downs and I was miles away? That man's a terrible gossip and he's always getting things wrong, though he can run rings around a steer, I'll give him that. Take no notice. You know I'd never make any decision without talking with you first.'

She thought about their honeymoon. It was true he'd consulted with her about that and, although he'd rather pushed her into coming to Australia, she had no regrets, even after all that had happened here. She thought about the job at Dimbulah Downs. He'd consulted her about that too, and he'd been right that it would distract her from her grief.

Henry said, 'I'm counting the days until we leave, Sarah. All we have to decide on is where we should go.'

'Southern New South Wales, I think.'

'Thank heaven we agree on that at last.'

It was only after Henry had fallen asleep beside her that she realised with surprise that she'd forgotten to tell him about the baby. There would be time enough for that tomorrow.

Chapter 36

Her Eyes Were as Dry as the Desert

'What was Harriet doing, wandering about on her own?' Henry said, as he and Sarah strolled towards the empty stockyards. In the distance she could see the billabong reflecting the luminous sky, and beyond that the darker smudge of the ranges. 'I told Mick and Bob to keep an eye on her at all times.'

'You can't blame her. Really, Henry, you must be more tactful. You can't expect to keep us locked up either. I know this is worrying you, but you shouldn't blame her.' She guessed he was reproaching himself as well. 'The sole person to blame is Brady. But I have some other news for you too.'

'Good news, I hope?' He looked at her, his expression anxious.

'Yes. It's very good news, Henry. Or at least I think so, and I hope you will as well.'

'Whatever makes you happy makes me happy too.'

Not always, she thought, remembering the enthusiasm with which he'd accepted working for Mr Arnott when they'd first arrived in Sydney, even though he'd known it would mean leaving her behind in Sydney. There was no point reminding him of this, however. She took his hand. Resting it on her stomach, she watched him closely as his expression changed from apprehension to surprise.

'Are you pregnant, Sarah?'

'Yes.'

'Oh my dear clever thing, this is wonderful news!' He put

his arm around her and held her close. 'I'm the happiest man alive!' He tilted up the brim of her hat and kissed the tip of her nose, before whisking her around in a few steps of a waltz. Suddenly he stopped and his expression became serious. 'But shouldn't you be taking things quietly? Goodness me, to think that you've been working hard all the weeks I have been away on that bally cattle drive. How could I have left you alone? What if something happened to you?'

'Something did happen to us, and we coped.'

'I know that, darling, but I meant the pregnancy. There's no doctor or midwife anywhere between here and Port Darwin.'

'I'm only five months pregnant. There's plenty of time. A pregnancy lasts nine months.'

'I'll have to start making plans. We'll have to decide where you want to have the baby. And are you eating enough?' He stood back to inspect her. 'You're looking well,' he said, 'although maybe you're a little bit thin for someone who's pregnant. We don't want you starving our child, do we?'

'Oh, do stop fretting Henry,' she said, smiling. 'Ah Soy always makes sure we all eat well. Look, here's Mick to see us.'

* * *

Sarah leaned on the top rail of the stockyard, one shoulder touching Henry's arm. Since his euphoria about her pregnancy had quickly been followed by a concern that bordered on fussing, it was as well that other responsibilities were competing for his attention. Mick, for instance, who was standing on Henry's other side.

'You don't think leaving here now is jumping the gun a bit, do you?' Henry said to Mick. An instant later Sarah could see that he was regretting his choice of words.

Mick didn't bother answering Henry's question, which

anyway was probably rhetorical. Henry began to pull off loose splinters of wood from the weathered railing, as if by removing the outer layers he could reveal some unsullied core.

Sarah felt that, if she were in Mick's position, probably about to be set up by Brady for a murder he hadn't committed, in a place where he was guilty until proved innocent – and where proving his innocence was well-nigh impossible – she too would be looking for a way out. A stiff upper lip was all very well for rich white fellows whose rights were guarded by the system. But there was no reason for Mick to have faith in a system in which his people were on the wrong side, squeezed out to the very margins of their own land.

Henry sighed and rested his head on his hands. After Henry's second sigh, Mick said, 'Don't worry, boss.'

'Carruthers was an animal,' Henry said. 'I know that, you know that. But we have to respect the law.'

What law? Sarah thought. Tribal law or white fellows' law? And anyway white fellows' law was imperfectly administered in the Territory. A handful of troopers and a few men scattered across this vast leasehold of land. Was it surprising that the justice system was full of flaws? There was no white rule of law here and individuals were not constrained.

'Sure, boss,' Mick said. 'We have to respect black fellers' law too.'

In the way that Sarah found so endearing, Henry made his goldfish mouth. A few seconds passed before he managed to speak. 'You're right, you should go. Go walkabout. Tribal business.'

'Not tribal business. Own business. Avoiding the gun is better than jumping the gun.'

'When will you leave?' Henry picked a few more splinters of wood from the railing.

'One day, two days.'

'Thank you for looking after things so well here,' Henry said a trifle awkwardly. 'I know Miss Cameron is sometimes difficult.'

Sarah winced. 'Really, Henry. That's too harsh about dear Harriet.'

'Missus Harriet good feller white feller,' Mick said, his voice faltering slightly.

Henry regarded him with surprise. 'She has a strong sense of justice,' he conceded. The dinner bell reverberated through the evening air. 'Chow bell,' said Henry. He cleared his throat, the usual signal that there was something he wanted to say. Before he had a chance to speak, Mick nodded at them both. Then he did what Sarah described to herself as his vanishing trick and evaporated into the fading afternoon light.

Chapter 37

Teetering on the Brink

Harriet, brushing her hair in her bedroom, wished the clock could be turned back. Until Brady had tried to rape her, she'd felt happier than she'd been for years, but all that optimism was trickling away. She twisted her slippery hair into a roll and secured it with hairpins. The dinner bell rang as she peered absently at her reflection in the miniature cheval mirror. Wisps of hair were already escaping from the chignon, but her attention was on other matters: the nature of chance preoccupied her, and how a whole sorry sequence of events could be triggered by a random encounter.

Her friendship with Mick was like a small ball resting on a glassy table surface. If you were to give the ball a little touch, a little push, it would begin to travel in one direction and it would continue, unless something else deflected it, until it had run its course. Until it either came to a rest or plummeted off the edge.

Yet her friendship with Mick might not have formed if she'd never met Brady. If Brady hadn't been following her at Palmerston, she and Mick would never have spoken more than a few words. If Brady hadn't gone to work at Empty Creek Station, Carruthers wouldn't have upset her when he visited. It was in reaction to this that she'd unburdened herself to Mick that night, and afterwards he'd invited her to the gorge. Their friendship had dated from this, had developed from this. It was Brady who'd brought them together. And Brady who was going to drive them apart again, before she could discover if her feelings for Mick were reciprocated.

She went outside. The leaves of the gum trees by the stockyards were twisting in the gentle breeze, so that they appeared to shimmer in the slanting evening light, like slivers of glass reflecting the setting sun. A hard beauty, she'd thought at first. But now she recognised it for what it was: a different beauty.

'You look sad,' said Sarah, when she appeared a moment later.

'No,' Harriet said quickly. 'I'm just a little homesick.' Yet that was not what she meant at all. Faced with the unattainable, one simply made adjustments and carried on. Her life had been a series of chance events, but soon she would have to make a choice about how she would spend the time remaining to her.

'Don't be upset, Hattie.' Sarah put an arm around her shoulders.

'My eyes are as dry as the desert.' Harriet took Sarah's proffered handkerchief though and slipped it under the cuff of her sleeve. As she did so, she noticed for the first time the dress that Sarah was wearing. The fine white fabric was gathered under her bosom and fell in soft folds over the slight bump that was the baby. How lovely she was; how graceful. I've been blind not to notice this change before, she thought. Her sister had metamorphosed into a Madonna. 'You look beautiful,' she said and lightly touched the white fabric of the dress. 'Where did this come from?'

'I've been remaking it for the past week. It was one of my trousseau dresses. I told you earlier but you've been so preoccupied with gallivanting about recording nature that you took no notice.'

'Recording nature was what it's been. Science and not art, at least on my part.'

'I was teasing, Hattie. I wasn't implying it wasn't art. You always seek out the worst in yourself.'

Sarah was right, Harriet thought. She did seek to identify the worst in her own character. But wasn't it human nature to do so? Without that capacity, would men be unable to better themselves? She said, 'I seek out the worst in *everyone*, Sarah. Isn't that what you said to me at the cricket match in Palmerston?'

As she spoke, she wondered if Brady would ever reproach himself for what he'd done. She doubted it somehow. 'Regret nothing' would be his motto. Perhaps she might benefit from such a philosophy. She would carry on with her life, one day after the other, until they had all run through, and each day she would endeavour to regret nothing.

'Did I really say that?' Sarah gave Harriet a little hug. 'Perhaps it's true. You are very critical of people.'

'Maybe I bring out the worst in people. Look at Brady!'

'You couldn't be blamed for that. I'm sorry I've upset you, Hattie. Being critical is good most of the time. You're right to stand up against injustice and Henry thinks so too.'

The little glow of pleasure Harriet felt at this surprised her. Perhaps the distance between her and her brother-in-law had been partly her fault. For years she'd blamed him for taking Sarah away from her. For years she'd thought he wasn't good enough for Sarah.

The dinner bell sounded for the second time. 'We must go,' Sarah said. 'We don't want to upset Ah Soy.'

Harriet said, 'When we were growing up, I used to think you were so dreamy.'

'I was.'

'Now you're so strong. I wonder if all that dreaminess was a way of escaping.'

'Perhaps. What do you think I was escaping?'

'The endless rationality, all that channelling. Never intentional of course, but it was there.'

'Music *is* a wonderful escape but I never felt channelled. That's because Father didn't love me in the same way he loved you. In that I was lucky. I'm not an intellectual and I could get away from all that logic in my music. Henry understands that. Father didn't.'

'I'm different from Father,' Harriet said. 'I've learned that here.'

'You're logical like him. But you're artistic too. You're doubly gifted. But pulled in different directions, I think.'

'Father believed painting was something people did when they couldn't do anything more useful.'

'Do you think so? Perhaps that's true. But you don't need to feel the same way, do you?'

'You can't help being influenced by your parents' attitudes.'

Sarah smiled. 'It's certainly the case that you've always felt that being artistic isn't enough. You think too much, Hattie. Just *do*. Just be who you are.'

'I'm only just discovering who I am.'

'Let me help you, Hattie. You're fiercely intelligent. You're analytical. You're unfettered by stupid social conventions. And you've got an amazing gift for painting landscapes in a new way. A *new* way, did you hear me? You can be really proud of that. I certainly am.'

At that moment Ah Soy appeared carrying a tray, and put an end to their conversation.

* * *

At last dinner was over. Once the table had been cleared, Harriet set off on her evening walk to the boundary fence of the home paddock. Though there was no one in sight, the homestead felt crowded; the sound of raucous laughter and shouting from the stockmen's quarters seemed strange after the peace during the men's absence. Yet tonight she was glad of their loud voices; they kept at bay the nervousness she'd frequently felt since the encounter with Brady.

Away from the lamplight illuminating the homestead buildings, she trod carefully, avoiding tussocks of grass and occasional stones. When she was almost at the boundary fence she saw the gleam of moonlight reflecting from a white shirt, all she could immediately discern of the black fellow standing there.

'I knew you'd come.' As Mick turned to face her, his shirt seemed almost incandescent, and she could see the whites of his eyes and his teeth when he smiled. 'You always do. But today you're a little bit late.'

She stopped a couple of yards away from him and leaned on a fence post. 'Ah Soy made a special effort because of Henry's return. I couldn't get away any earlier.' She wanted to move closer, she wanted to touch him, to rest her head on his chest. But she stayed where she was, shoulder against the post.

'When will you leave here?' he said.

'Soon, when Henry's contract ends.'

'Before the wet season. So nothing has changed.'

'Everything has changed,' she said sadly. 'But we will leave after the troopers. They will believe Sarah and me rather than Brady.'

But if only it wouldn't come to that, she thought. If only Brady would take off somewhere before then. Yet she feared there would still be reprisals. Someone would have to pay for Carruthers' death.

'I hope they'll believe you. Where will you go?'

'Down south with Sarah and Henry. Then I'll have to decide what to do.'

'Will you go back to your country?'

She hesitated. Probably she wouldn't go back to England. She didn't want to marry Charles, and Sarah and Henry would be staying in New South Wales. There was her work for the Women's Franchise League, but that was not really enough to make her think of crossing the ocean again. She could work on those issues in Australia and she could work for Indigenous rights too. She could write articles, she could write letters, she could attend meetings, she could lobby politicians. Her place was here and not in the old country, that small, green, damp island all those thousands of miles away.

'Where will you go, Harriet?'

'I'll stay in Australia.'

'Where?'

'Sydney, probably.'

'You must continue painting, Harriet. You're very good.'

She flushed with a pleasure that she wouldn't have felt so keenly just a few weeks ago.

'We see the same things but we paint differently,' Mick continued. 'You see the light; I see the structure.'

'You must continue too, Mick.'

'Yes, missus.' It was the first time for days Mick had called her this. It was as if there were already a vast distance between them. After a moment, he added, 'Can you keep my paintings?'

'Of course I'll keep them.' There might be a noose around her neck so tight was her larynx. She coughed before saying, her voice unnaturally high, 'I'll look after them until you return.'

'I'd like you to have them. A gift to keep.'

So she would never see him again. 'Thank you, Mick. You couldn't give me anything I'd like more.'

Although she couldn't see the expression on his face, she heard the gentleness in his voice when he said, 'Missus Hattie keepem goodfeller paintings.'

'I'll keep them safe. Would you like me to leave you the

paints? Not for now, but later when things have settled down. You could hide them somewhere.'

'No, you take them.'

She didn't ask him why. It was his affair if he wanted to travel light through life, or if he would never paint again. But she couldn't bear to think of the latter.

'Anyway, they're nearly all gone,' he added.

She smiled. It seemed there was nothing more to say, but the evening was far from silent. From the men's quarters came the sound of laughter. At the campsite a corroboree was starting. The didgeridoo mimicked bullfrogs, or perhaps it was kookaburras, she couldn't decide which. The clap sticks beat out a slightly syncopated rhythm, a background to the story the didgeridoo was relating, and occasionally there was a bang, almost like a drum.

The narrative proceeded and life went on. The past few weeks had brought great happiness but now that was at an end, and she and Mick were teetering on the brink of something new.

But it was not something they would share.

'Time for me to go,' Harriet said at last. In the distance Sarah was calling her, Sarah who had been inclined to worry ever since the incident with Brady.

'We'll see each other again.'

'Yes,' she said, although she knew this wouldn't happen.

'Good night, Harriet.'

'Good night, Mick.' She reached up to kiss his lips. A butterfly touch before she turned away. Afraid to see his reaction. Afraid her kiss might be unwelcome.

Resolutely she made her way back to the homestead. Halfway across the paddock, stumbling over the uneven ground, she stopped and looked around. Mick was nowhere to be seen.

Above her stretched the Milky Way. The river of stars. The big mob stars that were Mick's ancestors.

Chapter 38

Perhaps It Was the Cockatoos that Had Awoken Her

The sunlight, angling through the trees, cast long shadows on the red earth. In her nightdress and shawl, Harriet sat on the verandah and watched the morning metamorphose. Perhaps it was the cockatoos that had awoken her, screeching as they left their tree by the billabong and wheeled through the sky. The air was cool and she pulled her shawl more closely around her shoulders and tucked it into the neck of her nightdress.

Something caught her eye: a patch of bright red on the table. It was a red cloth wrapped around a small object that weighed down a stack of paper. On picking it up, she saw that it was one of Mick's red kerchiefs, tied around a stone. Underneath were his pictures, about a dozen of them. This must mean that Mick was going today. She felt an arrow of sadness pierce her heart.

She picked up his painting of the gorge: he could reduce a scene to its essentials. She remembered the spears of light striking sparks from the quartz in the cliffs, and that brief hour when the world seemed ablaze with a brilliant pink glow.

Mick was going today; the place would be impossible without him. Possibly gone already, gone away at first light. She looked around but there was no sign of him, no sign of anyone apart from the plumes of smoke rising from the encampment.

She carried the paintings into her room and placed them on

the chest of drawers. Soon she would have to work out how to store them, how to protect them.

* * *

Several evenings later, Harriet was sitting with Sarah and Henry at the verandah table when Bob rode up to the homestead carrying a bundle attached to the back of his saddle. Harriet assumed it was his swag until Bob dropped it on to the verandah table and unnrolled it, revealing a white cotton shirt, worn moleskin trousers and a pair of riding boots. Harriet's chest constricted and she had trouble breathing. Sarah leaned towards her with a glass of water, and said, 'Drink this, Hattie. You look as if you might faint.' Harriet's hand trembled so much she could not take it, and Sarah held it to her lips.

'Where did you find these?' Henry said to Bob.

'Next to the lagoon eighteen miles down river. They were folded up at the campsite.'

'Whose are they?' Sarah said.

Henry shook out the trousers and retrieved from one of the pockets a red bandana of the sort worn by some of the stockmen. A red kerchief like the one wrapped around the stone weighing down Mick's paintings, the kerchief that Harriet had put in her paint satchel two days before.

'They're Mick's,' Henry said. 'And they're not damaged. If they were found folded, I think we can assume that Mick just took them off and left them there. You know how neat he is. If you're going walkabout you don't need a stockman's kit.' Henry checked the pockets of the shirt and pulled out from one a piece of paper folded into four. He unfolded it and held it up for the others to see.

It was a pencil sketch of Port Darwin. The crude caricature that Harriet had given Mick on the day of the cricket match, the day he was dispatched by Henry to look after her at Palmerston.

'It's one of mine,' Harriet said. 'I gave it to him.' She was beginning to feel hope. Mick must have simply abandoned his clothes as he travelled further from Dimbulah Downs. And he'd been carrying her drawing all this time. She looked away from the sketch and towards the billabong and blinked rapidly. The late afternoon glare was hurting her eyes and her relief made them water.

'Oh,' said Sarah. 'It's rougher than your usual.'

'I did it hurriedly.' Harriet averted her face so her sister wouldn't see her expression. Mick had sent her a message. She would never have guessed that he might keep her drawing, that he might have been carrying it with him all this time. Although he'd discarded his clothes and with them the sketch, he must have known that they would be found; the lagoon was a regular resting place for the stockmen.

'You didn't find anything else with Mick's clothes, Bob?' Henry said.

'No. Just what I brought you. He could be dead.'

'Drowned or shot maybe,' said Henry slowly. 'That would be a most convenient story to tell the troopers if they come looking for him.'

I've misjudged Henry all this time, Harriet thought. He is kind, which I am not always, and he's been a good friend to Mick. She knew, as Henry did, that Mick wouldn't have drowned. While he was mission-educated, he hadn't lost his Aboriginal culture and he knew how to look after himself. He was a good swimmer too; Harriet remembered that afternoon she'd seen Mick swimming in one of the rock pools while Sarah was telling her about Carruthers killing an Aborigine.

Mick would have floated downriver, leaving no tracks. He would head for the Kimberley and lie low there. 'Drowning would be the better explanation,' she said. 'And rumour has it that the crocodiles have been terrible this year.'

After Bob left for the men's quarters, Henry put the drawing of Port Darwin on top of the pile of clothing on the table and stared thoughtfully into the distance.

'Perhaps Mick's gone to Adelaide,' Sarah said.

Henry put an arm around Sarah's shoulders, whether to protect her or himself was unclear. 'If Brady tells the troopers Mick speared Carruthers, there's no harm in them thinking he's dead.'

'Drowned,' suggested Sarah. 'I believe he was a poor swimmer.'

'If anyone asks,' Henry said, 'we'll tell them he's vanished, presumed drowned. The water's deep down from the lagoon where Bob found his clothes.'

Harriet picked up the dog-eared drawing and examined it. There was nowhere to conceal such an object when one wished to travel light. 'I'll keep this,' she said. 'Although it's not very good.' She folded it carefully and put it into her skirt pocket before heading off, rather earlier than usual, for her walk across the home paddock.

Chapter 39

'If I Come Upon It Suddenly, I Might Take It by Surprise'

Several days later, Harriet set up her easel behind the shed where the horse feed and tack were kept. There was a patch of shade there, cast by the shed and a pair of salmon gums, where she was unlikely to be interrupted. The homestead was peaceful; the only sounds were a few bird calls and Ah Soy whistling somewhere nearby. She put her oil paints and palette on a kerosene tin and sat on a folding stool that she'd taken from the verandah. To the top of the easel she pegged her sketches and notes from that first visit with Mick to the gorge. The moment when the sunlight struck the rock face and set the colours on fire had been obsessing her ever since she'd learned of Mick's departure. It was like a mosquito bite that she'd find no relief from, unless she could scratch at it, although she knew she might bleed as a result.

Flexing her fingers, she shut her eyes. Once more she could see the gorge, in that fleeting hour when she'd witnessed the transformation of the rock face into colours and pulsing light. When she opened her eyes again, the image was still with her and she picked up one of her brushes. All morning her hand and her brushes worked as if divorced from her head. Almost autonomously, tiny daubs of paint appeared on the canvas: yellow ochre, pink, carmine, rose madder, burnt umber, purple, and mauve too, their incandescence reflected in the pool of water below the cliff and their colours in the pale sky above. The canvas became a luminous united whole that had a profound meaning that she couldn't verbally articulate but could recognise as something far bigger than she.

When she had finished, she felt drained. She stood and walked a few hundred yards away before wheeling around and returning to the easel. If I come upon it suddenly, she thought, I might take it by surprise, it might be as if I'm seeing it for the first time. Brilliant or awful, she could not yet tell but she had to find out. Holding her breath, digging her fingernails into the palms of her hands, she stopped in front of the picture and looked at it through half-closed eyes. The canvas was ablaze with light and colour, it was as she had remembered the rock face, it was everything she had hoped it would be. Widening her eyes, she recognised in that moment that it was her best work ever. It was as if here, at Dimbulah Downs, she had discovered her vision, her voice, her own unique view of the world.

She sat down on the small folding stool and gazed again at the painting, this time with her head rather than her heart. The picture was good. It was very good. What made it work was that somehow – with her little dashes of many-hued paints – she had made the light look temporary, the way it had been in the gorge, when you knew it would go as soon as the sun moved across the sky, as soon as the shadows from the cliffs cast the gorge into darkness. The scene looked transient in a way that she could not analyse, and in this transience it had acquired the sort of dynamism that characterised each day with the passing of the hours and the movement of the sun across the heavens.

A crunching of leaves behind her made her start. Turning, she saw her sister, who stood with her hands on her hips, staring at the easel.

'That's beautiful, Hattie,' Sarah said at last.

'Thank you.'

'It's your best ever.'

'I think so too.'

Sarah smiled and Harriet felt her sister's arm rest lightly on her shoulder. Her cotton sleeve smelt faintly of wood smoke. 'Do you know, Hattie, that is the first time you have ever said anything nice about your own work?'

'There is a reason for that.'

'What is it?'

'My earlier work was banal.'

'Hattie, you're so hard on yourself.'

'There is something about the light here,' Harriet said, her voice so soft that Sarah had to lean forward to catch the words. 'In Australia and in the Territory.'

But even as Harriet spoke, she knew that it wasn't only the light that had led her to what she suspected was a metamorphosis. Something had happened at the gorge, something had happened since then with Mick, that had moved her forward. It had given her a shove along the trajectory that she knew now she would follow in the future. Yet she did not want to vocalise this thought, even to Sarah. It might vanish if she voiced it. She needed more time to know if she was right.

* * *

It was the mailman Frank O'Connor who brought the news. Heralded by a cloud of red dust, he arrived one afternoon with his string of packhorses and the bags of mail and newspapers that they had been looking forward to for weeks. Bringing the local gossip too, collected from every cattle station and every telegraph repeater station that Frank had visited along the way. Sarah asked Ah Soy to bring some tea to the part of the verandah protected by mosquito netting. After the usual talk of this and that – the polite stuff that had to be sat through before moving on to what was on all their minds – Henry was quick to ask Frank what he'd heard of Carruthers.

'Carruthers' and Brady's names have been on everyone's lips,' Frank said. 'And a grand set of rumours have been flying around about them, so I count myself lucky that I heard the truth about what happened straight from the horse's mouth. You see, I'd stopped at the repeater station not far south of Pine Creek and was yarning with one of the telegraph boys, and he told me that the troopers had recently been through and found Brady's body not that far from Empty Creek Station. Brady had fallen off his horse, you see, and broken his neck. His body was pretty badly decomposed by the time they got to him, it's this terrible heat, that's the thing.'

Sarah glanced at Harriet, who was staring into the distance, almost as if she wasn't listening to anything Frank was saying. Her shoulders were hunched forward. That and a vertical line between her eyebrows and her jiggling leg gave her agitation away. Sarah herself felt no guilt. She'd saved her sister from Brady's attack and in so doing had only lightly wounded him. She was not responsible for his demise.

Frank took a swig of tea before continuing. 'And you know they could find no trace of Carruthers, none at all, although Brady had somehow sent a telegram to Port Darwin to say he'd been murdered. The blacks had all gone walkabout, apparently, and there was no sign of the stockmen either. They'd all cleared off with the horses, by the look of things.'

'Was there anything else about Carruthers?' Henry said.

'It turned out that Carruthers was wanted by the police in Melbourne,' Frank replied. 'It was for the murder of a white feller in a pub brawl a few years back. So, what with one thing and another, it seems that no one is to be charged with Carruthers' murder.'

Again Sarah looked at her sister. Her shoulders were no longer folded inwards, her face had relaxed, and that vertical line between her eyebrows had quite vanished.

'I don't want to speak ill of the dead,' Frank said, before proceeding to do precisely that. 'But I never liked Carruthers much, he had such an unkind manner on him. Someone must have dropped him on his head when he was a baby. Happen that's the thing about being a big man. With all that strength, you have to learn how to hold back.'

Frank now launched into a tale about his uncle. 'Six foot three in his socks and all on a diet of milk and cheese and potatoes and cabbage. Bejesus, that's a grand diet for good health if only you can eat enough of it, and he was the gentlest man in the world. His strength was to protect others, he always said, not to get them to do his bidding.'

At this point Ah Soy reappeared with a smile and a cake and a pot of steaming water to replenish the teapot. The afternoon was beginning to feel cold, and Sarah knew that shortly the white cockatoos would come squawking in to jockey for position in the old gum tree down by the billabong. She felt peace descend on her as she watched the plumes of smoke arising from the Aboriginal camp. The sky was lightening, the cobalt blue fading to the palest shade, with a blaze of orange and gold at the horizon. In only a few more weeks the regular manager of Dimbulah Downs would return – with a new wife, it seemed, and Sarah hoped she knew what she was letting herself in for – and their sojourn in the Territory would be over before the start of the wet season.

EPILOGUE

Sydney, 1897

Tiny brushstrokes, a multiplicity of colours. A fractured, flickering, scintillating interpretation of Mosman Bay sparkles from the canvas. This is not by Harriet, but next to it is one of hers: a painting of the gorge that Mick took her to. She has four pictures in this Sydney exhibition. They hang side by side with some great names of Sydney and Melbourne impressionists. She can't believe her good fortune.

It is opening night. The gallery doors have just been unlocked. A couple of dozen people are already here, attaching themselves to the known artists, connected to one another by little threads of conversation, everyone talking at once. Someone says something that is imperfectly heard; someone else throws back something that is loosely related, or perhaps not related at all. And so it goes on: threads of conversations becoming hopelessly tangled.

And so far, no one is looking at the canvases.

Turning away from the crowd she again examines the view of Mosman Bay. The voices grow even louder as more people arrive. Get away, she thinks, her heart now a panicking caged bird. Get away fast. Soon these people will look at the paintings and she can't bear to hear the comments when they see hers. They will cut right into her and excise whatever impulse it is that makes her expose herself on canvas.

Be sensible, she tells herself sternly, wiping her sticky palms on her mustard yellow skirt and easing the neck of her high-collared white blouse. You can't leave, that will never do. It's a great honour to have your work selected for this exhibition and you've got to stay.

Turning abruptly away from the Mosman Bay painting, she finds herself staring at a familiar face. 'Mick Spencer!' Although she tries to make her voice sound normal, it emerges half-strangled. 'How wonderful to see you.'

'Mick Yarrapunga.'

'Yarrapunga?'

'Yes.' He spells it out for her. 'That is my name.'

'So that's why I couldn't trace you.'

'You tried to trace me?'

'Of course. In Adelaide and in Darwin and in Sydney and in Melbourne. And in Brisbane. No one had heard of Mick Spencer. After a while I began to think you might be dead.'

'But here I am.' In his smiling face she recognises something timeless that makes her catch her breath.

'I should have guessed you'd changed your name. I remember what you said when I asked for your last name, do you remember? "Too many syllables," you said. "They give me civilised name."'

'I remember. That was the day I asked you if you'd like to see the gorge.'

'I still have your paintings.'

'I'm glad. I hoped you'd keep them.'

'Would you like them back?'

'They were a gift for you.'

'I've had them framed.'

'Did you get your sketch of Port Darwin, the one I left with my clothes?'

'Yes. I still have it.' She carries it around with her like a talisman. It is folded up in an envelope in her bag.

'It was a message for you.'

296

'I know.'

'Are you that Harry Cameron exhibited here?'

'Yes.'

'I hoped it might be you. That's why I agreed to come. I'm in Sydney for a few weeks. I work for the Aborigines' Friends' Association and some friends told me about this exhibition.'

'I'm so glad you came.' The silence expands while she slowly sweats.

Eventually he says, 'But Harry Cameron is your working name. Have you married?'

'No.' Charles, with whom she still corresponds, has married someone else, a friend of Violet's, and she is glad of it. 'And you, Mick – are you married?'

'No.'

'What happened to you after you left Dimbulah Downs?'

'I made my way to the Kimberley and took a boat down to Perth. Then I did some odd-jobs before going back to the Coorong. Stayed there for a bit until I found out what had happened and then I got the job in Adelaide.'

She explains how she wrote to the Aborigines' Friends' Association asking if they knew anything about Mick Spencer, and received a reply saying they had no record of anyone of that name. She does not yet tell him how sad that made her. Instead, she says, 'So you know that Brady died in a fall from his horse without having a chance to blame you for Carruthers' death?'

'Yes.'

'In the end no one was blamed for Carruthers' death. He had a bad reputation, everyone agreed. He was wanted for a murder down south, he'd killed a white fellow there after a pub brawl, but the police had lost track of him.'

'I saw that in the *Adelaide Advertiser*. In a tiny article on page 6. Where are Henry and your sister?'

'Farming north of Bega. Sheep mainly but some dairy

too. They have a son and a second child on the way. They're very happy. Sarah has a piano again – I don't know how she managed for so long without one. And she shoots. She's very good at it. She wins competitions at country shows.'

Mick smiles. 'And you, Harriet – are you happy?'

'I'm contented enough. And I'm especially happy to see you again.'

There is a moment of stillness against the background roar of the gallery visitors. She must take a risk; she can't bear the thought of losing track of Mick again. She feels her face burn as she says, 'Do you have plans for tonight? We could have dinner after this opening's over.'

'That depends on whether we can find a place that will serve a white woman dining with a black fellow.'

'We can do that. We'll avoid the *proper* places. We'll find somewhere.'

'Yes.'

There is a pause. She sees on the far side of the gallery a couple standing in front of one of her paintings.

He says, 'Are you willing to go down this track, Harriet? It won't be easy.'

She looks into his dark eyes that miss nothing and feels like she's come home. 'I know it won't be easy,' she says. 'But I think we should give it a try.'

Acknowledgements

The Philosopher's Daughters is a work of fiction embedded in historical fact. Although at times I have altered minor details to fit the narrative, the story reflects the period of the 1890s as seen through the eyes of the two protagonists, the daughters of moral philosopher James Cameron. Readers may find some of the dialogue confronting, since it occasionally reflects some of the attitudes and expressions of the period. All characters and incidents in the book are fictitious.

I owe special thanks to my late father, Norman Booth, whose tales of his years in the Northern Territory awakened my interest in that part of the world. Warm thanks to RedDoor Press for stewarding this book into production, and also to first readers Heather Boisseau, Karen Colston, Tom Flood, Maggie Hamand, Tim Hatton, Ann McGrath, Kathy Mossop and Lyn Tranter. Historian Nicole McLennan was a wonderful person to discuss the 1890s with, and I much appreciate her meticulous research and insights. I am also grateful to Ana Baeza, who accompanied me on that long train journey from Darwin to Adelaide. Last but not least I thank Justine Small, who guided me on wonderful trips through the Northern Territory, and Alex Lee Small, who brokered some unforgettable visits to remote Northern Territory communities.

I am grateful to Varuna the Writers' House for the opportunity to write with no interruptions when this was most needed. Thanks also to the Northern Territory Library in Darwin, to the National Library of Australia, to the libraries of the Australian National University, and especially to the collection of the Northern Australia Research Unit that was held in the basement of the Chifley Library at the Australian National University until early 2018. I was fortunate to have browsed its contents before it was destroyed in a terrible flood in early 2018.

I am indebted to many books and newspapers of the time. Below is a selection of relevant books that readers might find interesting.

Blakeley, Fred, (1938), *Hard Liberty*. London: George G Harrap & Co. Ltd.

Booth, Norman W (2002), *Up the Dusty Track*. Darwin: Charles Darwin University Press. Reprinted 2006.

Dixon, Val (ed.) (1988), *Looking Back: The Northern Territory in 1888*. Casuarina. NT: Historical Society of the Northern Territory.

Gunn, Jeannie (Mrs Æneas) (1907), *We of the Never-Never*. London: Hutchinson.

Headon, David (ed.) (1991), *North of the Ten Commandments: A Collection of Northern Territory Literature*. London: Hodder and Stoughton.

Knight, J G (1880) (ed.), *The Northern Territory of South Australia*. Adelaide: E. Spiller, Government Printer.

Leichhardt, Ludwig (1847), *Ludwig Leichhardt's Journal of an Overland Expedition in Australia, 1844–5*. First published 1847, London: T & W Boone. This edition: Adelaide: Corkwood Press, 1996.

Masson, Elsie R. (1915), *An Untamed Territory: The Northern Territory of Australia*. London: Macmillan and Co.

McGrath, Ann (1987), *'Born in the Cattle': Aborigines in the Cattle Country*. Sydney: Allen and Unwin.

Searcy, Alfred (1911), *By Flood and Field*, London: G Bell and Sons, 1912.

Stevens, Frank S, *Aborigines in the Northern Territory Cattle Industry*. Canberra: Australian National University Press, 1974.

Also by Alison Booth

A

Perfect

Marriage

Alison Booth

Chapter 1

THEN

The body lay on a gurney in the middle of the room. When the coroner's assistant uncovered the head, my heart began to knock against my ribcage and I could feel the thump-thump-thump of a migraine starting.

The assistant stood back and I stepped forward.

The body was his all right. They must have cleaned him up. I put out a hand to touch the pale forehead. It was icy cold from the refrigeration. There were fine lines around his eyes and his blond hair was tousled. He was beautiful still, in spite of what had happened to him.

I waited as the minutes passed by, almost expecting to see his chest rise and fall, almost expecting to see the eyelids flutter open. I forgot about the coroner's assistant until she gave a discreet cough. Turning away from the body, I nodded to her. As I walked past, she took a step towards me and lightly patted my forearm.

Outside, sadness and relief wavered through my head like paper kites tossed about in a high wind. I bought a copy of the *Evening Standard* from the newsvendor on the corner. On the front page there was yet another picture of that woman. Behind the piles of newspapers was a wire rack with yesterday's headlines that I knew I'd never forget.

A blast of diesel fumes from a passing bus precipitated my migraine. I leaned against the mottled trunk of a plane tree.

When the nausea came, I stood at the edge of the pavement and threw up in the gutter. No one appeared to notice, certainly no one stopped.

I carried on retching until my stomach hurt. After a while, a smartly dressed woman asked if I needed help. Her kindness made me weep, hot silent tears. 'Is there someone I can call?' she said, her arm around my shoulders.

I hiccoughed a couple of times and accepted the tissues she was holding out. 'I'm fine, thanks,' I said, after wiping my eyes.

And I was. That part of my life was well and truly behind me now. I could do with a drop of water though. My mouth felt parched and I could barely swallow. But before I could get on with my life there was the coroner to deal with. She was waiting for me on the steps to the mortuary building.

All I wanted was some peace for Charlie and me. But there was no guarantee that would come easily.

About the Author

© StudioVogue, Canberra, Australia

Alison Booth was born in Melbourne, brought up in Sydney and worked for many years in the UK. Her most recent novel, *A Perfect Marriage*, is in the genre of contemporary fiction, while her first three novels (*Stillwater Creek*, *The Indigo Sky*, and *A Distant Land*) are historical fiction spanning the decades 1950s through to the early 1970s. Alison's work has been translated into French and has also been published by *Reader's Digest Select Editions* in both Asia and Europe. Alison's debut novel, *Stillwater Creek*, was Highly Commended in the 2011 ACT Book of the Year Award. Her fiction website is at:
http:// www.alisonbooth.net
and her Facebook page is at:
https:// www.facebook.com/AlisonBoothAuthor/ .

Find out more about RedDoor Press and sign up to our newsletter to hear about our **latest releases, author events,** exciting **competitions** and more at

reddoorpress.co.uk

YOU CAN ALSO FOLLOW US:

 @RedDoorBooks

 Facebook.com/RedDoorPress

 @RedDoorBooks